WITHDRAWN

D0953031

Go to My Grave

Go to My Grave

Catriona McPherson

Minotaur Books
New York

GO TO MY GRAVE. Copyright © 2018 by Catriona McPherson. All rights reserved. Printed in the United States of America. For information, address St. Martin's Press, 175 Fifth Avenue, New York, N.Y. 10010.

www.minotaurbooks.com

Library of Congress Cataloging-in-Publication Data

Names: McPherson, Catriona, 1965– author.
Title: Go to my grave / Catriona McPherson.
Description: First U.S. edition. | New York : Minotaur Books, 2018.
Identifiers: LCCN 2018020148 | ISBN 9781250070005 (hardcover) |
    ISBN 9781466879904 (ebook)
Subjects: | GSAFD: Mystery fiction. | Suspense fiction.
Classification: LCC PR6113.C586 G63 2018 | DDC 823/.92—dc23
LC record available at https://lccn.loc.gov/2018020148

Our books may be purchased in bulk for promotional, educational, or business use. Please contact your local bookseller or the Macmillan Corporate and Premium Sales Department at 1-800-221-7945, extension 5442, or by email at MacmillanSpecialMarkets@macmillan.com.

First published in Great Britain by Constable, an imprint of Little, Brown Book Group, an Hachette UK company

First U.S. Edition: October 2018

10 9 8 7 6 5 4 3 2 1

For Catherine and Oliver Lepreux,
with love and thanks.

Prologue

This is the story of three days last September when eight old friends gathered in a beautiful house by the sea. There was food, wine and laughter, and then the friends went their separate ways. That's the truth and nothing but the truth. The story is over. We have locked the box, swallowed the key and stitched our lips shut. Will that be enough? I don't know. It took twenty-five years, after last time, for the stitches to unravel, the key to burn through our guts, the box to rust and weaken. But this time's different. There's so much more to lose. I can't speak for the others but I'll keep this secret and go to my grave.

Chapter 1

The house was a held breath. Its ten empty rooms waited, polished like a bowl of apples. There were flowers in the hall and in the big bay windows of the drawing room and dining room. There were logs in the baskets and candles in the holders. The snooker balls were framed and the magazines were fanned and every window was open an inch at the top, not enough to make the curtains tremble but enough to let in the sound of the sea.

The sea. You couldn't get away from it even if you wanted to. From every room you could hear it, thrashing up on the beach and rattling the pebbles as it drew back again. You could smell it under the lemon cleaner and beeswax polish, under the lilies and freesias and the eucalyptus. You could see it in a film on the west-facing windows, little dots of wet salt back again hours after washing them. And in the shiver of damp when the sun sank and the squabble of gulls when it rose again, there was the sea.

Of course I'd grown up on an island so I was used to it.

Although we'd never lived right on the seafront on Skye, because those houses are worth more rented to tourists than sold to locals. Which was exactly the point: the hard cash value of the sound of the sea.

I walked up the stairs one last time, in and out of the five bedrooms. Pillows plumped, blankets smooth, tissues folded into fans. More flowers. In and out of the five bathrooms. Thick towels laid over warmed rails. Big bars of good soap unwrapped in every glittering dish. Not a drop of water or a speck of dust in the baths.

The house had seventeen rooms really, but the kitchen didn't count and the breakfast room attached to it was the 'staff lounge'. In other words, the dumping ground for supplies. The two smallest bedrooms didn't count either, because the nearest bathroom was down the back stairs, past the laundry facilities. We couldn't rent beds without en suites. Not at the prices we were charging. So they were 'staff accommodation' too.

And that was why the little room at the top of the stairs was called a snug in the brochure, even though it had a sofabed for overflow. Or – as my mum said – for flouncing off to after arguments.

I spent two late nights on Amazon choosing jigsaws and board games. My mum raised her eyebrows at the bill but she didn't argue. Hospitality was my end of this little venture, along with catering. I know my stuff and she trusts me.

I had to blink at the cost of the high-speed Wi-Fi, not to mention the fax and scanner and the extra-fast colour-printer down in the study, but I trusted her too. Holidays would be our bread and butter, she told me, but corporate retreats were the geese that shat the golden shit, second only to weddings.

And Galloway's cheap property and dark night skies with the excellent star-gazing – we had provided binoculars and a telescope – went hand-in-hand with pitiful connectivity. 'But I can outwit all that,' she said. 'By the time I'm finished we'll have download speeds like a bank in Manhattan.'

She spent a lot longer than two late nights setting the search terms so that corporations, brides and holiday-makers would all find us, no matter what they thought they were looking for. She knows her stuff too. The website had been live less than a day when we got the first booking.

It was a tenth wedding anniversary. Eight old friends coming down from Glasgow, over from Edinburgh, up from England for a reunion. They bought the full-catered package: Friday tea till Monday breakfast, with a big dinner on the Saturday night. Which was why I was wearing black trousers and a starched white shirt with an apron on top as I padded round the rooms.

If only my mum had been there too I'd have been padding round without my knees knocking. As it was, I was doing this whole weekend – eight people, four meals a day, five counting drinks and nibbles – on my lonesome.

'It sucks hard and blows back out again,' my mum agreed, when the news broke, 'and if you say no, it's no. So . . . what do you say?'

Because the thing is we had entered every competition going – as you would, starting up on a shoestring – and we had won one. The prize was free registration and a corner stand on the central aisle at Scotland's biggest wedding fair, at the SECC in Glasgow. We were still pinching ourselves.

'I'm more the business end anyway,' she'd said. True, but she can wash dishes and scrub toilets and she's great with names. It's always been my worst weakness, despite all the tricks and hacks in the book. It's the reason I prefer high-end, where you can 'sir' and 'madam' your way through everything.

'I promise I'll keep up with the bookings online in the quiet minutes,' she'd told me. 'But it's your call, Donna. Coal face and all that.'

'I can do it,' I announced. 'If we ditch the pan-seared scallops and soufflés, I can do it. But are you sure you can do the expo? You'll be more knackered than me.'

'We can *both* do it,' she said. 'We're unstoppable.'

A car door slammed, out on the gravel. I nipped to the side of the window and looked down. A navy-blue Range Rover had pulled up, slantwise, right across the front door, and a man was standing there with his head thrown back, staring so the house was reflected in his sunglasses.

He had to be one of the guests. He was dressed exactly like a townie dresses for a country weekend: brand-new cords, brand-new waxed jacket the same colour as his car, an inch of a checked collar showing above the neck of his cashmere. I edged in closer to the glass for a better look and, as I did, the passenger door opened and a girl stepped out. A woman. She matched him like the other side of the cuckoo clock: long legs in dark red jeans, tall boots, a sheepskin gilet over her angora. She was beaming and her hair bounced and shone as she skipped round the back of the car to stand beside the man. She took his arm and squeezed, then reached up onto her tiptoes and pecked his cheek.

It happened too fast for me to be sure. One minute she was kissing him, holding onto his arm, and the next she was sprawled on her arse. I'd have said she overbalanced, if he had stooped to help her up again. If she was still beaming.

But he was back in the car and she scrambled to her feet, rubbing her hands on her red jeans. Heels of your hands on the gravel like that, they had to be stinging. The car was moving and she hopped and hobbled after it. She managed to get the door open and herself into the seat as he gunned the engine and squealed away.

I trotted down the stairs without touching the banister. It gleamed like an eel, with not a single fingermark along its length. Even though that had been a false alarm, I thought I should get the scones in the oven. The smell of baking when the guests arrive is a basic move. There's nothing complicated about a batch of cherry scones, but knowing they've been baked fresh just for you works wonders on the toughest guest.

And doing it calmed me too. I stepped outside afterwards, wiping my hands on my apron, and found – as I'd suspected – that the sunglasses man had left a scar on the gravel when he peeled away. I took the rake from where it was leaning half behind the ivy on the long front porch and started scraping the ruts flat again. There was the print of her skinny bum and the two small dents from her hands. I smoothed them away with two swipes of my rake. Then I stopped. I nudged at the little bit of granite until it turned back again, showing the speck of red. She had fallen hard enough to break the skin and bleed.

I picked it up – that one red chip in the sea of perfect silver-grey – and put it in my pocket, beside the petals I'd tidied from a table-top and the white thread I'd lifted from a black hand-towel. Then I raised my head at the sound of an engine round the bend of the drive. They were coming back, or someone was arriving.

I didn't have time to get out of sight unless I took the rake with me so I stashed it back among the ivy and waited on the step like a welcome party.

It was a different car. This one was a red hatchback, sitting low on its suspension. The driver tooted a tune – *Tum-tiddly-aye-la!* – as it got close and someone waved at me from the passenger seat. I wiggled my fingers in reply as the car slowed and stopped.

It was another couple. Or maybe not, I thought as they climbed out, since both of them had the same short legs and thick waists, the same brown eyes. His hair was clumsily cut into a divot and hers had highlighted spikes, but it was the same hair.

'Unbe-fucking-lievable!' said the man. He was standing staring up at the house like the Range Rover guy, knuckling his back and pushing his paunch out like a pregnancy.

'It's not,' said the woman. 'It can't be. Glancing similarity.' Then she smiled at me. 'You must be Kim.' She scurried forward, trying to get her bag, coat, phone and a bunch of flowers out of the way to shake my hand. 'It's so lovely to meet you at long last.'

'I'm Donna Weaver,' I said. 'Welcome to The Breakers. You're the first to arrive.'

'Donna?' said the man. 'What the hell happened to Kim?' His voice swooped with concern, but his eyes were twinkling.

'Shut up, Buck,' the woman said. 'Ow.' An earring had caught on her fluffy jumper and her head jerked to the side as she fiddled with it.

'Here,' I said, stepping forward. 'Let me. I'm Donna from Home From Home. I'm going to be looking after you for the weekend.'

'Oh, you're a sweetheart,' the woman said, working her neck round, now the earring was free again. 'I'm Peach Plummer.'

'Peach,' I repeated, staring hard at her. I was trying to get her name into my head. She misread me.

'God, don't I know!' she said. 'But my real name's *Morag*. And this is my brother, Buck.'

Peach, I told myself. Round and fuzzy. And sweary Buck. Rhymes with—

'Buchanan Leslie,' the man said, shaking my hand. 'The curse of my mother's maiden name. If you're trying to tick us off on your sheet, you should know that my wife's not coming. One of the ankle-biters has come down with tonsillitis and she drew the short straw.'

'Hmm,' said Peach. 'We'll measure the straws on Sunday, shall we?'

'Right then, Donna-from-Home-from-Home,' Buck said, after a moment's silence. 'When you say you're looking after us, are you unpacking the car and ironing our jimmy-jams or should we—'

'Shut up, Buck.'

'I'll show you to your rooms and then leave you to unpa—' I began, but he spoke over me.

'No need to show us anything, Donna. Every nook and cranny is seared into our brains, despite all the therapy.'

'We think we've been here before, you see,' Peach said. 'But it wasn't called The Breakers then.'

'That's right,' I told them. 'It had a name-change. It used to be . . . Knockbreak House, I think.'

'That's right enough, then,' said Buck. 'God almighty.'

'Welcome back!' I spread my arms.

9

'I'd still love to see over it,' said Peach. 'It was a right old dump when we were kids. And look at it now.'

'But don't look at it with a black light,' Buck said. 'Just kidding,' he added. He even gave me a wink.

But I didn't miss the way he hesitated on the porch before he walked through into the vestibule. I was holding the inner glass door for him and, as he passed, I could see his arm where his sleeve was rucked up and the gooseflesh that bristled there.

———

I still enjoyed showing off the house. The corridor stretched its length, with the stairs at one end and the front door in the middle, so it would have been a bit much to cover everything. But we had a quick neb at the two rooms we passed. First, the library with its sage-green walls and carpet, dark green button-back wing-chairs, its long, pale, chesterfield couch; the bookcases were only MDF with beading tacked on, but we'd stained them and varnished them and I'd insisted on hardbacks. The black and yellow dining room was my favourite. All set for dinner, it took my breath away but even now the high polish on the bare table swelled me with pride. Home From Home had worked so hard and scrimped so much. I had been scared the plain black curtains with the patterns used for tiebacks and toppers would be too obviously thrifty but they weren't. They looked elegant and confident – the more so for a bit of restraint, maybe.

'Oops,' the Peach woman said, looking at a towering arrangement of allium and lilies in the dining-room window, then down at her cellophaned bunch of chrysanths. 'Maybe I could put these in my bedroom.'

'There are flowers in the bedrooms too,' I told her. 'But I'll find a jug and there'll be a perfect spot somewhere. They're lovely.'

'Oh, aren't you nice!' she said.

Buck was coming along the corridor with a couple of Tesco bags in each hand. 'Kitchen still in the same place, I'm guessing?'

'Oh!' I said. 'The food's all laid on, actually. Chef on duty all day every day.'

'Chef?' said Peach. 'Kim said we didn't need to, but I thought she was just being polite.'

'Shite,' said Buck. 'Don't tell me I dragged my arse round that supermarket for nothing!'

I took the bags from him and glanced into them. 'Good bread and English apples. These won't go to waste.'

'Oh, God, really? Aren't you *nice*!' Peach said. 'Will the chef get offended, though?'

'You're looking at her,' I said, nodding to my apron. 'And no. Come upstairs and I'll show you your bedrooms.'

The corridor stretched the length of the house up here too. The rooms off to the left had their doors ajar and the light poured through, dappling the long run of carpet. To the right, the door to the back rooms and back stair was closed and bolted on the other side.

'So I'm sharing with Jennifer, am I?' Peach said, when she saw the sign on the door. 'Fair enough.'

Buck whistled through his teeth, as we all trooped in. 'I have to say, this is pretty fantoosh.'

It really was. The couple who'd booked the weekend were getting one corner room and the other was reserved for a 'Paul and Rosalie' but this was the next best and it was charming. It was big enough for two Scotch doubles and the blue and white wallpaper was perfect with the cherry-wood suite – antiques from an auction in Glasgow. The curtains were white muslin and there was a white carpet that felt like velvet under your bare toes. It had the bathroom with the proper window too. Blue and white tiles and a roll-top bath.

'There's a lovely view,' I said. You could see the sea from all the front upstairs windows. Not the beach, because of the steep drop beyond the garden wall where a switchback path of leaf mould and tree roots led to the edge of the sand. But there was a clear sightline to the broad grey ribbon of sea filling the bay.

In a few years, our plan was to turn that treacherous path into a set of steps with a handrail so that The Breakers would be good for families as well as gatherings like this one. Until then, clients got warnings in their booking emails and there was a little plaque on the gate and a basket of torches on the hat-stand in the vestibule.

They'd walked over to the window as I gestured and now they were standing in silence, looking out. Three waves thrashed up and rattled back and still they stood there.

'The trees have grown,' Peach said at last. Buck put an arm out and hugged her.

'You're along at the end, Buck,' I said. 'Pretty much in the nursery, I'm afraid, but it's the only family room, and we thought you were bringing . . .' They hadn't turned round as I spoke and talking at their backs like this was starting to feel weird. 'I'm afraid you don't have a sea view,' I added. 'But you'll still be able to hear the waves.'

They both turned then and whatever the expression they had on their faces – I couldn't name it – they looked more alike than ever as they stared at me.

12

Chapter 2

The rooms on this side were dark, from how the hill rose up, ten feet across from the kitchen door, and how the trees crowded round, hugging the house. Yews, like in a churchyard.

'If there's a bed with no wife in it, and no kids in it, and no bloody *dog* in it, it'll do me,' Buck said, strenuously hearty, following me into the room with the four single beds in a row, like an old-fashioned dormitory. 'Jesus, though, that's a lot of tartan.'

'"Ooooh, Campbeltown Loch, I wish you were whisky",' Peach sang, doing a few Highland-dance steps. I kept the smile on my face without even trying. I've worked in hospitality since my first Saturday job when I was sixteen. And she had a point. Home From Home reckoned downstairs should have a 'cohesive country style' but the bedroom suites should give people a choice: one was pony-skin and silver, with those basins that look like mixing bowls left out on a counter-top; one was stone-coloured hessian, with photos of pebbles; the blue and white and cherry-wood was the pretty room; and this was over-the-top Scottish, with tartan throws, tartan tiebacks for the tweedy curtains, and a painting of stags and mountains.

'I'll leave you to get settled in,' I said. 'I think I hear someone else arriving.'

A woman was waiting in the hall when I got back downstairs. The light from the front door made her look like a shadow puppet striking a pose there. She had high-heeled black boots on and a tailored black suit so snug under her armpits it rucked up when she bent her arms. She was hunched over her phone

'Soundofthesea,' I said. 'All one word. You'll struggle for a signal unless you log in to ours.'

But she surprised me.

'And . . . off!' She twirled the phone like a Wild West pistol and dropped it into the laptop-bag she had over one shoulder. 'Is there a safe?'

'Safe?'

'Sorry,' said the woman, spiking towards me on her impossible heels. 'Still in work mode. I'm Rosalie. You must be Donna. Is there a safe I can put my devices in for the weekend?'

'How did you know my name?' I said. 'Never mind. No, there's no safe, Rosalie, I'm afraid.' Rosalie remembers me, I thought. Rosalie for remembrance. 'It's pretty low-crime around here. I could . . .' Nothing came to mind immediately, and before I could really apply myself to the problem, Rosalie was laughing.

'Oh, God, no!' she said. 'Not for the *safety*. To keep me off them and to keep him off his, even more so.' She jerked her head back towards the door. 'Conference call,' she said, with

14

an eye-roll. 'I know you because Kim bcc'd me in, by the way. No mystery there.'

'There's a cupboard that locks,' I said. 'If you're serious.'

'Deadly,' said Rosalie. 'I've told work. I've told the aged parents. The dogs are at the kennel. The kennel's got the landline – Kim gave it me – and everyone I might want to talk to is going to be here.' She handed me her laptop bag and then mimed floating away, grabbing the newel post to keep one toe on the floor. 'I need this weekend,' she said. 'Cliff walks and beach bonfires.'

'And my plan is, by Monday you'll feel it was a fortnight,' I told her. 'Let me start by showing you to your room.'

'What's that heavenly smell?' she said, as we passed the kitchen.

'Scones.' Which would burn in three minutes if I got sidetracked again.

She groaned with delight. More delight than a batch of scones deserved. I wondered if maybe she was in customer relations too and couldn't switch it off as easily as a smartphone. Me, I can switch it off as soon as I blow through the swing doors marked 'Staff Only'.

'Ro?' A voice came from outside. 'Rosie?'

'He's finally noticed I'm not there,' she said, as a tall man came hurrying in, looking down at a phone, showing the bald spot his short hair was supposed to disguise. Like her, he was dressed for business: jacket off, a good pink shirt I reckoned had been professionally laundered, the way its creases were still sharp at the end of the day. His tie was pulled down but it had started out in a Windsor knot that morning, and his shoes were those stupid, extra-long, square-tipped things that made me think of clown's feet. His watch was clunky and ugly and no doubt cost more than my car.

'How's Tokyo?' Rosalie said.

'What?' He frowned.

'Just a guess,' Rosalie said, winking at me. 'Paul, this is Donna.'

Tall Paul, I thought as I smiled at him.

'There's a delivery van here,' he said, pointing. 'Outside. Something needs a signature.'

'You've done remarkably well in life for a man who can't write his own name,' said Rosalie, marching back to the door and outside again.

I started my standard introduction but she was back before I got through it. She had a gift basket in her arms, a hamper propped open and covered with squeaky plastic gathered at the top in a bow.

'Not you too!' Peach had reappeared, on the landing, still in the fluffy jumper, but now with a chenille cardigan and furry slippers too. If she dressed like that all weekend I'd be laughing. 'We brought a *ton* of food and turns out it's all laid on!'

'Cousin Peach!' said Rosalie. 'No, this is a present for the happy couple, I assume.' She thrust the hamper into her husband's arms and started searching for a message envelope among the folds of cellophane and froth of ribbon.

'Oh, clever,' said Peach, coming down. 'Look, it's tins. Tin of foie gras, tin of caviar. Gentleman's Relish.'

'Pretty generic if you ask me,' Paul said. 'And heavy.'

'No, but it's *tins*,' said Peach. 'The tenth anniversary is the tin anniversary, see?'

'Load of nonsense,' Paul said. 'Silver's the first one you need to bother with. Then gold. Christ, we'll need to make sure and be busy when it's silver and gold. Cost a fortune.'

'Clearly you've never coughed up for a couple's massage

gift voucher,' Peach said. 'Some random silver napkin rings would be a snip.'

'Let me take the hamper off your hands,' I said. I hadn't missed the way the man – Paul – was frowning as his wife rummaged. 'I'll hold on to it till you decide when the big present-opening's going to be.'

'Big pres—' said Paul. 'Oh, for God's sake, is this whole weekend going to be nothing but speeches and toasts and heartwarming moments? Just stick it in their bedroom and let them find it when they get here.'

'Who's pissed on your chips?' said Peach. 'You're usually up for a party.'

'Ignore him,' said Rosalie. 'He lost a case this morning. Husband dear, we are having a free weekend in pretty swish digs, so toasting our host with the champers *he* bought is a small price to pay. Anyway, I think this is from Sasha's work – it's his name only on the card here – so he won't want it in his bedroom for his romantic anniversary.'

Paul's face twisted. 'Christ, that's right,' he said. 'They've only been married ten years. Hope we're not through the wall from it.'

'You're not, Face-ache,' said Peach. 'But I am. Unless I switch the name cards. Quick, Rosie, help me shift my stuff before anyone else gets here.'

I couldn't tell if she was serious. 'If you can show your friends their room anyway,' I said, 'I'll stash the hamper.'

'No friends of mine,' said Peach. 'We're all cousins.'

'And some siblings,' said Rosalie. She handed me the gift card and took Peach's arm. 'Let's make sure we've got the rooms we want before the rest arrive.' They scampered up the stairs, giggling like children.

'I dare you to take the master suite and see if Kim says anything,' was the last thing I heard from Peach as they disappeared round the landing.

A flutter of unease must have crossed my face. If they mucked up the room allocations, Home From Home would get the blame.

'I can't help you,' Tall Paul said, once they were gone. 'Not if you're wondering how my cousin, the respected doctor, and my wife, the lawyer everyone's terrified of, can turn into naughty toddlers in under two minutes. I knew this weekend would tip everyone into hysterics.'

'It's a big house,' I assured him, ignoring most of what he'd said. 'There are more than enough rooms to escape into.'

He looked to one end of the corridor, at the six-foot marble statue of Venus framed in the arched window, and then at the other end, where a matching Adonis stood on the deep sill of the tall landing window.

'Oh, I know exactly how big the house is,' he said. 'My wife might not have twigged yet, or she might be pretending not to have twigged, but I remember this place very well.'

'Why would she pret—' I began, then I pasted the professional smile on again and started backing away.

'Because Sasha's up to something, isn't he? Bringing us all back here to relive our golden memories. And if there's one thing Rosalie's good at, it's making sure her brother's little ploys are strangled at birth.'

'Families!' I said, to lighten the mood.

'Blood's thicker than water,' said Paul. 'Blood's thicker than concrete, actually. Good place to bury things.'

I opened my mouth to answer but nothing came out.

'However,' he added, 'a good malt dissolves anything.

18

Drinks tray still in the drawing room, is it?' He gave me a tight smile and walked away, leaving his luggage in the hallway.

I dumped the hamper on the breakfast table, tucked the little envelope back into the cellophane, and got the scones out of the oven without a second to spare.

A chorus of 'Mamma Mia' started at my hip and I dug my phone out.

'Anybody there yet?' my mum said.

'Four,' I said. 'We're halfway. Peach, Buck, Paul and Rosalie.'

'Well done!'

'How's things your end? You sound like you're down a well.'

'Yeah, it's a big barn of a place. But the pitch is great. Dead central. I'll send you a picture when I'm finished setting up. And the girl on the booth next door says she'll mind mine if I mind hers. For pee breaks.'

I dusted the scones with a bit more flour than they needed and decided they'd pass for well-fired. 'Sounds like you're on top of it all,' I said. 'I nearly burned the scones, showing folk round.'

'What are they like?'

'Small, round, studded with fruit. I know! I was kidding.' I thought about the couple in the navy-blue Range Rover and decided not to mention them. 'The client's not here yet. One of the men's a bit of a misery-guts but his wife's dead nice, and their two fat cousins are lovely. Mouths like dockers, mind you.'

It had surprised me when I stopped working in the bistro bit of the hotel in Portree, and went to London to learn the trade in the deep end. I thought posh people would be politer

19

than us but they swore all the time. And the really posh ones never said 'pardon' when they burped. Women in pearl chokers and diamond earrings would let a right old tonsil rattler go and just carry on eating.

'I think that's another car,' I said, cutting in on my mum wittering about the price of the coffee.

'Good luck,' she told me. 'And remember, if you get overwhelmed, just open more wine.'

'Yep,' I said, although that would hardly help if I got overwhelmed at breakfast time. A full fry-up's one of the hardest meals to get the timings right on. But we had already agreed the menus with the client by the time the wedding fair happened. We'd added daily specials and hoped no one would realize how much easier omelettes are.

When I got through to the hall, sure enough, another of them had arrived and was lugging in two duffels and a messenger bag.

'Ramsay Buchanan,' he said, when he noticed me. He was dressed head-to-toe in Gore-Tex: those trousers that unzip to make shorts and a coat you could cook a chicken in. 'I'm Paul's brother. I see his car out there.'

'Oh, yes,' I said. 'There's a resembl—' His look stopped me. He was definitely related to the lawyer with the watch, just as tall and even slimmer. Rangy from triathlons was my guess. But his face was scarred all over from old acne. It wasn't ugly exactly. It was as if he'd been made out of different material from other people, like an alligator bag instead of calf-skin.

'I mean Buck's cousin. Hence the name,' I said. 'Welcome to The Breakers, Ramsay. I'm Donna, from –' I remembered Buck teasing me and turned it '– the holiday company. I'll be looking after you for the weekend.'

'Oh, no, you won't,' Ramsay said. 'I'm low maintenance. You'll be looking after Paul and Rosalie from dawn till midnight, and when Sasha gets here you might need back-up. All I need from you is the Wi-Fi code.'

I started to tell him, but a bellow from the far end of the corridor stopped me. 'Amun-Ramsay! King of the gods!' Buck had appeared round a half-open door and came loping along to wrap the newcomer in one of those violent, thumping hugs men give each other.

'Buckaroo!' Ramsay said. 'Have you been painting a ceiling? You've got white bits all over your hair.'

'Fuck off,' said Buck. 'At least I've *got* hair. St Paul's through here.'

They disappeared into the billiards room and a noise went up like something from a troop of primates in the jungle. It made me happy. You couldn't work in this business if you didn't like the sound of people having fun. I worked the sleeper from London to Inverness one summer, stag and hen parties every weekend, and *that* was a bit much. But ordinarily the sound of people in high spirits lifted me too.

'Ramsay must get clamsy in his plastic clothes,' I said. 'Ramsay with the ravaged face. Paul's brother.' I grabbed his luggage to put it in his room and annoy him. I knew his type: uncomfortable with service. He'd deny he wanted a drink, then try to make his own and spill ice cubes on the good furniture. And he wasn't going to be the worst. Peach was going to be the worst. She'd be putting towels in the wash at the wrong settings, wandering through to the kitchen with stacks of plates, mucking up my system.

The room with the pale walls and hessian had an en suite that was the back half of the bathroom next door so there was no window. We had found a great extractor fan, though. Silent and powerful. I set his messenger bag on the desk in front of the window, put the bigger duffel down in front of the wardrobe and, after a peek, took the smaller one in there. I wondered what he would say if I opened everything up and laid it out, spirited his bags away, like they did at real country houses with butlers. But all I did was fold a towel onto the marble shelf near the washbasin and leave his vanity-case (to give it its name) on top. Guests always think you're being respectful of their belongings, setting them on towels like that. Really it stops the dye from their cheap bags staining the counters.

I was going to enjoy this weekend, I decided, steering such a ragbag through the diceyest kind of party – a family reunion – and making sure they all had a marvellous time without any of them knowing it was me making it happen. Call me a puppet master, but that's why I love hospitality. I smiled at myself in the mirror and turned to go.

There was a woman standing in the middle of the room, hands on hips, glaring round.

'What the— Who are you?' she said.

'Hi, I'm Donna,' I began, coming forward with my hand out.

'It says "Ramsay" on the door,' she said. 'Did he pick you up en route? You're young enough to be his daughter!'

'I'm the Home From Home representative,' I said, taking a step back. 'I was just checking your cousin's—'

'Oh,' she said. 'Right. Well, he's not my cousin. He's nothing at all to me. Why does he get his own room?'

I took a breath. She wasn't joking. She had to be forty if a day but she was moaning about sharing a room with . . . Was *Peach* her cousin?

22

'Have you seen your own?' I said. 'You must be Jennifer, aren't you?' I swelled a little with pride. I wasn't just keeping up with the names, I was getting ahead of them. 'Yours is my favourite.' I pointed the way. 'The bath's humungous and the hot-water system can fill it twice over. There's a wonderful view of—'

She hadn't moved. 'What makes you think I'm not Kim?' she said. Her voice was dead and cold. 'Or Peach or Rosalie?'

The names swam and I hesitated. What made me think she wasn't Kim, the rich wife who'd rented the house and chosen the menu and the flowers, was that her plastic costume jewellery picked out the brightest colours in her striped tights. And her tights were pilled and stretched at the ankles. And the thin belt on her homemade dress made her look like a sack of potatoes.

'I've been corresponding with Kim.' That was a lie. My mum did all the emails. 'And the others are already here.'

'Where?' she demanded.

'Here!' said Peach, breezing in and throwing her arms around Jennifer. 'Jellifer! We're roomies. Did you know? We're having a midnight feast tonight and no arguments. Hey, Donna, do chefs do midnight feasts or do we sneak down?'

'*Jennifer*,' the woman said, her voice colder than ever. 'And I wasn't told I'd be sharing a room. If I'd known that, I wouldn't be here.'

'Well, aren't we a happy family!' It was Rosalie. She had taken her jacket and heels off, but still wore the pencil skirt of her business suit, with a tight white shirt tucked in. 'Donna, I was wondering about baths. Is it still a Rayburn downstairs? Will you be able to cook if I run off hot water?'

'What do you mean "still" a Rayburn?' Jennifer said. 'Have you been here before? Are you all down here together every other weekend? Why add me this time?'

'God almighty, Jell— Jennifer,' Peach said. 'Don't you *remember* this place?'

'What are you talking about?'

'Don't you remember the party?' said Rosalie.

'What party? If you lot are going to spend the whole weekend reliv—' She stopped and I think she changed colour. 'Are you talking about Sasha's birthday party?'

'Of course, that's right,' Peach said. 'We were all staying and you only came for that one day, didn't you?'

Jennifer swallowed. There was a sheen of sweat on her brow. 'But that was at the beach,' she said.

'Right there.' Peach pointed out the window. 'The trees have grown up. It threw me too.'

I thought I could see droplets forming on Jennifer's top lip and she was the colour of pistachio ice-cream.

'Are you all right?' said Rosalie. 'Do you need to sit down?'

'You need your feet up and a cup of tea.' I steered her out of the stone-coloured room and into her own. Rosalie and Peach came bustling after us.

'You've had the longest drive of us all, Jelly-Belly,' Rosalie said. 'And I bet you set straight off after work without so much as a mochaccino. Jennifer's a teacher,' she added to me.

Of course she was. I would have put good money on it. Teachers were hands-down the worst guests possible. They're always knackered and they sulk if they don't get told how hard they work every ten minutes. Not to mention the fact that they're used to being the boss of the room and they never stop telling everyone else what to do. The worst week of my entire life was being the chalet-maid for five teachers at Aviemore one wet November.

Back in the cherry-wood room, I manhandled Jennifer onto the chaise longue, then put an extra cushion at her back and one under her knees. I twitched the cover off one of the beds and tucked it round her. 'Sweet tea and a plain biscuit coming up,' I said. 'Try to close your eyes.'

'Can you shut the window?' she asked, in the wan voice of an invalid.

'Well,' I said. 'Maybe the fresh air?'

'It's that noise.'

I cocked my head but all I could hear was the sea.

'Let me,' said Rosalie.

'And I'll move out and bunk in with my brother,' Peach said. 'No arguments. It'll be a laugh for us. You can have this place to yourself, Jelly.'

'I'm sorry,' Jennifer said. The fuss had reached her required minimum. 'It's just I can't sleep if there's someone else in the room. I'm sorry I got upset. Forgetting things throws me into a panic. Mum started when she wasn't even seventy and I'm seriously thinking about a care home for her now.'

We all shushed and murmured and withdrew ourselves to the corridor. I closed the door.

'There's a little room at the end with a sofa-bed,' I said to Peach. 'If you're determined to move.'

'I'm determined not to catch whatever classroom bug she's incubating,' Peach said. 'No way she panicked at forgetting she'd been here.'

'I think she panicked at remembering,' Rosalie said. Then she glanced at me. 'Although Aunt Verve is completely gaga, it's true. My poor old pa's started to go too, you know.'

'No!' said Peach. 'Has he?'

We were along at the head of the stair now. I pushed open the door of the snug. 'What do you think?' I said. 'It's a full double with a good mattress.'

Peach wandered in and looked around, lost in memories.

'Are Jennifer's mum and your dad related, then?' I asked Rosalie. 'Only Jennifer just told me Ramsay's not her cousin.'

'We're all related,' she said. 'But not all by blood.' Paul's words came back to me and I felt a tickle at the back of my neck. 'Oh, I get it now!' Rosalie went on. 'That's why she's here. She's on the pull and Ramsay's fair game. She never usually bothers with us. Don't you think, Peach?'

Peach, still looking out of the window, was gripping the edge of the velvet curtain so tightly she was crushing it and making the curtain rings, six feet above her head, squeak against the pole.

'What?' she said, turning.

'Didn't you wonder why Jelly suddenly decided she loved us again? It's strictly Christmas cards and funerals normally.'

Peach didn't answer. I don't think she'd heard a word. 'I'm not going to use this room,' she said. She wasn't green, like Jennifer, but she wasn't as rosy as she'd been five minutes ago. 'It'll be a laugh, in with the Buck. Despite all the farting.'

'It *is* a gloomy room,' I said. 'We thought of it as a winter snug, really.'

'*You?*' said Peach. I bit my lip. There was no advantage in letting them know we owned the business, that we were responsible for the house as well as the weekend. I had learned that in my first job, only finding out 'the manager' was really 'the proprietor' when she sold up and moved away. It kept the complaints down like a dream, her saying she would inform the owner. I'd remembered it and advised my mum to do the same when we struck out on our own. She'd lapped it up.

'See?' she'd said. 'I'm not doing you the favour. You're doing me the favour. You're the one that's going to make this work.'

She was being kind. Truth was, I'd come badly unstuck. I was trying to build a hospitality empire before I was thirty when I found out the emperor, my beloved boyfriend, had no clothes. At least, not when I found him in our best rentable bedroom with one of the barmaids. I was too embarrassed to be heartbroken, but a bit too heartbroken to be business-like.

The upshot was I fled without a penny of the dosh I'd forked over and went back to Skye. Back to a one-street town where the shop had closed down decades back and the café was open Thursday night to Sunday night, Easter to October only.

I thought I could move in with my mum and lick my wounds awhile. That was embarrassing too, but I wasn't the only one from my class living at home nearly ten years after school had ended. And I wasn't too proud to pick up some waitressing – even kitchen-work – in a hotel in Portree.

But I'd landed in the middle of my mum's big plan. I'd always thought she was happy with the online world. Sometimes I'd even got the sense she looked down on me, mixing drinks and making beds. But she'd caught the bug now and no mistake. My grandpa had left her a wedge when he shuffled off, The Breakers was on the market, and she was on fire.

'Why Galloway?' was all I'd said. My whole life, my family had lived right there, on Skye, in the middle of a massive tourist trap.

'Cheap,' my mum had said. 'Half the price we'd pay up here. Closer to cities too, for short breaks. Closer to the M74, for the English.'

'Home From Home call it a snug,' I corrected myself. 'I just can't help feeling a bit . . . What's the word?'

'Invested, committed, possessive?' said Rosalie. 'Proprietorial!'

'It's such a lovely house,' I said. 'And I love houses.'

'Yes, it's not a bad old pile,' said Rosalie. 'And it's certainly very adaptable. So . . . if Peach is adamant, is there any chance Jennifer could have Ramsay's room and Ramsay could have hers? With the two beds? Thing is, if there's a big dinner planned, I'll have eight hours of warthog.'

'What?' I said.

'Paul. He snores like Henry the Eighth when he's been drinking.'

Peach was staring at Rosalie. 'Seriously?' she said. 'You're going to sling him out?'

'Oh, don't judge me,' said Rosalie. 'First it was the Jack and Jill bathrooms and they – let me tell you – changed my life. Then we roped an extra bedroom into the master suite. And I don't care what you think. I sleep like a baby and, if he comes to visit me, it's another honeymoon. Speaking of which,' she went on, holding her foot up and twisting her ankle this way and that, 'I need to shave my legs.'

'That's not what you meant, is it?' I said to Peach, when she was gone.

Peach shivered but she managed to give me a smile. 'No,' she said. 'I don't actually believe in ghosts, but I wouldn't sleep on my own in this house if you paid me.'

Chapter 3

1991

'Mu-um!' I can feel tears threaten, but if there's anything she comes down on harder than 'language' it's 'waterworks'.

'Don't "Mum" me, Carmen,' she says. Her lips are pressed together hard enough to turn them white. She's peeling potatoes, swiping at them as if they've offended her. 'You wanted to go and you're going. Can't see any loose ends there.'

'What's the point of going if I have to babysit?'

'If the older ones don't mind babysitting *you*, you shouldn't mind babysitting Lynsey.'

'How are they...?' But it's not worth finishing. She's smirking down at her potato now, as if she's made some brilliant point. I turn on the ball of my foot, making the sole of my bee-bob squeak on the vinyl, knowing I'm leaving a black mark there that she'll have to rub off with her slipper because otherwise it'll drive her nuts. I wrench open the kitchen door and, in my head, I slam it shut so hard it shakes the whole house and gives Mum such a fright she bites her tongue. In my head that's what I do. Actually, I leave it swinging behind me, making a draught. That'll bug her too but not so much she'll come out waving her potato peeler and shouting at me for everyone to hear. We live two doors down from the pub, and on a sunny Saturday at the end of August, the beer garden's probably full of lucky kids from my school who get crisps and Coke while their parents have a glass of wine. They'd love to hear Mum screeching at me, in her slippers, with her potato peeler.

Because, of course, we're having spuds with our chops for tea. Never mind that it's the hottest day of the year, hotter than any day the whole of the summer holidays, and everyone else is in the beer garden, in sandals. Mum's got her pink slippers with the sheepskin linings on, and she's peeling spuds to boil till they fall apart, and making sure there's no draughts in her kitchen.

Then I remember. The potatoes aren't for me. Because I'm going to a party. I slip round behind the back of the shed to Lynsey's swing set and sit straddling the leather seat, scuffing my bee-bobs in the bark Dad put down for a soft landing. I've done it! Even with my little sister tagging along, I'm still going. The sun's dazzling through the leaves of our magnolia tree and the bits of chaff and midges look like gold dust. Even the smell of the grass clippings Dad tipped out over the back fence can't bother me.

I've seen just one of them only once and the sun was dazzling that day too, spangling the water so it looked like sequins. I always go to the beach to sunbathe, because if I try it in the back garden, Mum's always nipping at me to pull my straps up and put some shorts on over my bikini bottoms. And there's never anyone there once the Scottish schools go back.

30

I don't know when I first noticed a dark blob out in the bay that could have been a seal, or a piece of driftwood with weed tangled round it. He was no good at surfing, that was for sure. I never saw him stand up all the time I was lying there. I didn't even know he was a person until a car parked up on the headland and someone leaned on the horn. Then he let himself be carried in on the next wave and clambered out of the tide.

He flicked his head to get his wet hair out of his eyes and reached behind him to pull his wetsuit tag down so his brown back showed between the two sides of the open zip. That's when I was sure he'd seen me. Then he was walking up the beach with his surfboard under his arm, while whoever it was up there kept jabbing at the car horn.

He wasn't looking at me, but the way he was headed to the steps, he was going to pass within a metre, and the way he was scuffing big gouts of sand up ahead of him, he was going to cover me in it.

'Hey,' I said when he was close.

He did this big fake startle, putting his hand against his chest like Mum when someone swears on the telly. His fingers were purple with the cold.

'Are you a lifeguard?' he said. I was squinting up and he moved so he was blocking the sun from my eyes. His head was in silhouette, with bright gold drips swelling on the rats' tails of his hair, then dropping and shattering into specks of glitter, like mercury, on the black rubber of his wetsuit shoulders. 'Are you a sand monitor? You're not a mermaid.' I was sure he was looking at my legs when he said that last bit.

'I'm just trying to sunbathe without getting stood on.' I knew I sounded like I couldn't take a joke but I couldn't think of anything else to say.

'Wait a minute,' he said. 'I know exactly who you are.' The person in the car leaned on the horn for so long it ran out and sort of hiccuped, and the boy in the wetsuit waved and started walking away, taking a big elaborate swerve around me and placing his feet as if he had snowshoes on so he didn't disturb a single grain of sand.

'Wait. What do you mean?' I called after him. 'Who am I?'

He turned round and ran backwards for a few steps, grinning at me. Now he was facing the sun I could see his snaggle teeth and perfect skin. I put a hand up to cover my chin where I'd squeezed a spot until it turned scabby. He slicked his hair back with one hand and grinned even wider. Maybe if you had skin like that, the teeth didn't matter. 'You've got your mum's eyes,' he said, turned round again and ran away.

I lay down on my stomach and watched him, with his board on his head, scampering up the wooden steps to where the car was parked. A man got out of the driver's seat. They didn't tie the board onto a roof rack. They just shoved it on the back seat and left one pointy end sticking out the window. The boy shrugged off the top bit of his wetsuit, then peeled it down over his hips. He was far away and I couldn't really see but he was the same colour all the way down except for a round dark patch. I flipped over on my back and put my arm across my eyes and I heard faint laughter over the sound of the engine and slamming doors. He thought I was looking at him in the noody. Well, I *was* looking at him in the noody, but only because he'd taken his wetsuit off and didn't have a cozzie on. Or maybe it peeled off by accident. Maybe he was mortified. Maybe the man was laughing at him and the boy wasn't laughing at all. And neither of them was laughing at me. Maybe.

I know what Mum would say. She's full of them every night when she comes home. 'Typical towners,' she tells us. 'Never catch a glimpse before ten and then they're slopping around in their pyjamas till lunchtime. Not a one of them owns a dressing-gown. I don't know where to look some mornings.'

'It has been a bit warm,' I say. 'And if they're all family.'

'Your guess is as good as mine on that, Carmen. There's six kids and goodness only knows *who* they are. There's only one dose of parents there, I know. And you'd never think they had six to look after. Lying around drinking wine and letting them all run wild.'

I say nothing. It sounds like heaven. Mum wakes us up every morning at the same time, schooldays and weekends, summers too.

'And the mess they leave! The bathrooms would make you weep. Some days it takes me all morning to clear that kitchen! I asked if they wanted me to stop on and make a dinner, because near as I can tell they're all just going their own way. Packets and tins and everything in the microwave. Never cover anything. There's sauce and cheese and gravy spattered all over it. I had to throw a dish out yesterday.'

'Shocking,' I say. But under my breath so she won't hear me.

'A good enamelled oven dish, but there was nothing for it. Spare ribs, I reckon. Barbecue sauce. I found the bones out on the patio. And it would be me called for all sorts if they got rats coming round, wouldn't it?'

'Hard to say.' But she's right. She cleans that holiday house until you could eat off the bog seat, but if anything ever goes wrong – bird's nests, blown fuses, fluff fire in the dryer – they

33

always phone up with that same injured tone in their voice, expecting her to drop everything.

'Heaven knows what it'll be like after a party,' she's saying now.

'They might clear up for a party,' I say. Any time we've got relations coming to visit Mum never lets go of the bleach bottle for days beforehand.

'Not that kind of party,' Mum says. She's wiping the fronts of the radiators with a fistful of white bread – one of the things I pray no one else will ever see her do – but she stops and gives me a hard stare. I'm not wearing eyeliner or strips of lace in my hair or anything. There's nothing for her to object to.

'What?' I say.

But she just resettles herself and goes back to dragging that stupid lump of sliced white down the ridges of the radiator, kneeling there on the carpet, with a cushion in a carrier bag under her knees. I wonder if she does that at Knockbreak House. If those six kids saw her slip a plastic bag over a cushion before she put it down on a clean carpet they'd think she was some kind of maniac.

It's not till later that night I find out why she was staring at me. I'm passing the top of the stairs on my way for a pee and I hear my name.

'We've never even met these people. How do they know Carmen? How do they even know we've got girls at all?'

I sit down on the top step, holding onto both banisters and lowering my weight carefully so the stair doesn't creak.

'I do chat, Rob,' Mum says. 'I do pass the time of day. And you met the parents when you dropped me off that morning.'

'And this is one of the kids, is it? That's having the party?'

'It's a sixteenth birthday party. They're everywhere from

34

twelve to . . . Well, I think the oldest cousin's coming down from college. But the birthday boy wants a proper kid's party. Cake and games. Sweet, really, this day and age. And so they wanted more children there, I think. For the games. Six isn't enough for Pass the Parcel and The Farmer's in His Den.'

'They're hardly going to be playing that! Crowd of teenagers? Are you sure they don't want our girls there to fetch and carry?'

'Oh, Rob!' Mum's been bitching them up left and right the whole two weeks they've been at Knockbreak but that's one thing. Anyone else saying a cross word about them and she's turning on a sixpence to defend them with her dying breath. I know what's going on. She's already told them I'd love to go to their stupid party and she can't back out now. Dad'll never work that out, though. He thinks they're talking it over before they decide, like he always thinks when they never are. 'Anyway, it's not "our girls". It was just Carmen got mentioned. She ran into the one with the birthday. Met him on the beach and he took a shine.'

I feel a flutter in the top of my stomach. He took a *shine*? That boy with the surfboard? I heave myself to my feet, hanging from the banisters again, then step up carefully from the top stair to the landing. The floorboards don't make a sound.

Back from the bathroom, I put the light on in my end of the wardrobe and lie looking at the sad selection of clothes hanging there, wondering what outfit I could put together in a million years that would be good enough.

When I hear Mum getting a lift home the next day, I'm sure it's him. I'm on my own in the bedroom, trying things on. If Mum would let me wear my faded jeans – if I could get out of the house without her seeing that a threadbare patch

35

has worn right through on one knee – I could pair them with my hankie-point top and pull it down off one shoulder. And I could paint my fingers and toes to match. Only trouble is I've got the top on right now, checking what it looks like, so I can't go downstairs or he'll see it.

I sidle to the edge of the window and put my eye close to the gauzy folds of the net curtains, watching. It's the big black car, almost too wide for our lane but he still wiggles it round so the passenger side is closest to the kerb and Mum's got less far to dash in the rain. Even so, he gets out and comes round, holding up a golf umbrella. I can't see anything except the bottoms of black jeans, rolled up, and green bee-bobs, the same as mine but a different colour.

Mum gets out, scrambling and awkward, trying to put her own scootery wee brolly up as she digs around for her keys. They disappear from view under the windowsill as they come up the path, him taking long strides, ignoring the way the puddles on our crazy-paving splash up the sides of his ankles. I lean forward until my head's against the window, sliding a bit on the net. Lynsey's shell-covered crap shifts and I move back. She's commandeered the whole windowsill and filled it with bowls and frames and ashtrays, all dipped in Polyfilla and studded with shells from the beach. They crumble in the damp and she's always having to superglue the shells back on, so they get uglier and uglier. And they're hideous to start with. I've given up arguing about them.

From downstairs I can hear the front door opening and the sound of Mum making a fuss about something. She's probably offering tea and biscuits or maybe even petrol money. I wouldn't put it past her. I can't pick out the words as he answers but I can tell from his tone he's saying no, trying to get away.

36

'Oh, Mum,' I say, under my breath.

'Carmen!' Her voice comes up the stairs like a squawk.

I freeze, my heart thumping. No way I'm going down there, not only revealing my party outfit but letting him see my hair in a scrunchie too. She won't come up, will she? She won't send *him* up? No, she wouldn't send him up. We're not allowed boys in our bedroom.

The front door's opening again.

'No, no, not at all.' His voice is louder now as he tries to get out of Mum's clutches. There's a laugh in it somewhere and I can imagine him telling the rest of them when he gets home and all of them giggling. Sniggering about her. The door closes and then he's hopping and splashing down the path again. I draw back so he won't see my ghost face through the net. He opens the back door of the big black car and shoots the umbrella in like a javelin. And then I can see what I should have known, if I had a brain in my head. It's not even *him*! It's a totally different person. And of course it is, because he's just going to have his sixteenth birthday and this boy's old enough to drive a car.

'Didn't you hear me shouting?' Mum's standing in my doorway. She's upstairs in her outdoor shoes. 'I wanted to introduce you to one of the youngsters who's going to be at the party. He drove me home, because of the rain. Lovely manners. Buchanan, he's called. Buchanan Leslie.'

'What a daft name.'

I watch her struggle for a bit but in the end the pull of gossip wins and the backward drag of politeness loses. 'That's nothing,' she says. 'There's one called Sasha too. The birthday boy, actually.'

Sasha, I say to myself. Sasha and Carmen sound good

together. And for once I'm glad to have a name that's usuan, just a magnet for wind-ups. When Mum was having me she said Dad could name a girl and she would name a boy. She was sure she *was* having a boy and she didn't want to call him Arnold after Grandpa, like Dad kept saying. Then when I popped out – when it turned out my auntie's swinging pocket-watch and Mum eating pickles and treacle had been wrong – Dad said, 'Carmen,' and they were stuck with it. Next time it was Mum's shot and Lynsey was Lynsey. We're more of a Lynsey family, really. Our dog's called Laddie, our cat was called Snowy and the goldfish are called Bit and Bob. I stick out like a sore thumb. But put me in a party in a big house, with *Sasha*, and I'll finally be right at home.

'Is sixteen too old for Airfix models, do you think?' Mum's saying.

'What? Yes!' I say. 'Jeez, don't make me walk in there with a *toy* for him, Mum.'

'Don't "Jeez" me,' Mum says. 'And don't go talking like that at the party and showing me up. They've got lovely manners.'

She hasn't got a clue, I think. But then, as it turns out, neither have I.

Chapter 4

Most of the food supplies were still sitting on the big oval table in the breakfast bit of the kitchen. Looking at them made me feel weary, and feeling weary made me feel scared. If I was tired already with three days and fourteen different food services to go I was sunk before I'd left harbour.

Or maybe I could blame the room. Why had I let my mum talk me into bottle-green wallpaper for a north-facing aspect? This was our only living space when the house was full. She had argued it was a waste of time trying to lighten such a gloomy place, with its low ceiling and its one window looking out over a few feet of cobbled yard to the sheds set into the looming bulk of the hill. She said we should embrace it and accentuate it. So the walls were nearly black and she'd chosen a black tablecloth and chair covers to match.

She was wrong. It should have been sunshine and gingham and strong lights left on all day. If we had a good late season we'd plough some cash into it during the dead time after New Year and take a second run.

At least she hadn't tried to dictate the kitchen. I had chosen the teak worktops that would stand up to a knife, and the rubber floor, comfy underfoot. There was a good light over the stove and two sinks for different jobs. I'd added a few touches to entice the clients who wanted the house self-catering – a row of jugs and copper jelly moulds – but it had the bones of a proper cook's kitchen.

I started poking around in the bags and boxes. Normally, I'd unwrap the good cheese and redo it in greaseproof sheets and foil, but it was only till tomorrow and it would be fine as it was. And the grapes I'd planned to dip in sugar crust and chill could go straight into the fruit bowl. Healthier as well as quicker. In fact, I thought, as I looked at the hamper sitting there, maybe I could use the foie gras, caviar, Gentleman's Relish and smoked oysters for the hors d'oeuvres. Save myself fiddling away at cheese straws and tartlets.

Maybe it was going to be okay. I walked to the French windows that led out the side of the house to the long straight stretch that would be a croquet lawn again once we had the funds to re-turf it. That and the tennis court. A few winter-breaks and a lucky Christmas would put us close to the black and no one would care much about the garden until spring, even down here in balmy Galloway. By next June we'd have a summerhouse and brick barbecue at least. If the couple of years after that went as well as I was dreaming, there was a perfect spot for a hot-tub too. In five years at the most, we'd buy a wee cottage somewhere close by and wouldn't have to shift out to the static caravan hidden round the back when the whole house was let self-catering.

I turned from my daydream and back to my work. This kitchen was a long way from the guests. Nipping back and forward to see they had everything they wanted was going to cut in hard to my cooking time. I glanced over at the deep shelf beside the stove where the pot of wooden spoons sat and the oven gloves were clipped to the hot pipes with magnets.

I had stared at my mum when she suggested it. I'd thought she was joking.

'An intercom?'

'More like a baby monitor. You'll hear them but they won't hear you. It's just for this one weekend. If they're sitting moaning about the tea being finished – hey presto, you appear with a fresh pot. They'll be happy with the service and what they don't know can't hurt them.'

'But we can't be listening in to them!' It was the first time my mum's total lack of experience with face-to-face customer service had come up.

'We're scrubbing their toilets and changing their sheets,' she said. 'And I wasn't thinking of the bedrooms. The dining room and drawing room. Just this weekend, like I said. Or I can tell the wedding fair to give it to the runner-up.'

In the end, I'd let her put in the receiver and two discreet transmitters, but I'd made a pact with myself that I wouldn't use them and I was determined to stick to it. I washed my hands, put a clean apron on and started the cucumber sandwiches. The freshest of fresh white bread, the best unsalted butter whipped and light, wafer thin cucumber slices cut with a mandolin and pressed between cloths. A sprinkle of pepper, a few drops of sherry vinegar to make it pop, crusts off and perfect triangles. I beamed at the plate when it was finished. The scones were cool enough to load onto another plate. Two kinds of homemade jam and I was done.

I shot another look at the baby monitor. Were they all in the drawing room? Were they ready for tea? I reached out, rummaged behind the oven gloves and flipped the switch.

'Just light it. We can hardly ring a bell. She's not a housemaid.' That was probably Paul, the grumpy one. Or the one who hated service, maybe.

'Yeah, you're right. Why would they lay it if it wasn't for lighting?' That was Buck.

'Maybe tea's not in here.' That was definitely Peach. 'No point wasting a load of logs if we're going to be sitting in the library, is there?'

I switched it off and shot along to the drawing room, with the tray of teacups.

'Would you like a fire?' I said, edging round the door. 'It's getting chilly.'

'You're an angel,' said Peach. She was in one end of the smallest sofa with her furry slippers kicked off and her feet up in Buck's lap. He had his arms folded above them.

'A poppet, a treasure, a godsend, a brick and a boon,' said Rosalie. She had bagged the comfiest couch and was curled up in it, still in her tight shirt and pencil skirt.

Paul was leaning against the fireplace with a whisky in his hand. He had taken his tie off and rolled up his sleeves, but he hadn't changed either. That's the sign of really good clothes, I always reckon. You're not dying to shuck them as soon as you can. One day . . .

Ramsay looked up from his phone. He had peeled off the Gore-Tex and was down to a thin nylon top and cycle shorts. 'How's Jennifer?'

I opened my eyes wide. 'I forgot to take her tea!'

'Do her good,' said Paul, stepping out of my way. 'There's

never been a family gathering in the history of the Mowbray-Buchanan-Leslie clan when Jennifer didn't come down with something invisible and inconvenient.'

'Oh, Paul, have some pity,' said Peach.

'You didn't see the "migraine" she pulled at Sasha and Kim's wedding,' said Rosalie.

'I know you were in labour,' said Buck, 'but, honestly, Peach, if you'd come along and pushed the kid out at the reception you'd have been less of a spectacle than Jelly with a headache.'

'Donna, ask Jennifer if she sent the hamper,' said Ramsay. 'Since no one else will admit to it.'

'I've never bum-dialled Fortnum's,' Buck said. 'Although I suppose there's a first time for everything.'

'Isn't that how the KGB infiltrated dissident groups?' said Ramsay. 'Bugged gifts?'

I tried to laugh along but 'bugging' was a bit too close to what was rigged up in the kitchen.

'Stop it, you lot,' Rosalie said. 'You're making Donna uncomfortable.' She must be pretty eagle-eyed to have seen it. I ducked my head and carried on unloading the tray.

'I'll light the fire,' said Buck, heaving his sister's feet off his lap and standing. 'Anything to get Peach's trotters away from my nostrils.'

'Cheeky bastard,' said Peach. 'I was hoping for a foot massage.'

'Well, you shouldn't have got divorced, then. I'm off the hook for the whole weekend when it comes to doing chores for womankind.' He knelt on the hearthrug and reached for the box of matches.

'Although Donna's got you on your knees pretty quick,'

Paul said. I didn't join in the laughter this time. I was almost out the door anyway, not sure whether I was meant to hear the joke or not. I put on a spurt to make sure I didn't catch whatever they said next.

Back in the kitchen, the kettle was beginning to rumble. I splashed some of the water in on top of a chamomile teabag, grabbed a plate, a biscuit and one of the small trays and headed for the stairs.

Jennifer had dozed off. I stood over her, looking at the rapid darting of her eyes under her closed lids. She was dreaming about the sea, I thought. Or at least the sound of it had got into her sleep. Every time a wave crashed, her eyes fluttered.

I bent and eased the little tray onto the table at the side of the chaise. 'Jennifer,' I said softly.

She rose up out of sleep and out of the chaise in one movement, sending the table flying. An arc of pale yellow tea caught me from neck to knee. After one wide-eyed moment of complete blankness, she spoke. 'Oh! It's you. I'm. Oh, my gosh. Are you okay?'

'I'm fine,' I said, pulling my shirt away from my front.

'Has it scalded you?'

'I'm fine,' I repeated. I didn't want to tell her I hadn't made her tea with boiling water. 'I'm sorry I gave you a fright.'

She sank down again. 'You didn't. I was having a bad dream.'

'I'll get you another cup.' I was trying not to be annoyed that she hadn't matched my apology with one of her own. Not a word about my white shirt or the white carpet. 'Although, if you're feeling better, real tea is served any minute in the drawing room. Nothing too heavy or rich.'

'Who's down there?' She shrank into herself a little, as if she didn't really want to hear. So I gave her a full answer. It let me run through the names again. Two birds, one stone.

'Buck and Peach, Paul and Rosalie. Ramsay. We just need you to complete the welcome party for the happy couple.'

Jennifer hauled herself back to her feet. She seemed twice as heavy as the woman who had sprung from lying to standing a minute ago. 'Sasha making a big entrance as usual,' she said, as she picked up a briefcase and made for the door.

'And don't worry about this.'

'This what? Oh, the floor, you mean?' She gave the long stain a casual glance. 'Surely you've got it Scotchgarded. I mean, a white carpet in a holiday home?'

I stuck my tongue out once she'd gone and used her big bath sheet to mop the stain. She didn't need it to cover her modesty anyway, since she'd wangled a room of her own.

———————

I had three changes of black and whites, but I hadn't expected to trash a set before tea on the first day. I shrugged out of them and held my shirt up to the meagre light coming in my bedroom window. It was a goner and I threw it in the wash, but I hung the trousers on the back of the door by a belt loop. Once they dried they'd be fine again. I skipped down the back stairs.

Tea looked perfect. Snowy mounds of food and the jams sparkling like jewels. Enormous pots of tea and hot water.

I scanned the room as I entered. All there, except Rosalie. All sprawled on couches, except Jennifer, who was in the bay window with a pile of papers in front of her and a laptop open, and Buck sitting on his heels at the fire. The paper had burned away but the twigs weren't even charred.

'Let me take care of that,' I said, putting out a hand to help him to his feet. He took it and leaned heavily, groaned too, as he stood.

'Don't let Ro-Ro see you,' Paul said, going over to Jennifer.

'See me marking?' said Jennifer. 'Does she really think a teacher can take a weekend off marking?'

'She's going for us handing over our devices to live like Bushmen.'

'*Bushmen?*' said Jennifer, turning and looking at Paul over the tops of her reading glasses. 'I can't believe you said that word.'

'San, if you'd rather,' said Paul. 'Or Basarwa. !Kung in Namibia, of course. I have actually been to Africa, Jennifer. Have you?'

'Shut up, Paul,' said Peach.

'Hey, look!' said Buck, pointing out of the window. 'Aw!'

I craned but couldn't see over the high back of the couch. I knew what he was pointing at, though.

'Aw, look!' said Peach. 'A black rabbit. Oh, it's adorable. Is it a baby?'

The black rabbits had been nibbling the grass of the front lawn all summer. They were the first thing that had made me glad of Galloway. I still missed the otters and dolphins, the eagles most of all, but black bunny rabbits right there on the doorstep was something. In the evenings, the sinking sun shone through the long hairs on their backs so they glowed.

'I think they're adults,' Ramsay said. 'The same genes are responsible for them being small and being black. Cute, though.'

'Do you mind us calling them *black* rabbits, Jennifer?' said Buck.

'Shut up,' Peach told him. She went back to the couch and lifted the teapot. 'I'll be Mother.'

'We're perfectly capable of pouring our own,' Jennifer said, joining her. She sat so heavily that a dribble of tea came out of the spout.

'Christ's sake, Jelly,' said Paul. 'If Buck can cope with being emasculated by this slip of a girl fixing his fire you can let Peach pour some tea without your ovaries shrivelling. It's only an expression.'

I was facing the hearth, undoing the pile of twigs to put new paper in, so I didn't have to look at any of their faces, but the silence was long and cold and broken only by a miserable sniff from Jennifer.

'I can't believe I agreed to come,' she said. 'I can't believe I set myself up to be attacked by you all again. I mean, I've given up hoping for any actual gratitude ...'

'"You all"? Who all?' said Buck. 'I didn't attack you. Ramsay didn't attack you.'

'I didn't attack her either,' said Paul. 'I criticized her. She criticized me and then I criticized her. I'm sick of the way everyone bleats about being attacked and being b—'

'Why are you talking about me as if I'm not here?' Jennifer said.

'Well, if we're not allowed to talk *to* you ...' Paul said.

'And we're not allowed to talk *about* you ...' Buck added.

'And something tells me you wouldn't like being ignored either ...' said Ramsay.

'Why are you all so determined to bully me?' Jennifer sounded close to tears.

'Bullied!' said Paul. 'Bingo. That's what I was going to say. Bleating about being attacked and *bullied*.'

'Oh, come on, everyone,' said Peach. 'Let's—'

'Does "everyone" include me?' said Jennifer.

'Of course,' Peach said. 'Come on, eh? We all know better than this.'

'I can't believe you're including me. I didn't say anything.' Jennifer sniffed and turned back to her marking.

'I'm the one who didn't say anything,' said Ramsay. 'You snapped at Peach for pouring the tea.'

'Right,' I said, standing up. 'Ready for another try.'

The silence told me they'd forgotten I was kneeling there.

'What must you think of us all?' said Peach. 'Reverting to our fractious childhood games as soon as we're together again.'

'Who's doing the honours?' I said, holding out the big box of household matches.

'Go for it,' said Buck. 'I can't stand any more emasculation.'

'It was nothing to do with your fire-lighting powers,' I said, kneeling again. 'The flue wasn't open. You have to pull on this wee chain to lower it and get a draught going.'

'Well, that's completely different,' said Ramsay. 'There's no shame in a man not understanding engineering!'

'Fuck off,' said Buck. 'Donna, these little sandwiches are to die for,' he added in a camp lisp.

'And another thing,' Jennifer said. 'I don't care for that kind of language.'

'So don't use it,' said Paul.

Peach gave a long groan. 'Oh, Jell! We were pals again.'

I heard Jennifer slam her laptop shut and flounce out, but the fire was taking every bit of my concentration. We'd got the chimneys swept and we'd done a clear test run, but something was wrong now. None of the smoke was going upwards and when the twigs caught, the little ribbons that were coiling out into the room turned into thick dark rolls. I batted at the flames with both hands and then with a folded newspaper tugged out of the kindling basket. All that did was make more smoke. It belched out and I coughed.

'I'm starting to feel better about myself,' Buck said. Then he coughed too.

I opened a double sheet of newspaper and held it over the mouth of the fireplace trying to get the chimney to draw, but the smoke curled out around its edges.

'Uh, I might need my inhaler,' said Peach.

'I'll open a window.' It was either Paul or Ramsay speaking, hard to tell, although it didn't seem like Paul to be so caring.

'I'm really sorry about this,' I said. I took the poker and pushed the bigger logs off the kindling then stirred the kindling sticks out of shape to kill the fire quickly. Now there were scraps of charred paper in with the smoke that billowed out. I could feel myself changing colour and tears pricking behind my eyes. Unless it was the smoke doing that too.

'Shit,' I muttered. I bent closer in and angled the poker upwards, jabbing it to see if the flue was really open. It banged against something that shouldn't have been there. That was it! The flue cover was stuck. Only the hollow 'pock, pock' didn't sound like a poker hitting metal.

Behind me, the guests were opening windows and fanning the door to the hall, and they were all coughing. They weren't complaining or blaming me but still I felt like howling. What a fiasco! I found the edge of the obstruction with the hook on the end of the poker and gave it a good tug. A square black object fell into the hearth, puffing out the last of the red embers and sending a cloud of smoke and ash three feet into the room.

'What's that?' said Ramsay.

'A box!' said Buck. 'Secret treasure?'

'It wasn't there yesterday,' I said. 'Don't!' I added, as Paul reached out. 'It'll be hot.'

He gave me a screwball look and kept reaching, as he had been, for the fire tongs. He picked the box up and turned it this way and that. Smoke still curled off it.

'What the hell?' It was Rosalie, appearing in the door fresh from her bath. She had a black sweater and leggings on and her hair was slicked back in a ponytail. She looked ready for the catwalk, even without make-up. 'What happened?'

'Did you put this box up the chimney?' Paul said, holding it out in the tongs.

'Wha'?' said Rosalie. She lifted one of her long cuffs and covered her mouth and nose. 'God, what a stink. Why am I getting the blame, out of interest?'

'Because everyone else was here and would have stopped the fire being lit,' Ramsay said.

'Actually . . .' said Paul. He was turning it this way and that, looking at it closely. I wished he wouldn't because he might as well have been waving a smudge stick around. I coughed, not exactly authentically but hoping he'd get the idea. 'Actually, I don't think it *is* a box. I think it's just a lump. There's no opening. No hinge. No way to get into it.'

'Give it here,' said Ramsay. He took the tongs out of Paul's hands and shook them. 'It must be a box. It's hollow and there's something inside it.'

'Ooh, very mysterious,' Peach said. 'Soldered shut, is it?'

'Aw, wait!' said Buck. 'How dumb can we get? It's a locked box!'

There was a silence then. I don't know where the look started, because I couldn't be watching everyone at once. But it skittered across all of them, like a daddy-long-legs bumping and rattling its way round the edge of a ceiling, looking for a way out and never finding one.

Paul spoke first. 'Donna, do you have anything like a sledge-hammer we could use to open it?'

'Do we actually want to open it?' said Peach.

'I'm not quite—' I began.

'Private joke,' said Rosalie. 'Very childish. Best ignored.'

'Best left to cool down before we try to open it anyway,' said Buck.

'And besides,' said Rosalie, 'I'm gasping for a cuppa.' She coughed. 'But I don't think I could—'

'Tea in the library!' I announced. 'I'll gather a couple of extra chairs if one of you brings the tray. This place needs to air awhile. I'm sorry for the disruption, everyone.'

They all hurried to hush me and reassure me that it was nothing, Rosalie starting a long story about food poisoning at a picnic, when they'd gone to an island in rowing boats. Peach bustled back and forwards with the teapots and the men insisted on carrying the armchairs. The whole operation took two minutes.

I reached up the library chimney with the long poker and, feeling nothing there but the four sides of the brick flue, I lit

51

the twigs and had the fire roaring by the time the pot was refreshed and everyone settled.

'This is much cosier, anyway,' Peach said. The library would have been a decent-sized living room in any ordinary house. Even with the extra seats it wasn't exactly cramped. That and the smoke disappearing up the chimney with only a trace of apple-wood scent left behind it straightened my face out at last.

'I agree,' said Rosalie. 'We're as snug as bunnies in a burrow.'

'Oh, hey, Ro-Ro,' Peach said, 'that reminds me. Look out the front. We saw the most adorable little black baby rabbit on the lawn. Like something from Disney.'

Rosalie unwound herself from the couch and went over to peer out. 'Oh dear,' she said, as the rest of us heard the sound of a car.

'Is that Sasha at last?' said Ramsay.

'Uh, no.' Rosalie stood back and let us see. A battered blue Escort was disappearing around the bend of the drive, as the rabbits scattered. 'We've lost Jennifer.'

'That was quick,' said Buck. 'Last time it took—'

'Shut up, Buck,' Peach said.

There was another silence and then Paul spoke. 'So. No Jennifer. This weekend might turn out to be fun after all.'

'And you get a room of your own!' said Buck to Peach, sounding hearty.

'I'll stick,' Peach said. 'I mean, I'll use the good bathroom, but when will you and I ever get the chance again?'

'Seriously?' said Rosalie. 'You're a better sister than I am.'

Peach shrugged but I caught her eye and thought again about the way she'd clutched the edge of the curtain in the snug. 'So shall we gather all the presents before they get here?' she said, and her voice was not quite steady.

'Oh, let's wait till tomorrow,' said Rosalie. 'That's the actual day.'

'You're right,' said Peach. 'If they don't like what we've bought it's less time they'll have to pretend. What did you get them, Rosie?'

'I managed to find a set of nesting vintage tins online. No idea if they're Kim's thing, though.'

'Who knows what Kim's thing is?' Buck said.

'Well, she likes money,' said Paul. 'And older men.'

'Shouldn't we maybe stop bitching her up before she even—' said Peach, then stopped at the sound of a car coming up the drive.

'We've brought them forth,' said Paul, 'with the pure power of our own snark. Here they are!'

I knew what I would see when I stood up straight and looked: a navy-blue Range Rover. A tall man in cashmere and cords getting out of the driver's side. A long-legged woman in red jeans and sheepskin stepping down and coming round to stand beside him.

'I'll go and welcome them, shall I?' I said. 'Tell them where you all are?'

It wasn't even so much that none of the guests was rushing to the door to greet their host. It was more that no one said a word. Ramsay, with his hands locked between his knees, stared at the carpet. Buck glanced at Peach, then quickly looked away. Rosalie was the only one who appeared calm. Her face was a mask, like she'd been freeze-framed. It was probably an expression she'd learned dealing with bolshy clients. But she was holding on tight to Peach's hand.

And suddenly it all made sense. Paul wasn't really sour. His griping and slagging, like Buck's bad jokes, Peach sleeping near her brother, Rosalie so bright and determined she was close to snapping, Jennifer running away. They were terrified. Every last one of them.

Chapter 5

They were still by the car when I got to the front door. I watched them, standing in the shadows where they wouldn't see me. He was beaming and had an arm slung round her neck, pointing at the house with his free hand as if he was showing it off. She nodded and smiled, but when he grabbed her and pulled her forward, she couldn't help wincing. I winced too, thinking about the graze on her palm pressed against his skin. I felt in the pocket of my trousers for the little nugget of blood-stained gravel there, then remembered I'd changed them.

'Hello,' I said, walking out into the light of the vestibule. 'Mrs and Mrs Mowbray!'

'Kim and Sasha,' the woman said. I knew she would, but it's a nice touch to show some deference every now and then.

'I'm Donna. I've been cc'd in on some of your emails. Welcome to The Breakers.'

'Changed its name, eh?' Sasha said. He'd packed in the beaming. And he'd dropped her hand too. 'Knockbreak

55

House not swanky enough to part gullible tourists from their cash?' He was handsome, with his thick hair and gym-figure, his good bones and his perfect teeth that were whiter than the gum he was working them on. But the scowl on his face ruined the dark eyes and the smooth skin.

I smiled at him and shrugged. 'Couldn't tell you. I just know it's The Breakers now.'

'Named after a nearby historic junkyard? Famous local dance championship?' Sasha had strolled in and was looking around. I ushered Kim inside to join him.

'The sea,' I said, holding up a finger and tilting my head as a wave came crashing in.

'Well, that's one mystery solved.' He still wasn't smiling.

'Right, then, everyone's in the library,' I said. 'I'll get a fresh pot of tea and . . . Would you like to unpack for yourselves or can I take your bags to your room?'

'I'll unpack,' Kim said. Blurted, really.

'Which one are we in?' said Sasha.

'The master suite.' At his frown, I added, 'Turn left at the far end of the corridor.'

He strode over to the door that opened onto the back rooms and we both listened to him pounding up the stairs. Kim let out a shaky breath and pushed her sunglasses up with her knuckles, revealing red eyes and dried mascara tracks down her cheeks.

'I've really sodded this up,' she said. 'And I don't even understand why.'

I hesitated. She looked about my age – much younger than her horrible husband – and she'd reached out like we were friends. I knew she'd regret it once she'd cheered up. I also knew me acting the same way back would turn into a two-star review for 'pushy staff'. I'd seen it before. So I tried to find a middle ground.

'Don't worry,' I said. 'It's stressful being the one who plans everything, but you can let go now and Home From Home will take care of it all.' She looked at me as if I was talking Greek. 'Come and splash your face,' I tried instead.

'I knew his family spent a summer in Galloway when he was wee,' she said, as I led her through to the staff loo. 'I thought that would make it extra-special. Even if I'd known he'd stayed at this very house before, I'd have thought that was brilliant. I don't know why he's so angry.'

'Men are weird.' She let out a snottery little laugh and then sniffed hard. 'Help yourself to any of that,' I added, pointing to my make-up that was lined up on the shelf behind the basin.

She wrinkled her nose at it.

'I haven't got any disgusting diseases,' I said. Then I realized she was pouting at the brands, not at the thought of sharing. She had that deep-down rich look about her. The long boots, the lambskin, ten shades of professional red in her hair and those big loose curls you get from a salon blow-dry. A knuckleful of diamonds and platinum on her wedding finger. She took off the solitaire and the half-hoop before she wetted her hands but even her wedding ring was a beast of a thing. I supposed that was the usual way middle-aged men like Sasha Mowbray got young wives like Kim.

She stood up and looked at herself in the mirror. 'Happy anniversary, you clueless bitch.'

'Hey!' I said. 'Don't speak to yourself like that.'

'You're right,' she said. 'That's my husband's job, isn't it?'

I gave an awkward laugh and backed away

'All present and correct,' I told my mum's voicemail, when I was back in the kitchen. 'The client and hubs have arrived. Four women, four men, one big happy . . . She doesn't look old enough to be having a tenth wedding anniversary, mind you, and I wouldn't bet on an eleventh.'

I hung up and headed back to the library with more tea. I hadn't agreed with my mum that we needed so much china, but she was right. This was slick and professional-looking, walking in with a replacement, not making them wait.

I paused just outside. There was total silence from the other side of the door, except for the logs crackling. Had they all gone upstairs to say hello at last? To thump Sasha's back and call him by old nicknames? I still thought it was weird they hadn't done it right away. I pushed the door open and froze.

Sasha stood with his back to me, the rest of them staring up at him from their seats. I squinted to make out what he was holding. Some big bulky armload. I came further into the room and the firelight twinkled in the folds of the cellophane. The hamper.

'Who did it?' Sasha said. 'What joker wrote that name on this card?' He was holding the little envelope that had come with the gift. It was twisted in his fist from him gripping it so hard as he shook it – actually shook it – in their faces.

Peach looked over his shoulder towards me and swallowed. Sasha followed her gaze.

'Get out!' he said, swinging round. Then: 'Oh, it's you. Can *you* cast any light on this? Do you know whose idea of a hilarious joke this is? Do you know who put it on my bed for me to find?'

'On your bed?' I said. 'I left it in the kitchen.'

'Sasha, it's probably a mistake,' Rosalie said. 'And if Kim hasn't seen it, then it doesn't matter. It'll be a client or someone, working off an old address book.'

'What are you twatting on about?' Sasha said.

'Hey,' said Paul.

'Oh, spare me!' Sasha said. 'Look, if I laugh like a good little boy at your priceless wheeze, will you at least tell me which one of you did it?'

I stood like a pillock just inside the door. I couldn't get past him to put the teapots down without shoving him aside.

'Christ, Sasha,' Paul said. 'We like a laugh but none of us would put your ex-wife's name on an anniversary present! We're not total arseholes.'

'Who said anything about my ex-wife?'

'What?' said Peach. '*You* did. You minced in here like Zorro and accused us of writing the wrong name on an anniversary present. Are you drunk? Are you high?'

'It's not addressed to Marina and me,' Sasha said. 'And this is no client with an old address book. This is for me alone: "Dear Sasha, Happy anniversary and—"'

'And what?' said Buck.

'And welcome back,' said Sasha, spitting the words. 'So much for your claims to be astonished at finding yourselves here.'

'Whose claims?' Ramsay said. 'Who sent it?'

'Not the person whose name's on the card,' Sasha said grimly.

'Sash, none of *us* brought it,' Paul said. 'I swear.'

'You *swear*?'

'I swear too,' said Rosalie. 'I don't know anything about it.'

'Do you swear on a locked box?' said Sasha. Everyone was quiet then.

'Locked box isn't for swears,' said Peach at last. She sounded like a child. 'It's for secrets.'

Buck got to his feet and walked over to stand in front of Sasha, his face inches away. 'What are you playing at?' he said. 'Why are we all here again?'

In the silence that followed, we could hear footsteps outside in the passageway. Kim was approaching.

'Here!' I shoved the teapots down on the end of a bookcase and held out my arms. 'Give it to me. I'll use it up in the kitchen.' Sasha thrust the hamper at me, then flung the little card into the back of the fireplace as Kim entered the room.

'There she is!' he said. 'My bride!' She had pulled herself together and in the low light there was no trace of her crying.

'Darling Kim,' said Rosalie, getting to her feet and wrapping her arms round the girl.

'Budge up, bruv,' Peach said, elbowing Buck in the ribs. 'Come and sit by me, Kimmie. We've got to get to know each other from scratch. Let's start now.'

'And let's hear three cheers for Sasha,' said Paul. 'Now we're all here.' Like me, he had forgotten Jennifer already. 'So, Sasha, how did you do it?'

'How did I do what?'

'How did you get this organized?' said Peach. 'None of us could have found it again if we'd tried. How did you even know it was still a holiday home? We couldn't believe it when we rolled up, could we?'

'I did nothing,' Sasha said. 'Kim did it all. Found the house, booked it, got the staff, did the flowers, got you all here, got me here.'

'So ...' said Paul, sending a look round the others '. . . you're saying it's a coincidence.'

'Gift from the universe we decided to call it, didn't we?' Sasha said, walking round behind the couch and planting a kiss on Kim's head.

'Wow,' said Rosalie, her voice like a stone in a pool.

'Spooky,' said Buck. 'Hey, Kim, since you've got some kind of witchcraft going on, to take us back to old times, you didn't by any chance plant a little surprise for us, did you? Rosie, go and get the box. It must have cooled down enough by now.'

'I could ...' I said. It was weird for me still to be standing there, but there hadn't been a good moment to slip away. Suddenly this room seemed kind of cramped after all.

'Shut up, Buck,' Peach said. 'Oh, but, actually, Kim, did you?'

'Box?' said Kim.

'What do you mean "cooled down"?' said Sasha.

Rosalie was on her feet and gone. We heard her light steps along the length of the corridor, then silence, then 'Shit!' faintly.

'Don't burn yourself, you daft moo,' Paul shouted, as we heard the footsteps coming back again.

'It's gone,' Rosalie said, coming back into the room. 'Someone's moved it.'

'Who?' said Ramsay.

'Same joker who moved the hamper,' Sasha said, letting his gaze travel over everyone. 'Come on, don't thrash it to death. Whose little joke is this?'

Whoever it was was a good actor. It's easy to avoid looking guilty if you're hiding something. Where people get it wrong is they forget to look curious. But all of this lot were looking pretty sharply at all the others, as if waiting for someone to crack.

'No?' said Sasha. 'More to come, maybe? Oh, goody. What a treat we have in store.'

'Moving on, then,' said Paul. 'A lovely weekend beckons. And my wife has had one of her rare good ideas.'

'Kick him for me, Peach,' said Rosalie. 'And, Paul, take a gold star for subtlety, casualness, adroitness and stealth, why don't you?'

'What do you think to the idea of handing over our phones and laptops?' Paul went on, ignoring her. 'Until . . . say, Sunday morning. Have a proper break?'

'What a marvellous idea,' said Sasha. His voice was dripping with scorn. 'Since we're here anyway, why don't we go back in time? Shall we all listen to Madonna singles all weekend and start smoking again?'

'No,' said Buck, 'it wasn't Madonna. God, what *was* that song we all got so sick of?'

'*I'm* for switching off,' Ramsay said. 'There's mounting data from research in this area. Well-designed longitudinal studies.'

'Oh, do tell us more,' said Sasha.

'I've got a friend who works on it.' Either Ramsay didn't hear the sarcasm or didn't care. 'They're finding that for every hour online, and Ezli says it's unrelated to click freque—'

'What's EZLI?' said Peach.

'Ezli's his name,' said Ramsay.

'Oh, well, if your *boyfriend* thinks we should all surrender our phones,' Sasha said, 'who am I to argue?'

'And then you say he's not your boyfriend,' Paul said, in a bored drawl, 'and then Sasha asks why you broke up and Kim wonders why she married such a prick . . .'

'What is *wrong* with you today?' Rosalie said.

'I floated your suggestion,' said Paul. 'Be happy with that.'

Rosalie gave him a long look, then shrugged. 'So how about it?' she said. 'I go three days without my online Scrabble, you go three days without . . . I draw a veil.'

'Put them outside your bedroom doors tonight,' I said, 'and they'll be gone by morning.' With that, I managed at last to edge my way to the door and leave.

———

I threw the hamper back down on the breakfast table. 'You are fair game, little basket of goodies,' I said. 'If no one else wants you, I'll happily plunder you. Ooh! Snails. Lovely. But for tonight, sausage, beans and chips.'

They were my homemade game sausages and my homemade borlotti beans stewed for hours with duck fat and bacon bones. And the chips were quartered spuds tossed in olive oil, garlic and rosemary, glittering with salt chips like a frosty morning. It was the best Friday night comfort food I could do on my own.

And maybe they'd all had a rough week and really needed the comfort. For whatever reason, supper went down a storm. When I took the wine in, every single one of them had a hunk of bread to mop up the juices. That's always a giveaway. The only bum note came because I'd set too many places.

'Are you joining us?' Sasha said. 'This table seats eight and there seems to be someone missing.'

'Oh, no, that's terrible!' said Peach, with an uncomfortable giggle. 'We forgot about her. Sasha, Jennifer's not here.'

'She came,' said Rosalie, 'but then she went.'

'You only missed her by a hair,' Ramsay said. 'Surprised you didn't lock bumpers at the gate, actually.'

'She had some kind of stomach bug, poor soul,' said Peach. 'And she was kind enough to take it away instead of staying and passing it round.'

'I'll bet,' said Sasha. 'I imagine finding herself back here *would* make Jennifer pretty sick. So, *are* you joining us?'

I gave a polite laugh and told them I had work to do on the pudding.

'I wish you could,' Kim said. 'We were balanced with Jennifer. We're short of a female now.'

No one spoke but that pinball look went ricocheting round again.

'God, who cares about all that shit, these days?' said Paul at last. 'Turn to your other partner after the fish and ladies leave the men to their port.'

'I wouldn't mind,' said Rosalie. 'What do you say, Kim? Peach? Will we go and loll after dinner? Leave this hairy lot to drone on about golf clubs and stock options?'

Kim glanced up the table at Sasha. They were sitting at head and foot, yards apart.

'Perhaps not quite the right note for an anniversary,' Sasha said.

I left them to it, clicked the monitor on so's I'd know when to take second helpings through and rolled up my sleeves to get a jump on the dishes.

It was hard to tell the voices apart in the hubbub of a dinner table. As Peach got louder she sounded more and more like

Buck, both of them cracking jokes. The Buchanan brothers were identical except that Ramsay offered information, while Paul cut in at the end of stories and capped them. Even Sasha and Rosalie sounded alike: the brother's light voice and the sister's professionally lowered pitch ending up in the same key. Only Kim stood out.

It had almost got to where I thought I was listening to a radio play when all of a sudden: 'Don't go scampering through to the kitchen like a skivvy,' Sasha said. 'We're paying through the nose for an actual skivvy. Let her do her job.'

'You get more charming with age, brother mine,' Rosalie said. 'But he's right, Kim. The servants won't thank you for going into their kitchens and interfering.'

'Ring for Jeeves!' said Peach. She really was drunk. 'Bread, Jeeves, and plenty of it!'

And now I would appear and watch them squirm. I put a fresh napkin in a basket, took a second loaf out of the warming oven and started sawing it into hunks. I've noticed people hate breaching a loaf for themselves. But I couldn't hear properly with the sound of the knife on the crust so I stopped to listen. Kim was speaking.

'. . . don't want to get all New Agey on you, but some of the techniques that sound daftest of all are the most useful.'

'Om!' said Paul.

'Not crystals,' said Peach. 'And I'm not going to fork over hard cash to have someone wave their hands over me. A good deep-tissue massage is one thing.'

'And a happy ending?'

'Shut up, Buck.'

I started in on the bread again. I could have heard Peach

over a blender. 'But a little something to calm me down when I actually have to go and face him in the courtroom.'

'Should you really be talking about your divorce at Sasha and Kim's anniversary?' That was Paul.

'It's not catching!' Peach said. 'You sound like an etiquette guide.'

I headed back through, and by the time I lost the sound of the monitor, I could hear their voices for real.

'Our senior partner gave us all a lecture on the plane on the way to Beijing this one time,' Paul said. '"Dinner party rules," he told us. "No sex, religion or politics." Some boring dinner parties he must go to. And then he *had* sex in a fountain at the conference hotel.'

'More bread!' I said, backing into the room. 'And more wine if you're getting low, which I see you are.'

'I'll take another glass,' said Sasha, reaching back with his closest hand. I put the bottle into it. If the gesture had been him reaching out to draw me towards his chair, I didn't want to think about it. I couldn't help a look up to the other end of the table, though, to see if Kim had noticed.

'But I really think I can help you, Peach,' she was saying, and something about the way her face was turned so hard towards the other woman told me everything. 'There's no need for anything elaborate or costly. Have you ever heard of holding another's fear?'

'Holding another's what?' said Buck. 'Filthy!'

'Tell me later when we withdraw and leave them to their rough talk,' Peach said.

'No, go on, Kim, I'm sorry,' Buck said. I was halfway down one side of the table now, offering the bread and topping up the wine.

Kim shook her head to both as I got to her. 'You find your fear – locate it in your body – and you draw it into your lungs by breathing in hard, then you cough it up. You literally cough it up.'

'"Literally" abuse!' said Ramsay. 'Ten-pound fine.'

'Cough it up into your hand,' Kim said. She was leaning forward to talk directly to Peach past Paul and Ramsay and Jennifer's empty chair. 'And roll it up into a little ball.'

'Or you could go with the crystals after all,' said Sasha. There was an odd note in his voice.

'And that's where I come in,' Kim said.

'This is hardly a topic for the table, Kim,' Sasha said.

'Does this mean we can all have sex in a fountain?' said Buck. I wondered if I should have filled his glass.

'Shut up, Buck,' said Peach, but she was looking at Sasha.

'You give it to me to hold!' Kim said. 'It's not my fear so it does me no harm and you really do feel as if it's gone. I hold it as long as you need and then I give it back.'

'Who told her?' Sasha muttered, half under his breath.

'It works!' said Kim. Paul drained his glass as I reached him, then held it up to be filled. 'It really does work. It lightens the one who gives it away and it physically weighs down the one who takes it to hold. It's amazing.'

'It *would* be,' said Ramsay. 'It sounds like a basic placebo effect.'

Sasha was rising to his feet. He dropped his napkin on the seat of his chair and walked, slowly and deliberately, to the other end of the table. 'Where did you hear that?' he said.

'I saw it online, I think,' said Kim. She glanced at the others and then at me as he came right up to her and put his hands down on the carved arms of her dining chair.

'Same website that sold you the hamper?'

'What?' said Kim. She was recoiling from him. She was physically shrinking into her chair as he loomed over her. The others were transfixed, not eating, not drinking, not even chewing. I could see a white lump of bread in Buck's open mouth.

Sasha leaned in close and Kim closed her eyes. Then he kissed her with a loud smack and stood up, laughing. 'You've been had, sweetheart,' he said, strolling back to his seat and flinging himself down in it. 'Which one of you jokers has been selling snake-oil to my bubble-head of a wife? Come on, out with it!'

I was at Peach's place now. She nodded, telling me to fill her glass.

'Sasha, get a grip!' said Rosalie.

'Yeah, gaslight someone your own size,' said Peach.

'Actually, now I think about it,' Sasha said, 'it was Jennifer's invention. But that's irrelevant. The question is who's been stuffing Kim up with it?'

Rosalie was sitting on his left side, and as she waved a hand at him to brush off his words, he caught her by the wrist and pulled her round to face him.

'Was it you?' he said. 'Is this *your* idea of fun? We've only got your word that the famous "box" disappeared.'

'Get your hand off my wife before I lay you out,' said Paul.

'Your wife?' said Sasha. 'My sister.'

'I'm not joking,' Paul said. Sasha dropped Rosalie's wrist. Flung her away, really.

I was near the door and I fled, putting the bottle down on the sideboard but taking the bloody bread out with me again, before I realized what I'd done.

'More burgundy, Vicar?' came Buck's voice – I think it was Buck's voice – through the monitor.

'You don't do séances as well as the crystals and other claptrap, do you, Kim?' said Paul.

'What?' Kim's voice was strained.

'Ouija board, maybe? Knock once for yes? We could go straight to the source.'

'Stop it,' said Rosalie. 'How can you?'

'And I thought this was going to be dull,' Buck said. 'You Mowbrays should sell tickets. You're the same as you ever were.'

'Shut up, Bu—' I clicked the switch and silenced them.

Chapter 6

1991

My shadow looks like a crossbow. I've been walking with my arms out from my sides all the way from the house and I can feel the sweat trickling down inside my top. We're nearly there, though. I'm going to stop at the mouth of the drive, wipe under my arms with a tissue, throw the tissue in the bushes, then ring the bell. Or, if it's a party, are you just supposed to walk in?

Ten paces behind me, Lynsey's still moaning. 'Why have we got to go? We don't even know them. I don't even like them. They're stupid. I want to go home.'

'How do you know they're stupid if you don't even know them?' I say. I don't twist round, in case my top sticks to me.

'They're old,' Lynsey says. 'They won't play proper games. They'll play stupid games.'

'One of them's the same age as you,' I tell her. Mum said the girl called Morag's thirteen and Lynsey's twelve.

'And they're snobby,' she says. 'My shoes hurt. Why have I

got to carry the stupid present? They'll make us do things. They'll make us do the dishes.'

I sigh. Loud enough so she'll hear me. And I wait for her to catch up and walk ahead of me. Her shoes hurt because I made her take her socks off. It's nearly September but hot enough for July, the bees lazy in the verges and the tractor ruts pale and crumbling after weeks of dry weather. Even so, Lynsey came downstairs with her grey school socks pulled up to her knees under her party dress.

'For ticks,' she said. 'If we're going over the fields.'

So we've come round by the road, all that extra way in the heat, because I knew she'd never take them off when we got there and then those girls Mum told me about – the one with the black hair and the one with the loud laugh and the other one that wasn't here yet – they'd all see me at a party with my twelve-year-old sister in her grey school socks and they'd point and then the boys would notice. The two tall ones and the short one and the one with the wetsuit.

Lynsey stops walking and bends to ease her sandal-straps off her heels then starts up again with them slapping against her soles like flip-flops. It makes me feel a bit bad to see a bright red mark across the back of each ankle. If Mum was here she'd tell her to put them back on before she wasted her good shoes that cost good money. Wasting good things that cost good money is the biggest sin going, in Mum's book. Showing her up is another.

'Don't show me up,' she said, as she watched us setting off. She didn't need to tell us what she meant. We know. Don't eat too much, don't chew with your mouth open, don't talk with your mouth full, don't drink with food in your mouth. Don't ask too many questions, don't tell everyone our business, remember to say please and thank you and thank you very much for having me. She added one thing, whispering to me: 'If you need to go to the toilet, Carmen, don't announce it. Don't ask where it is. Just go. There's one right at the back door on the left.'

'Why aren't you telling Lynsey this?' I wanted to know.

'Because she's only a wee girl,' Mum said. 'It's different.'

'Carmen!' Lynsey's voice breaks in on my thoughts. 'There's a car coming!' She grabs me and pulls me up onto the steep verge. I can feel a nettle against the back of one elbow. 'My shoe!' Lynsey says. One of her white sandals – good new shoes that cost good money – is still in the middle of the lane. Lynsey makes a lunge towards it, but the car's coming round the corner already, braking when the driver sees us. It stops with its front tyre right on top of Lynsey's shoe. A tiny piece of the back of the sole is still showing under it.

Lynsey lets out a high-pitched little noise, staring at her shoe as the window slides down. The man driving has got to be the dad of the boy with the wetsuit. He looks exactly the same except with white in his hair. A woman leans forward to see past him.

'You must be Carmen,' she says. 'And you've brought a little sister along, have you? Tosca? Mimi? Well, the more the merrier. I'm Anna and this is Oliver. We would turn round and give you a lift but we've been banished. There'd be hell to pay if we go back now. Have fun!'

She flicks a look down at Lynsey's one bare foot and her smile dims a tiny bit, but she doesn't say any more as the window slides up again. It's automatic. You can tell from the way the man sits so still while it's moving.

I'm expecting Lynsey to cry. Her sandal's flattened and

some of the white has come off the straps and got stuck to the ground in the pattern of the tyre. But she giggles instead.

'Ay'm Enna and thees ees Olivah!' she says, prancing out into the middle of the road. 'There'd be hell to pay if we gew beck nee-ow.'

I'm checking my top. I had to put my arms down when the woman was talking to me. I couldn't stand like a crossbow in front of them. Lynsey's foot was weird enough for both of us.

'Is that their mum?' Lynsey says. 'Is that their dad? Does Mum know there's not going to be a mum and dad there?'

I ignore her. My top's pale blue and now there's dark streaks under the arms. Maybe if I put a tissue in each armpit it'll soak up the stain. But what if I can't get it all out? The sleeves are wide and floaty and someone might see bits of tissue stuck there. Likes of if I'm dancing.

Anyway, before I can decide, Lynsey's whining again.

'The colour's coming off on my hand,' she says. We wrapped his present – an Eternity gift-set – in navy-blue crêpe paper and put silver ribbon on it, and now there's a perfect print of Lynsey's chubby fingers on the edge of the box and her right hand's deep purple from the blue dye on top of her pink palm.

'Don't touch your dress,' I say. 'We'll go in the back way and straight to the toilet to wash.' I'll be able to flush the tissues down the pan and check for bits.

'Or I could do this,' says Lynsey. She presses her index finger against one eyelid, leaving a smudge there. 'Eye-shadow.'

'Stop it!' I say, then I look at her properly. 'Do me! Do mine!' I've got lip gloss and blusher on and a bloom of blue from Lynsey's hot finger would be perfect.

'Can't make me,' she sings, and then she's skipping up the road, still with her sandals flapping, waving her hand in the air. 'It's drying! It's drying!'

'It's going to look like a black eye!' I call after her. 'I won't show you where the toilet is.'

So she wheels back, presses her fingers all over my eyes and does her other one too.

I've never come up the drive to the front of the house. I've been in Dad's car a few times when he dropped Mum off at the back, if she had bags of washed sheets to put on or if she'd ironed shirts and it was raining. It looked nothing at all from there. It's a plain brick wall with a door in it and the sloped roof of a row of sheds, then the back wall of the house with the same windows as our place, deep-set with peaks over them and the same crisscross panes.

It's totally different coming in the front way. This one house looks like the whole row of cottages where we live, five windows along the top upstairs, and downstairs windows you could walk in and out of at each end of a curve, the middle bit filled in with a deep porch full of seats and tables.

The front door's open and there's music pouring out. When we stand on the doorstep, I can feel the bass coming up through the soles of my feet. I can feel it all the way up my legs, if I'm honest, and it's making me tingle even though I hate that song. There's been nothing else on the radio for months except Bryan Adams wailing and mooing. And *Top of the Pops* is so boring, because you know the end of it's going to be him standing in that scruffy wood, like out the back of our house, looking old and ugly.

I push the doorbell, but there's no way anyone could hear

it with Bryan yodelling on and on. Lynsey puts her hand in mine.

'Let's go home,' she says. 'We can leave the present and say we felt sick. Mum would kill us for doing a sick in front of people. Carmen, no!'

I'm ploughing forward with her hand gripped tight in mine. Inside the hall itself the music's so loud I can feel it in my teeth. It's coming from the end of a long passageway that stretches miles in both directions, with pictures on the walls and a statue. It's not like the inside of someone's house at all. At the other end, halfway up the stairs, the curtains are shut, maybe pulled close to stop the sun coming in and fading the carpet, like Mum does in our front room too. But these curtains are so long they make me think of being at the pictures. I can imagine them suddenly going see-through with the black film-rating thingy behind them.

'What will we do?' Lynsey whispers in my ear, close enough to tickle. 'Where do you put the present if there are no mums and dads?'

'We need to find the party,' I say. 'Follow Bryan and find the party.'

I walk away from her, swishing my hips a bit as I head for the half-open door where the racket's coming from. It's so loud the tape machine's buzzing and squealing and, as I push the door wide and walk in, the music disappears completely and all I can hear is the feedback from the speakers.

It's a huge room with a full-sized pool table, like at a leisure club. But there are no balls or cues. The ghetto blaster sits on the green felt at one end and at the other end is a collection of bottles and those cut-glass decanters people put drinks in to pretend it's good stuff when it's not.

There's no one in here with the music and all the bottles. The beanbags and sofa-beds all round the walls are dented but empty.

From out in the corridor I hear a deep voice. 'Hello, little girl. What are you doing here all alone?'

'Car-*men*!' Lynsey shouts.

I go back out and there's a tall boy looming over her. He's got the worst skin I've ever seen. Three different kinds of acne all at once: the usual greasy teenage spots and blackheads in the creases of his nose and chin, plus so many red bumpy spots on his cheeks and forehead they're nearly joined up, and one huge angry boil on his neck.

'She's not alone,' I say. 'She's with me.'

When the boy speaks again his voice isn't deep at all. He was putting it on. He takes a step back. 'Sorry,' he says. 'I didn't mean to frighten her. I'm Ramsay.'

'You and whose army frightened me?' says Lynsey. 'Here. Happy birthday.' She shoves the box of Eternity at him and glares.

'It's not my birthday,' he says. 'It's *Sasha's* birthday. Come and jab *him* in the belly with your present if you want to jab somebody.'

'That's Lynsey and I'm Carmen,' I say.

'Carmen!' he says. 'Yes, I heard about *you*.'

'What's that supposed to mean?' says Lynsey.

Ramsay's face colours. At least it hides some of his spots. 'Sasha!' he shouts, throwing his head back 'There's a surprise for you!' He turns and leaves us, bounding up the stairs.

'I told you they'd be stupid,' Lynsey says. 'Let's go home.'

But someone else is coming now. It's the wetsuit boy. His hair looks even darker than it did when he came out of the sea that day. It's slicked back with so much gel I can smell it from a metre away. His face looks a bit less perfect. I think he's shaved – maybe for the first time, trying to be grown-up – and he's scraped too hard and left a red line on his jaw.

'Carmen,' he says. 'Who's this?'

'Lynsey,' says Lynsey. 'Who's asking?'

Sasha gives her a long, cool look. I know exactly what he's feeling. No one can be as annoying as Lynsey when she puts her mind to it. I'm kind of proud of her. 'I'm Sasha,' he says at last. 'This is my party. This is my house.'

'Yeah, for the week,' Lynsey says.

'We're all upstairs. Come and join in.'

'Happy birthday.' But this time she holds the present out instead of ramming it at him.

'You shouldn't have,' Sasha says. Lynsey giggles and I can feel a wave of heat taking over me as I try not to giggle too. He's a kid but he speaks like a teacher. Maybe when we get upstairs he'll say, 'Do sit down.'

Lynsey feels for my hand again as we follow him up, past the closed landing curtains to the dim upstairs corridor. I shake her off. At the top, the boy turns right and holds open a door for us. The room's pitch black. I shrug as if it's the kind of thing I do every day and stroll in.

'Ow!'

I've trodden on someone's legs and, tripping, kicked someone else's.

'Sasha, this is bloody stupid.' It's a girl's voice. 'We're crammed into the smallest room in the house and I'm getting stood on.'

I can hear someone moving and then a light's clicked on. There's a handful of them there, I think at the time. Seven, I learn later when I piece it together. All sitting on the floor of 'the smallest room in the house', which would be the biggest room in my house. They're teenagers, but that covers a lot. The oldest-looking one even though he's the shortest – the one that drove my mum home in the rain – has got a scruff of wispy beard that doesn't match his thick hair. The youngest-looking could be Lynsey's age, with his baby-face and his thin brown legs poking out of his shorts. Except they're not really shorts. They've been made by hacking into a pair of jeans and leaving the rough ends to fray and clump. I'd kill to do that to a pair of jeans, and have the nerve to wear them to a party after. Mum would drop dead, though.

'What game are you playing?' Lynsey says. She's the opposite of me in some ways. She was scared of coming, ready to run from the doorstep, but now she's here she'll hide her shyness. I've been looking forward to this all week but, now I'm here, standing looking down at four strange boys and feeling three strange girls' eyes all over me, I've got lockjaw.

'What and Who,' Sasha says. 'It'll be a lot more fun and a lot less incestuous now you're here to join in.'

I've never heard of it, but I can guess the basics from the way they're all sprawled on the floor with their legs meshed together.

'Let's go downstairs,' says one of the girls, staggering to her feet and pulling her clothes straight. 'I'm hungry.' She's short and thick and her hair's like a guinea pig's coat, but she's got a boat-neck top and a pair of 501s on. My hankie top and no-name jeans from the market suddenly feel like they're burning my skin. On the other hand, one of the girls is in a stiff, shiny dress and the grown-up one's got straggly hair

78

and really bad eyeliner. Anyway, even the one with the good jeans is friendly. 'Come down to the kitchen, you two,' she says to Lynsey and me. 'Aunt Anna's left enough grub to keep us going for a week.'

'Dining room first, Morag,' Sasha says, 'before you go face down in the trough. I promised Anna I'd get a picture of us all. She left the camera set up on a timer in the dining room.'

One by one they all get up. The girls drift into bedrooms and the boys clatter down the stairs. Mum would kill us for making so much noise. But, then, we'd never be up here in our shoes anyway.

It takes them ages to get organized for the photo. Lynsey and I hang around on the landing, not sure if we're supposed to be part of this or not. But the girl in the shiny dress scoops us up when she comes back. She's really pretty, even if her stupid homemade dress looks like the crackly paper you get round cheap chocolates and even if her French plait's finished off with a ribbon to match it.

'Of course you should be in it!' she says. 'Anna's got a million pictures of us lot this holiday. She wanted one of the party.'

'Yes, but that's probably about me, Rosalie,' says the big girl with the straggly hair. She hasn't done anything to tidy it, although she's taken a swipe at her eyeliner and managed to make it worse: still squint and now smudged too. 'Aunt Anna probably wanted to make sure I was in it. I haven't been here all the time.'

'Thank God,' both the other girls mouth behind her back, as if they've been practising. Then they get a fit of the giggles that Lynsey catches.

The boys are already in the dining room, but they've locked the door.

'What are you doing?' the big girl asks, banging on it.

'Some extra pictures,' one of them shouts. 'Won't be a minute!'

'We can come round and get in the front bay, you know,' shouts the chubby girl in the 501s.

'Don't!' says the other one, the one in the shiny dress. Rosalie. 'I know my brother. Don't you know yours?'

'No! They wouldn't. Not on Aunt Anna's camera.'

'Wouldn't they?'

'What?' says Lynsey.

'Sasha's school's next to Boots so he puts the photos in and picks them up. If Anna ever looked at the negatives, she'd have a fit.'

'What are they talking about, Carmen?' Lynsey asks.

'Those silly boys taking photos of their bare bottoms,' I tell her.

Lynsey opens her eyes wide. 'Boys *are* silly.'

Rosalie puts an arm around her and kisses her head. 'You're a darling,' she says. 'Your sister's a darling,' she says to me. I catch Lynsey's eye and we both struggle not to crack up again. They sound so daft with their compliments, like they're playing at grown-ups.

When Sasha opens the door at last he's breathing hard and his face is red all over, not just his jaw.

'Why are you panting?' says his sister. 'You're not right in the head.'

'I'm excited about my birthday. Look what Anna's left out for me.'

In the dining room a little extra table is set up in front of the fireplace and heaped with presents. Lynsey adds ours to the pile, glad to get rid of it at last.

'Can you believe Anna blew up balloons?' says Rosalie in the shiny dress, even though 'Anna' is her mum. 'And, oh, my God – look! Party hats.' She lifts one and puts it on Sasha's head, pulling it over one eye. He sticks his tongue out of the side of his mouth. 'Here,' she says, throwing one over to Lynsey. Lynsey puts it on and pulls her hair through so it sticks out the top like a pineapple.

'I go here,' says Sasha, sitting down behind the table. 'And you all cluster round me like backing singers.'

'I don't want to be in it,' says the boy with the terrible skin.

'No, you should be in the middle,' says Sasha. 'And *we*'ll be the backing singers. Pizza-face and the Clearasils.'

'That's not very nice,' says the grown-up girl.

'Crater-face and the Cover-sticks,' says Sasha.

'Ha-ha,' the boy says, but he's not laughing.

'God's sake, take a joke,' says Sasha, dropping down. 'Pull your party hat down and stand in the back row. Morag, sit beside me.'

Morag – the girl in the 501s – slides onto the other half of the chair he's sitting on. He puts a hand on the inside of her thigh and pulls her closer. She puts her hand down to prise his off her but he keeps smiling. He flicks a glance at me to see if I've noticed. Like I'm supposed to be jealous or something.

'Will I click the button?' I say.

'Anna's got a timer set up,' says Rosalie. 'We all need to get in position. Hurry up!'

The rest of them file in. The short boy on the other side of Sasha and the big girl and the tall brothers behind them. The spotty one looks miserable but it's the other who shakes a long piece of hair in front of his face. Rosalie fluffs out the skirt of her homemade dress and stands at the edge of the group, feet together and hands clasped. I take Lynsey by the shoulders and guide her to the other edge. 'One of us needs to squeeze the bulb on the end of the thing,' the big girl says. 'Oh, shut up! Grow up, all of you.'

But everyone's laughing now. The short boy with the scrubby beard goes loping over to the tripod and unloops a wire from the stand, unwinding it as he returns to the group. He bends his knees like a sharpshooter.

'Everyone say "Cheeeeeese Pizza Face",' Sasha says.

The flash goes off and blinds us.

'One more,' says the spotty boy. 'Everyone say "Raaaazor-burn"!'

'Razor-burn isn't smile-shaped,' says Lynsey.

The flash goes off again, not so bad this time when we're expecting it.

'And a third one for luck,' says Sasha. 'Everyone say, "Weeeeeeeeee'll see who chickens out tonight."'

When the third flash dies none of the boys is laughing.

'I don't get that,' says Lynsey.

'Let's go and see what Aunt Anna's left for the birthday tea,' says Morag. She gives Lynsey and me a friendly look and then she sort of shepherds us out in front of her, like the teachers when someone's spilled something sticky in the dinner hall and they're trying to make sure no one walks in it.

The other two girls come with us. When I look closer at the ribbon in Rosalie's French plait, I can see it's actually a piece of her dress fabric doubled over and hemmed.

'I know,' she says.

I try to mumble that I wasn't looking, but she just laughs and links arms with me.

The other girl's behind, talking to Lynsey like a grown-up,

asking her what year she's in at school and whether she's having a nice summer. Lynsey asks her back and the girl says she's left school and she's going to university next month. She's going to be a teacher.

'I'm going to university too,' Lynsey says. 'I'm going to be a vet.'

Then we're at the kitchen. I know it's scruffy because Mum's told us all about it – no workspace to speak of, no proper units, cupboard shelves lined with newspaper – but I expected it to be clean. Mum comes in every morning when there's people here and once a week when it's empty. And I know she works hard because I do the ironing for all of us and sometimes her clean tabards still smell under the armholes when the hot iron hits them. So it's a shock when I step through the kitchen door.

The sink's piled with dishes and there are chopping boards and mixing bowls everywhere, even on the floor. Egg shells, still trailing snot ribbons of raw egg, have been left all around a scraped-out jug of something congealing to the colour of mustard, and the food mixer's sitting with its head thrown back, its beaters crusted dark. Flies are everywhere, rising when we disturb them.

'Yum, yum,' says Morag. 'Nice one, Aunt Anna.'

But she's not looking at what I'm looking at and she's not joking. The kitchen's open to another room down a couple of steps to one side and the table in that half is crowded with bowls of food. Most of it's salads, I think. Different mixtures of chopped-up stuff covered in salad cream, with a cake on a raised stand in the middle. It's not a birthday cake. It's a plain sponge with jam in the middle and icing on the top. Not even any candles.

'Maybe we could throw a cloth over,' I say. 'Keep the flies off till we're ready to eat?'

'I'm ready to eat,' the grown-up girl says.

'Me too,' says Morag in the 501s.

Lynsey gives me a worried look. Are we supposed to wire in to the birthday spread when the birthday boy isn't even here?

'How can you, after that lunch we had?' says Rosalie. She shouldn't be as confident as she is. If I had to wear that get-up I'd be mortified, but she's not bothered.

'Lunch?' says the big girl. 'I wasn't invited to lunch.'

'We went out,' Morag says. 'That was the deal. We had to sit there in a hotel dining room and make polite conversation and they agreed to leave us alone to enjoy the party.'

'I was told to come at five.'

Lynsey and me were told the same thing, but it's different for us because we're strangers. That big girl's a cousin like all the others and I understand why she's pissed off.

'Oh, Jelly,' says Rosalie. 'You didn't *miss* anything.'

I'm staring at her and trying to decide if she can really be called 'Jelly' when noises upstairs make us all look up at the ceiling. There are thumps and shouts, then the thunder of feet on the stairs.

Sasha comes crashing into the kitchen with one of the other boys right after him, pulling at his shirt and dragging him down until they're both rolling on the floor.

'Fuck off, Paul!' Sasha says. Lynsey gasps but I'm the only one who hears her. Sasha is kicking out and struggling hard but he's laughing.

'God, what's that smell?' says the grown-up girl who can't be called Jelly, pulling her T-shirt neck up over her nose. The

84

boy Paul is shaking something over Sasha, both of them choking and coughing as a cloud of white dust puffs out. It's the talcum from our gift-set. I opened one end of it and sniffed before I wrapped it. They're wasting it.

'Drop your weapon!' The short boy with the beard is here now. He's got the cologne bottle in his hand. 'Freeze or I'll shoot!' He launches himself on top of Paul and Sasha, squirting long squirts of the cologne until the nozzle stops and he's got to let it go and start again. The smell's even stronger.

'You shitbags! It's in my eyes!' Sasha shouts, letting go of Paul and rolling away. 'It's in my fucking eyes.'

Paul's still trying to empty talcum powder over him, but as Sasha scrambles to his feet, he gives up and throws the talcum tin into the sink beside the dishes.

'Are you okay?' the squirting boy says, sniffing and laughing.

'No, I'm fucking blind,' says Sasha.

The other tall boy's in the room now. Ramsay with the acne. The girls – Lynsey included – are walking round the buffet table with their plates pretending they can't hear a thing.

'You stink like a pile of poofters,' says the beardy boy. Sasha's rubbing his eyes with his fists, ignoring him. He keeps ignoring him until the beardy one's standing close, then Sasha wraps him in a hug, smearing his face and hands all over.

'Ha-ha, look who's talking!' he shouts. Then he grabs Paul and rubs against him like a cat. 'There you go. If I'm honking like a cheap tart, we all are.'

Ramsay takes a step back but Sasha just laughs even louder. 'I'm not touching you, Pus-factory.'

'It's hard to believe you're sixteen, Sasha,' says Jelly. 'You'd be a backward six-year-old.'

'Oh, don't be such a drag, Jellifer,' Sasha says. He's still panting and his face is caked with a mixture of sweat and talc 'I mix much better cocktails than a six-year-old.'

'Big talk,' says Paul.

Sasha hawks and spits into the sink. 'That stuff tastes even worse than it smells,' he says. 'Bring sliced lime and a bucket of ice to the bar, my good man, and prepare to eat your words.'

I watch. They have got limes. And an ice bucket.

I help myself to some of the gluey salads – there's plain pasta and plain potato, but there's some weird mixture with eggs and olives and little scraps of the saltiest thing I've ever tasted in my life. Saltier than salt somehow and greasy too. And there's a big bowl of black shining balls I think are brambles till I see Rosalie scoop up a heap of them on a cracker. Lynsey takes another cracker, smeared with brown paste.

'This isn't Marmite,' she whispers, through a mouthful of crumbs. She picks two black olives out of the egg and potato and chews fast, to take the taste away. Her face screws up and she shudders. 'And there's something wrong with the grapes!'

'Ssh,' I tell her. 'Have some cake.'

'I want to go home.' She's scrubbing her tongue with a paper napkin.

'No, don't go!' Morag says. 'We're going to play games when we've eaten. Tell us your favourite game and I'll make sure we play it.'

So Lynsey goes out of the kitchen with the girls, trying to explain the rules of piggy-piggy-squeak-squeak and making them laugh. She's trying to be funny, but a bit of me reckons it's her accent cracking them up.

I go after them, more or less to get away from the smell of the gift-set and the sight of the flies, settled on the food now and laying eggs there.

Chapter 7

I took the chance to set out brandy and hot coffee in Thermos pots in the drawing room while they were eating their pudding. It was dark-chocolate lava cakes with white-chocolate sauce. Peach made that noise some women make about chocolate and most women only make in the bedroom. I'd wondered earlier if so much rich on top of rich would make them sick, but now I was hoping it would soften them up and slow them down. It had never occurred to me that the kind of people who could afford this place might be rough; that there might be trouble to navigate, fights to break up.

And whether or not it was my food, when they finally left the table – I was tidying the library and watched them pass – it seemed like they were pals again. Laughing and joking. I watched them all through the crack at the hinge side of the door. Sasha had his arm slung around Kim's neck, Paul held Rosalie's hand, Peach and Buck were arm and arm. Only Ramsay was alone. He brought up the rear a few paces behind the rest and, as he passed the door, he turned. Had he seen me? Would it matter?

I knelt at the fire again. It had died down enough to let me reset it for the next day, but I needed to do it quickly and get the table cleared before they started passing the dining room on their way up to bed.

Then I spotted something. A sharp corner of white behind the fire basket. The gift card that Sasha had hurled in there had overshot and escaped the flames. I took the tongs and reached in for it. The envelope was warm and smudged with soot but it had protected its contents except for one corner that had burned away.

'Happy anniversary, Sasha. And welcome back. Love from—'

But the name that had got so deep under Sasha's skin was burnt to ashes.

I laid it on the cleared grate and covered it with twists of paper. Then I imagined the fire failing to light and someone dismantling the kindling to try again, someone – maybe Sasha himself – finding it and getting angry all over again. I took it and slipped it into my back pocket to put in the recycling.

The library looked perfect when I was finished. The cushions were banged and plumped, the magazines re-fanned and the curtains drawn back to let in the morning light. I pulled the door over and went to tackle the dining room.

Peach had drunk more than everyone else. Of course I knew she had let all three of her own glasses be filled – I had filled them – but she had dragged Sasha's and Ramsay's glasses to her place setting and drained *them* too. Kim hadn't finished anything except her water and had only taken a

89

single bite of her pudding. It sat congealing on her plate, the chocolate lava that had oozed out warm now a cold sticky mess. Rosalie had eaten half of hers, then helped herself to grapes from the bowl on the sideboard. All the men had scraped their plates clean.

There were some spills, but the napkins were folded, not crumpled into the chocolate on their plates and they hadn't started mucking about with the centrepiece or the candlewax the way some people do if you leave them at a table for long enough. The worst was that Kim, maybe to keep her hands busy while she wasn't eating, had picked the label off the pudding wine and ripped it into confetti. It sat in a little pile beside her plate.

'We've got a hamster,' I told my mum, when she lifted the phone. The last tray-load was through and the kitchen door shut.

'If that's all . . .' I heard her groan and stretch.

'Are you in bed?' I said. 'All right for some. I've got a cake to ice yet.'

'I've got a mini-bar full of ten-quid Mars Bars to pretend don't exist. And an alarm clock set for five.'

'You win,' I said. 'Anyway, they only want one sentence on it. No roses or anything. One bag of icing and a single nozzle change.'

'What was it again?' said my mum. She had forwarded the email request, with a laughing emoji.

'*There's no love like your love*,' I said.

'Aww. Maybe all this wedding palaver's got me but I think that's nice now.'

'Most of it's nice,' I said. 'The Os are nice. Ks can be a bitch.'

She laughed and we said goodnight. But when I'd hung up I suddenly felt uneasy for the first time. I couldn't tell if it was her being so far away or me being on my own with that crowd. Or maybe it was only the quietness of the kitchen. I switched the monitor on but no sound came out of it. Maybe they'd all gone up already and I hadn't heard them.

As I walked along the corridor, though, I could hear the click of billiard balls and the knock and rumble as one of them dropped into a pocket and ran along the channel.

'*Goodness gracious, great cues of fire,*' sang Buck.

'You're absolutely insufferable when you're winning,' said Ramsay. 'Did you know that?'

'I wonder what I'm like when I'm losing,' said Buck. 'I wonder if I'll ever find out.'

In the drawing room, the silence was explained. Rosalie sat on the floor at Sasha's feet, a brandy snifter dangling from her fingertips and her head hanging down. Sasha himself sat back comfortably against the couch cushions. Paul was in an armchair by the fire, staring into the flames. Peach was either asleep or unconscious, half lying on the smallest of the sofas.

'More coffee?' I said.

Rosalie lifted her head. 'We've been reliving old times,' she said. She sounded even drunker than she looked. 'Kimmie went off to get her beauty sleep, so we thought we'd get our boring reminiscences out the way. Reminiscences,' she said again, and made a better job of it this time.

'Peach,' said Sasha. Then louder: 'Peach! Do you want coffee?'

Paul shushed him. 'Don't. It won't sober her up. It'll *wake* her up and then we'll have drunk Peach yakking all night.'

'Did you know why she's *called* Peach, Donna?' Sasha said.

'Peach Plummer,' I said, but even as I said it I realized Plummer was her married name and the nickname must have come long before it.

'Peach schnapps,' said Sasha. 'During our first family party here at The Breakers, Peach drank an entire bottle of schnapps. It was the start of a long and illustrious drinking career.'

'Sasha, you promised we wouldn't talk about it any more,' Rosalie said. 'It's a different house. Different name. Let's just forget.'

'Should I . . .?' I didn't know how to ask about plastic under-sheets and sick buckets without offending them.

'Lay some in for this weekend?' said Paul. 'No, no, no, she's never touched it since.'

'Ver' good thing,' said Rosalie. 'She had a complete black-out that night. I think if she took a sip of peach schnapps even now – even two and half years later – it would all come rushing back and she'd go stark raving bonkers.'

'Decades,' said Paul. 'Not years.'

'Twenty-five of them. That's what I said,' insisted Rosalie.

'Is this you not talking about it any more, dear sister?' Sasha's voice sounded sardonic but his face had not a whisker of a smile on it anywhere. 'Is that your best effort at locking the box?'

'No,' said Rosalie. 'Don't say that. It's a secret. It's a secret secret.'

'Come on, you drunken mare,' said Paul, getting himself to his feet and putting his hands out for his wife. 'To bed with you.' I stepped forward and relieved her of the brandy glass.

'Will you brush my hair?' Rosalie said, as they left the room.

'Well, if there's nothing else,' I said to Sasha and to Peach's closed eyes and open mouth.

'Aren't you dying to ask?' Sasha said. He stood up and put his glass on the mantelpiece. 'Great dinner, by the way. And excellent brandy.' He went to the door and called across the corridor. 'Come and scoop up your sister, Buckaroo!'

An answering shout of 'One last frame,' came back from the billiards room.

'Well, if—' I said again.

'*Locked in a box* is the first level of secrets, you see,' said Sasha, coming back and standing in front of the fire. He was rolling on the balls of his feet, his hands clasped behind him.

I've never known someone go from nasty to nice by drinking. Nice people get nicer and nasty people get nastier. Sometimes nice people get nasty. But here was Sasha not sneering or scoffing but just talking to me, with a hint of brandy softening some of the sounds.

'We were big on secrets when we were kids,' he was saying now. 'It was the first swear. "I will keep it locked in a box."'

'*Is* it you?' I said. 'Playing practical jokes. Did you put the box up the chimney?'

'The next was "I will keep it behind stitched lips",' Sasha said, ignoring me. 'I was never sure what was behind the stitched lips, mind you. I think it's the key that locked the box. Once it's been gulped down, you know. Or maybe it's the secret itself. If the box doesn't work. You see?'

'Not really.'

'Take Peach's black-out that night. We never told the grown-ups. We stitched our lips. And then the grown-ups stitched them even tighter, of course.'

'Gruesome,' I said. 'What was the third swear?'

Sasha looked at me out of bleary eyes. 'How did you know there was a third?'

'Of course there's a third swear. Three billy goats gruff, three wishes, three little pigs.'

Sasha shook himself like a dog. 'I'm going for a walk,' he said. 'Down to the beach. I might even swim. The last time we were all here we went swimming in the moonlight.'

'Was it late September?' I said.

He gave a soft laugh. 'It was not. But consider the Gulf Stream.'

'I think the Gulf Stream's overrated. But it's not just the cold. I don't think it's a good idea, in the dark, after a big dinner, and a glass of wine or two.'

He laughed again. 'You're right,' he said. 'A walk, then.'

To be honest, even that wasn't a great plan. It was black as hell outside and he was pretty hammered. He didn't even get a coat. He went straight over to the bay window and slipped out. I looked at Peach and at the coffee-table, crowded with chocolate papers and brandy glasses, then I hurried out after him.

'Sasha?' I called, in a kind of loud whisper. He had vanished, it seemed, then he turned and I saw his pale face. He was halfway across the lawn to the gate in the wall that led to the beach path.

'Look, why not take a turn down the drive to the road?' I said, when I drew up beside him. 'That path's a death trap. There's tree roots and it's steep as anything.'

'I remember,' Sasha said. 'It was a golden summer, Donna. And my sixteenth birthday party was supposed to be the jewel in the crown. The oldsters went off and left us. We had the house to ourselves. Keys to the cocktail cabinet.'

'How old were the others?' I said. I would have given Sasha a few years on Paul, although Ramsay was harder to pin down with his scarred face. But hadn't Rosalie called him 'Big Bruv' at one point?

'Old enough,' he said. He'd reached the gate but he turned and leaned against it instead of unlatching it and passing through. 'Not old enough to get served in a pub, but old enough to have one wild night to remember. Or forget, in Peach's case.'

I shivered. It wasn't winter cold yet, not the sharp cold that makes your eyes water and your nose run, but there's no mercy this close to the sea. Tonight it was a creeping foggy damp that got right in your bones. I hugged myself, the beads of mist on my thin shirt sleeves making me feel even colder as I pressed them to my skin.

'Here,' Sasha said. He shrugged out of his cashmere jumper and put it round my shoulders. It was warm from his body and slightly stale. 'I need to make it up to Kim in the morning,' he said. 'She chose the best house she could find in a place she knows I used to love.'

'Why did it bother you so much?' I asked. Maybe it was because I was wearing his jumper, but I had forgotten for the moment that he was a client. Maybe the close damp stealing round us made me feel cocooned or something. For whatever reason, I spoke like we were just two people, the way he'd been speaking to me.

'Who knows?' Sasha said. I waited. 'Yes, that's not much of an answer, is it? What can I tell you? The party got slightly out of hand, as these things do. Some locals came and joined in. Not skinheads or anything. Kids we knew vaguely from days on the beach. But . . . our family's idea of good fun for a crowd of teens wasn't the same as theirs.'

95

I knew exactly what he was talking about, of course. It was the same on the island. Worse maybe. People like them coming up for the summer, driving their big cars too fast on the single-track roads, talking too loud in the pubs, asking for couscous and Tabasco in the corner shops and laughing at the puzzlement they caused. I had watched crowds of them at Talisker Bay at sunset, laughing and shrieking, ruining the high tide for the beach fishermen.

'And it turned out they were right and we were wrong,' Sasha said. Then he sniffed and shook his head. 'Jesus, forget I said that, eh? I need a swim to sober me up. Come for a swim, Donatella. Come and be my little mermaid. Make me feel less of an old bull walrus.' He was through the gate and holding it open for me. I walked backwards across the lawn.

'No way,' I said, 'absolutely no way, and if you don't stop I'll go and wake everyone up.'

'Oh, come on. You can practically paddle to Belfast from here.' His voice was getting fainter. I walked over to the gate and peered after him.

'Sasha, please,' I said, then shrieked as he popped up from where he'd been crouching on the other side of the wall. 'Jeez-us!' I said.

'Do you happen to know what this kind of gate is called?' he said, opening it and closing it, clicking the latch back and forth.

'Isn't it just a garden gate?'

'No,' he said. 'If you look closely at the fastening mechanism . . .' I bent over the top to see what he was talking about '. . . it's a kissing gate.'

His lips brushed mine, dry and warm, and I pulled back after less than five seconds. But five seconds is a long time in kissing and we both got the message. I got the message of what it was that had hooked Kim ten years ago. And he got the message that he wasn't completely up a gum tree, trying it on with me. As well as that, I got a message from myself that my taste in men hadn't improved any.

When I saw the glare of headlights swinging round on us, my first thought was relief. But then there's a way people stand when they've just been kissing and might do it again, and as Jennifer's car came round the bend of the drive and lurched to a halt, her door was already opening.

'You fucking pig,' she screamed. 'You fucking goat. What are you playing at?'

'I thought you didn't like that kind of lang—' Sasha said. He wasn't even bothered. He was laughing. Me? I shot across the dark grass like one of the rabbits, darted into the drawing room and threw Sasha's jumper onto the back of an armchair.

'Twat!' I told myself, under my breath. 'Pillock!'

Peach opened her eyes and sat up blinking. 'Is that Jelly back?' Her voice was thick with sleep and booze.

'Nope,' said Sasha, entering the room behind me. 'You must have been dreaming.' Out of the corner of his mouth, he said to me, 'She's off again! She reversed all the way to the road. I didn't know she was a good enough driver.'

'I wasn't asleep,' Peach said. 'I heard every word everyone said. The stitched lips and the locked box and I've remembered the last one.'

'Never mind that now,' said Sasha. 'Time for bed. Up the wooden hill to Bedfordshire.'

Peach blinked up at him, working him into focus. 'Did you do this?' she said. 'Did you bring us all back here?'

'Upsy-daisy!' Sasha put out his hands and Peach took

97

them. 'Heave-ho!' She tottered a little but he grabbed her under her ribs and they made it out of the room. I took a deep breath and let it out in a whistle, then started tidying.

————————

By the time I got upstairs, all was quiet. A lamp glowed dimly on the half-moon table at the end of the long corridor, showing me the little heaps of phones, tablets, laptops and cables outside every door. I'd wait awhile until everyone was definitely asleep before I started creeping around, gathering them.

First, I settled down at the little writing table in my room and wrote my diary: food and drink notes; how many baskets of logs we'd got through; which chairs no one had sat in; which rooms had got the most use. I was disappointed no one had been in the study yet, if I was honest. I wondered if I should maybe start a jigsaw on the round table in there. It was a trick I'd learned to stop country-house-hotel guests mumping if their rooms weren't ready. Give them a tray of tea with buttered gingerbread and a jigsaw with the edge done and all the bits turned over the right way and they'd be sorry when their rooms *were* ready. Buttered gingerbread was the key. Or malt loaf. Banana bread at a push. So long as it wasn't biscuits from a packet. I looked at myself in the black glass of my window. This was going to work, I told my face. I knew what I was doing. I was going to cope with this single-handed weekend and my mum was going to promote us all weekend up in Glasgow. Everything was fine. There was nothing creepy about the house. This was just a strange crowd. I yawned at my reflection and then had to wipe spit-squirt off the open pages of my notebook before I started writing out their names to test my memory.

Fuzzy Peach, Sweary Buck, Jennifer, if she ever reappeared, Sasha the Snake, Kim the client, Tall Paul and his wife, the fragrant Rosalie. I didn't even need a mnemonic for her. I'd cracked it. There was just one left. I stared into the mirror. The one with the skin. I could look it up in Kim's emails, or nip out and read the label on his door, but I had a better way.

There's a trick that always works. I put my hands flat on my desk and told myself my left index finger was the first letter of his name and my right was the last. I closed my eyes and started reciting the alphabet. I'd only got to G, with no fingers moving, when a thud on my wall jolted my eyes open. Ramsay!

Good old subconscious, I thought, as I went to investigate.

Peach was making her unsteady way along towards the room she was supposed to be sharing with Jennifer. She must have stumbled and fallen against the wall.

'You okay?' I said softly. She looked at me out of one eye, the other screwed up. I had never been so drunk it was easier to focus with one eye but I'd seen it.

'Going to throw up in privacy,' she said. 'Don't want Buck taking the piss all weekend.' She must have seen my face, because she went on, 'Don't worry about your lovely bathroom. You don't get to be such a spectacular lush that your husband kicks you out and keeps the kids without learning how to be a civilized puker.'

'Oh, Peach,' I said. 'I'm sorry.'

'Me too,' she agreed. She burped, but didn't make a move. I wanted to encourage her to hurry but I didn't want to offend her.

'Anyway, I'm not as bad as they all think,' she said. 'I *didn't* black out tonight. I *didn't* fall asleep. I really did hear every word everyone said. *And* I remembered the third swear.'

'That doesn't matter now.'

She was swaying. 'No, but I remember,' she insisted. Her voice was getting low and thick. 'No one else remembered except me. For the deepest, darkest secrets of all, you have to swear *I'll go to my grave.*'

'And what's the deepest darkest secret of all?' I said.

Peach came very close to me and spoke in a whisper.

'She died, Donna. She drowned in the sea.'

Chapter 8

They were gone! The scene popped into my head the second I woke the next morning and I snapped upright. Last night, when I talked to Peach in the corridor, the laptops and phones were gone from outside the bedroom doors. I had watched her lurching along towards the bathroom. If they'd been on the floor I'd have been scared she'd step on one.

I bounded out of bed and put on a dressing-gown. A quick peek round the corner confirmed it. The hallway was empty.

If one of these jokers had hidden the devices, I'd get in trouble for not picking them up quick enough. I knew I would. Same way I once got blamed for some toffee-nosed madam breaking her crown on a goose drumstick. She said she'd thought the meat was all carved off the bone, which was pure crap, because who picks up a gob of meat that hasn't got a bone in it? She said I should have warned them as I served it and the arsehole manager backed her up and scolded me.

I had a hollow feeling in the pit of my stomach as I went

down the back stairs in my dressing-gown to start some coffee and get going on the hollandaise. And going through to lay out juice and cereal didn't help my mood. Whoever built this house couldn't get past the sea view to think about sunlight, and while a west-facing dining room's fine for evenings – because dinner's more about lamps and candles anyway – it's hopeless at breakfast time. We had done our best, with pale striped wallpaper and curtain poles long enough to keep the windows completely unobstructed, but it niggled at me.

I went to look at it from the bright end of the room, and decided it would do. They probably lived in city flats with no daylight to speak of at all. And, besides, out on the lawn a black rabbit was nibbling busily. I smiled. The Breakers was idyllic and I was mad to think otherwise. I should take a picture of those rabbits and get them on our website gallery, really. Then I heard a creak overhead – Paul and Rosalie's room – and hurried out to shower and dress before anyone saw me in my jammies and asked for a refund.

Something caught my eye as I was leaving the room but, with no coffee inside me, I was still too dull-witted to do more than flag it for later. Good thing too, because I barely got out of sight before Ramsay came bounding downstairs in a running vest and tiny shorts and went out the front door.

By the time I was dressed for the day with my hair scraped up in a ponytail and my face bare – no one wants to look at sticky lipstick first thing – I could hear various showers running and a hairdryer blasting away in Rosalie's room.

I took bowls of blackberries and blueberries in to set out on the sideboard, started in on a warm baguette and was ferrying in the first of the coffee when Paul appeared.

'Hi,' he said. Then: 'Oh, my God, I've completely forgotten your name.'

'Donna,' I said, with a smile. 'Don't worry about it.' Then for laughs, I added, 'I can't remember if you're Paul or Ramsay.' Because I'd smiled he had to smile too, but it nearly killed him. Either because he reckoned he was too cute to be mistaken for Ramsay with his ravaged face or just because he had no sense of humour before his coffee. For whatever reason, he sat down with his face like a skelped arse and asked what was for breakfast.

'Irish Florentine,' I said. 'Bacon instead of the spinach. Or a general fry-up if you'd rather.'

'I'll have the full heart-attack,' said Buck, coming in with his hair wet. 'Don't suppose there's black pudding, is there?'

'Some of the best black pudding you've ever tasted,' I said. 'We get it from a farm butcher in Castle Douglas.'

'I'll have the eggs,' Paul said, as if I'd forgotten him.

'One eggs F, one fry-up,' I said. I took the long way round to the kitchen, checking in the bank of linen cupboards along the back corridor. Sheets, towels, tablecloths . . . the same neat piles of linen I'd shelved there as soon as the paint was dry. No sign of the missing devices.

Back in the kitchen, I hit speed-dial and tucked my phone under my chin while I started the sausages.

'Hiya,' I said, when my mum answered. 'Are you at the convention centre already? It sounds packed.'

'I've sent you some pictures,' she said. 'It's pandemonium. Going really well, though. Those close-ups of the dining table and master bathroom are bride catnip. It was well worth the cost of blowing them up.'

'Cool,' I said. 'It's great publicity even if it doesn't cough up any actual bookings.'

'Eh? I've got two bookings for a recce – cake-tasting and all that – and a twenty-four-hour hold for an actual wedding. Don't you ever check the live calendar?'

'Wow!' I said. But I knew my voice sounded hollow. 'Listen, I've got a bit of a problem down here.'

'Tell me,' my mum said. Of course she did. She always said I could tell her anything.

'I've lost their devices.'

'What did you say?' The background noise had got even worse because someone was talking over a Tannoy. Or maybe she just wished she'd heard me wrong.

'They put them out on the corridor floor, like room-service trays, and I was supposed to take them and lock them in a cupboard so they'd have a proper break. But I forgot.'

'Well, obviously someone *else* took them. Isn't one of the guests a teacher? She'll be used to confiscating phones. I'll bet you it was her.'

'How did you know that?' I said.

'What? Kim told me in an email. Donna, I haven't got time to chat. How's it going in general?'

'Weird,' I said. 'Hostile. Fine, from our point of view. Except – like I'm trying to tell you – for about five computers and seven mobiles vanishing overnight.'

'Trust me,' said my mum. 'One of the women probably stepped in. My money's definitely on the teacher. Or is there a bossy one?'

'The teacher *is* the bossy one. But she left.'

'*What?*' She sounded bothered for the first time. 'One of the guests has left?'

'Like I told you. Hostile. They've driven one away already and the weekend's hardly started.'

'As long as it was nothing to do with Home From Home,' my mum said. I thought about what Jennifer had seen before she roared off and gave an uneasy little laugh. 'And as long as it wasn't the one who's paying the bill.'

'Nope and nope,' I said. 'This is more like old ghosts from the last time they were all together. They were right here, Mum. They stayed in this house. And – like I said – there are ghosts.'

'They're having you on,' my mum said. 'Maybe they think that's part of the fun for a house in the middle of nowhere. Hey! We should do that for Hallowe'en. Haunted-house weekends.'

'Except the one who said that most definitely wasn't having fun,' I said. 'She was dead drunk and she'd just woken up.'

'Probably had a nightmare.'

I nodded – as if she could see me. 'It's hard to explain.'

'Families,' my mum said. 'Bound to be undercurrents.'

But when I went back into the dining room to deliver breakfasts and take orders from the new arrivals, they were chatting away like a house on fire.

Everyone was there except Ramsay and Peach, but both arrived within minutes, Peach coming downstairs slowly with a glass of what looked like Alka-Seltzer and Ramsay loping along from the front door, breathing hard and dripping with sweat. His running top was stuck to his body and showed that he didn't have an ounce of spare flesh on him anywhere.

'Freak,' Paul said. 'There was a mix-up in the hospital. No way you're related to me.'

'Nor me,' Buck said. 'What are you in training for?'

'Sublimating your illicit proclivities, isn't it?' Sasha said.

'Don't choke on that dictionary,' said Buck. 'You're worse than Rosie.'

'Donna, if I spread a towel on the chair can I have my breakfast now?' Ramsay said. 'I'm starving.'

They sat in different seats from the night before, Sasha in front of the window and Kim at his side. They were holding hands on the table-top. Buck stayed close to the food laid out on the sideboard. Rosalie drew out the chair next to her and patted it for Peach to sit there.

I ferried in more plates of bacon and sausage, more mounds of velvety Florentine. Peach watched them pass and moaned in her throat.

'You should eat,' Ramsay said.

'After I've had my liver salts.' Peach raised her glass. Rosalie gave it an odd look, then quirked a smile at Sasha.

I saw Sasha's answering glance but didn't know what it meant.

'So, Buckaroo,' said Ramsay. 'I take it *you're* not in training any more?'

Buck laughed, rolled a sausage up in a slice of buttered bread and dipped it into a pool of tomato ketchup. 'One five-K was my whack,' he said. 'It nearly killed me. I raised twenty grand, though.' Ramsay gave a long sinking whistle. 'Anyway, I don't need to run. They recruited me for the phones. I do twenty hours a month cold-calling.'

'What's this?' said Kim.

'Operation Smile,' Buck said. 'Corrective surgery for harelips and cleft palates in the developing world.'

'Oh!' said Kim. 'Of course.' She gave him an awkward little grin.

106

Buck smoothed his moustache with his napkin and flashed his eyes at her. 'Don't feel bad,' he said. 'My handler at Smile's blootered through all my finer feelings. Then all my coarser feelings. Samundra. She's based in the Philippines. Every time I try to get out – pleading shiftwork and kids – she sends me a new photo of another sloe-eyed tot.'

'And now,' said Sasha, 'because *you*'ve lost all sense of what birth defects are suitable for table conversation, we all have to think about it whether we want to or not.'

'Suitable for *table* conversation?' said Buck. 'Have you done a body-swap with Miss Priss and her School for the Dainty?'

Peach waved a hand at him. 'Oh, please don't make me laugh yet,' she said.

Sasha flung himself out of his seat and strode to the sideboard, where he swiped up a fistful of blackberries. He headed back, throwing them into the air and catching them in his mouth. When he drew level with Peach and Rosalie, he tossed one, caught it, then stopped, his hand flying to his throat, choking sounds coming from him.

'Oh, God, Sasha!' said Rosalie. 'Jesus, you idiot. Does anyone know the Heimlich manoeuvre?'

'I do,' I said, banging down the plates I was carrying and rushing forward.

Sasha shook his head, put out a hand to stop me and groped on the table-top, picking up an empty coffee cup, then throwing it down.

'Here,' said Rosalie, grabbing Peach's glass.

Sasha knocked back a good glug of the fizzy liquid, then coughed hard and deep, finishing with a retch. A blackberry shot out of his mouth and landed on the marble skirt of the fireplace, sending up a cheer from the rest of them. Kim, who'd been hopping from foot to foot, sank down into her chair again.

'God almighty, Peach,' Sasha said, staring into the glass and coughing again. 'That's pure vodka.'

There was a long, silent moment and I wondered if Peach was going to grab the glass and douse him with it. In the end she just shrugged. 'Hair of the dog,' she said. 'Vodka, Perrier and Alka-Seltzer.'

'Your own recipe?' said Buck. He and Peach were the only ones who laughed. 'Oh, don't be so fucking sanctimonious, Sasha. This is supposed to be a party.'

'It's not as if I don't know I drink too much,' Peach said. 'I'm not an imbecile. But your anniversary shindig doesn't seem like the time to sign the pledge. Anyway, how'm I supposed to stay in touch with my sponsor when we've gone all Amish for the weekend?'

'How about a round of Buck's Fizz for everyone?' I said. 'I was going to serve them tomorrow but there's no reason I can't start today.'

'Lovely,' said Kim. 'Count me in.'

'Me too,' said Peach. 'But no orange juice, eh? It's full of sugar.'

They all laughed at that and were friends again. They were like children, I thought, the way they split and regrouped, made allies and enemies and five minutes later changed sides. As I went to the fireplace to retrieve the spat-out blackberry, Paul and Sasha were collaborating to tell a story about a stag weekend in Amsterdam, not a trace of coolness anywhere.

I was thinking just that – how childish they seemed – when I straightened and saw, at last, what I had half noticed earlier. There was something on the mantelpiece that I hadn't put there: in a silver frame, behind glass, a photograph of a crowd of kids. I looked closer and felt a smile spread across my face.

They were all there. Sasha was sitting at a table heaped with presents, a paper hat on his head and a huge grin showing unfixed teeth crowded in his mouth. His eyes were glittering. I had never seen a kid so excited about his birthday. Peach, just as cheerful, and even chubbier than today, was sitting next to him in a striped boatneck T-shirt that showed the beginning of her breast buds. Buck stood to one side, legs slightly bent as if he didn't know whether he'd be in the photo. He looked straight at the camera, grinning under a bum-fluff moustache and wispy goatee.

Behind them, Paul leaned forward, a long swipe of blow-dried hair hanging down, obscuring his gaze. Ramsay had the same no-nonsense haircut he wore today, with no attempt to hide the flare of acne all over his face. He was staring off to the side, ignoring Jennifer, who was pushed up against him, laughing as if someone had said something funny and she was checking to see if Ramsay got the joke. Right at the edge of the group stood Rosalie in a shiny dress with big sleeves and a wide skirt, her toes turned in and her hands clasped in front of her, her head on one side and her mouth pursed. She looked at the camera from the corner of her eye. What did she remind me of? An idea floated through my brain but was gone before I could catch it.

Anyway, I had been standing still far too long. 'Kim, Sasha,' I said. 'Look. Someone's left a surprise for you.'

Sasha flicked a glance at it, not pausing in his description of the brothel he and Paul had been stuck in, no credit cards, police on the way. Then his voice died and he rose, steadying himself with both hands on the table-top.

Kim got to it before him and picked it up. 'It's this room!' she said. 'Oh! It's the time you were all here before, isn't it?'

I hadn't noticed but she was right. Behind the kids in the picture was this fireplace and the mirror above it. The camera flash reflected there.

'What?' said Paul, coming over. 'Who brought this? Christ, look at my hair.'

Peach shrugged and Buck shook his head.

''Fess up, Kim,' Ramsay said. 'You planted it, didn't you?'

'Me?' said Kim. 'What makes—'

'Who else would have a photo of Sasha's birthday party?' Rosalie said.

'Uh, his sister?' said Kim. 'Anyway, what's the problem? It's a sweet thing to do. I would have wrapped it up and given it as a present, not left it here. That's kind of weird but . . . it's a lovely thought.'

'Oh, yes, it's darling,' said Rosalie. 'I'm *thrilled* to have a picture of me looking like Grayson Perry.'

I couldn't help a snort of laughter, because that was exactly the thought I'd been chasing.

'You are the most self-absorbed woman who was ever born,' said Sasha. He spoke coldly and stared at the photograph as if it was a cockroach. He was standing quite close to me – they all were, huddled round to study the picture – and I could see that his breathing was tight and fast. What was wrong with them all?

'Jellifer!' said Peach, suddenly. 'It must have been Jelly who put it there. And then she forgot to scoop it up again when she flounced off.'

110

'Or she stuck it there deliberately after she'd decided to flounce off,' Ramsay said.

'It can't have been Jennifer,' Sasha said. 'She doesn't know how to Photoshop people out of a picture. She barely knows how to email an attachment. Ramsay?'

'I've got the technical know-how but I'd have Paintshopped my face. I look like a rock bun.'

'Cherry and macadamia,' said Buck.

'Oh, puke,' Peach said.

'But who's been Photoshopped out?' said Kim.

No one answered. In the silence, I scrutinized the picture. It *was* an odd grouping, actually. The four in the front row were centred but the three in back row were off to one side, nothing but an empty wall filling up that quarter of the picture. And as I looked up and down, from picture to setting and back, I could see that the wall shouldn't have been empty. There was a bell-pull there and the edge of an alcove with a drinks cupboard below it. Someone had copied a section of plain wallpaper from the edge of the shot and repeated it.

'Who's gone?' Kim said again.

Sasha lifted the photo out of her hands. 'No one,' he said. 'Couple of random locals who wangled themselves an invitation.' He put an arm round Kim. 'I'm not angry with you,' he said, 'but I want you to stop this. Admit who it was that suggested this house as a venue. Was it Jennifer? Was it someone in this room?'

'What the hell?' said Rosalie. 'Sasha, we all *know* it was you. Stop messing about.'

'Look,' Sasha said, very calm, 'this is ridiculous. Someone knew we were coming back here, didn't they? It wasn't me. I'm not playing silly buggers with a photograph.' His voice was rising now. 'Kim, for God's sake, forget about your stupid weekend and all your stupid surprises and gimmicks, and tell the truth.' By the end he was shouting.

Kim's face drained until she looked as sick as Peach the night before on her way to the bathroom. She pushed past Ramsay and Buck, both of them trying and failing to catch her, and rushed out of the room. We heard her running upstairs and the soft thump of her feet on the bedroom corridor, before a door slammed faintly.

'Jesus,' said Peach, and took off after her.

'What a prize you are, Sasha,' said Rosalie. 'Why don't you believe your wife?'

'She found the house online,' Ramsay said. 'She booked it. She wanted to make you happy. Jennifer brought the picture, obviously. Since she's the only one who's not here. She Photoshopped out the . . . unhappy memories because *she* wanted to make you happy. For God's sake, Sasha!'

'Yes,' said Paul. 'For God's sake, Sasha. Stop being the same spoiled brat you were twenty-five years ago, can't you?'

Sasha was glaring around at them as he listened, every look like a flick-knife. Then he got to me. 'Why are *you* standing there listening to all this?'

'Good question,' I said, starting to move. 'It was just pretty interesting, I suppose. Sorry.'

Buck laughed. 'What the hell sort of operation is this?' he said, which stung me even though I suppose I deserved it.

'No, it's my fault,' Sasha said. 'You make the mistake of mingling with the staff and they lose all sense of their place.'

I speeded up, trying to get out of the room before I turned and told him where to go, but Rosalie came after me, grabbing my arm before I could get through the kitchen door.

112

'Mingling?' she said.

'What?' I wanted to shake her off but her grip was firm.

'Sasha and you have been mingling? Fraternizing? Consorting? Communing?'

'Give me a break,' I said. 'You don't need to warn me off him. He's forty-odd and I'm—'

'Oh, Donna, I'm not warning you off him,' she said. 'I'm telling you to be careful around him. You're, what . . . twenty? Twenty-one? That's right up Sasha's street, actually.'

'I'm older than *that*!' I said. 'And it's his anniversary! And he's your brother!'

'Which means I know him better than most. It's his tenth anniversary and his wife is twenty-six. His first wife was twenty-five when he traded her in.'

I knew my lip was curling but I couldn't help it. 'Jesus, poor Kim.'

She rolled her eyes and nodded. 'Go and get those Bucks Fizzes while I see how she's doing,' she said. 'We're going to need them. I'm traumatized from looking at that picture. What an insufferable little prig I was.'

I went into the kitchen and leaned against the closed door. They still weren't done. Voices rose up over the monitor.

It was Ramsay. 'Google it, for God's sake! Google "Holiday House in Galloway. Sleeps ten" and I bet this one comes up on the first page. You're paranoid!'

'The more I think about this the less sense it makes,' Sasha said. 'None of you knew you were coming here? None of you looked it up? None of you recognized the address?'

'Believe it or not,' Paul said, 'this weekend isn't the be-all and end-all of our lives, Sasha. I came as a favour to Ro, and Ramsay came as a favour to me. We haven't all been poring over the website for months in delicious anticipation.'

'Speak for yourself,' said Buck. 'I was thrilled to get away on a free jolly. But of course we didn't recognize the address. The house has changed its name! We put the postcode in the satnav and first we knew was when we rocked up on the drive same as you. Stop freaking out.'

'Why not phone Jennifer and ask her if she brought the photo?' Buck said. 'If it's bothering you that much.'

'Because we've all given our phones to Donna and she's spirited them away,' said Sasha. 'And Jennifer won't answer a landline number she doesn't recognize.'

'Right,' said Paul. 'We've all given our phones away. That was my suggestion, if you remember.'

'So?' Sasha snapped.

'Rosalie asked me to suggest it. Kim asked her. Kim wanted you to have a proper break but she knew you'd cut up rough. So I stepped in. See? We're not hiding anything. We're not playing games. For God's sake, calm down before—'

'She's crying her bloody eyes out,' Rosalie said. I hadn't heard her coming back. 'What is *wrong* with you?'

I knew I had to take the champagne in, not to mention three more plates of breakfast, but I knew if I went back through there now Sasha would ask for his phone and I'd have to admit I didn't know where it was.

'Now look,' Rosalie was saying, 'we all need to try to get this weekend back on track. For Kim's sake. It's her anniversary too, in case it escaped everyone's attention. This weekend isn't another instalment of *The Sasha Show*, like the last one. So what do you suggest? Quick, before Peach gets her back down here. Oh, and, Sasha? Lay off.'

'Lay off what?'

114

'Yeah, yeah, butter wouldn't melt in your bum crack,' Buck said. 'I second that. Lay off, Sasha.'

Communing, consorting, mingling. The words fizzed in my head. Fraternizing. Rosalie's breathy hiss in my ear. Another instalment of *The Sasha Show*.

'What's going on?' I asked my own reflection, bright and bulbous in the curved side of the chrome kettle. But, like me, my reflection didn't know.

Chapter 9

1991

'The bar' turns out to be the pool room. Bryan Adams is finished at last and there's a Bobby Brown on that nobody knows how to dance to, so they've turned it down a bit. It's still too loud to let you talk but at least the speakers aren't squealing and buzzing and I can only feel the hum in my body if I lean against the table.

Sasha's mugging away at the other end of it, shaking something in his two hands like someone trying to get a lucky throw of the dice, or like a Spanish dancer with her maracas. When he stops and unscrews the top of the canister I feel stupid for not knowing it was a cocktail shaker, but it's too dark in here for any of them to see me blushing.

He pours the drink he's been mixing into two glasses and hands them to Jellifer and the Rosalie girl in the homemade dress. They clink and drink, then raise their glasses to Sasha. He doesn't notice. He's already busy mixing more.

I never know what to do at a party if you're not dancing.

116

So I concentrate on eating my plate of food, even though the gluey salads taste disgusting. It's not salad cream sticking them all together. It's something like cold cheese sauce, claggy and bland, and it's beginning to melt and slide in greasy lumps off the chunks of potato and pasta. I keep eating anyway, wondering how to get any of this crowd to talk to me, wondering what I'm doing here, wondering how come Lynsey isn't beside me.

Then the music changes. I love Madonna. I wanted to dress like her when she had lace in her hair and leather knuckle gloves. I'd been putting one extra necklace on every day, thinking if I did it gradually enough Mum wouldn't notice. It lasted until I added the big cross, then I was back to square one and had to smuggle them out of the house in my bag, get ready on the bus and remember to take them off again at home time.

I put my plate down on the pool table and I'm thinking about maybe starting to move my feet and see if anyone joins in, when I notice what the rest of them are all laughing and whooping about. Lynsey's dancing. She's biting down on her bottom lip with her goofy little buck teeth and she's got her hands locked above her head as she gyrates her hips in time to the bass.

Suddenly Sasha's standing beside me. The smell of the cologne makes me sneeze and I blush again. But it's only because there's so much of it. It would smell fine if he'd worn it like you're supposed to.

'Thirsty?' he says.

'What is it?' I look at the glass he's holding. It's shallow and conical and it's got fruit in it as well as liquid.

'Pimm's,' he says. 'Mostly. It's a cordial.'

'Have you got any Coke?'

'I've never heard of putting it in Pimm's, to be honest.' He takes a sip from the glass, keeping his eyes on mine. 'I think it would be a waste, actually. It's pretty good as it is.'

'I meant instead.'

'Absolutely. You are my guest, and if you want a cup of cocoa, I will get you a cup of cocoa.'

'Coke!' I say, even though I know he's teasing me.

'All milk or a mix of milk and water? Do you take sugar?'

So I grab the glass out of his hand and take a swig of it.

It tastes like all booze tastes if people would be honest: like something that could have been nice but with a bit of medicine added that spoils it.

'See?' Sasha says, when I've swallowed the first mouthful. 'Wouldn't it be a sin to put Coke in that?'

'Or cocoa,' I say, and take another sip.

'Drink it down far enough so it doesn't spill and then we can have a dance,' he tells me.

It's not until I've been dancing with Sasha for two records that I notice Lynsey's got a glass in her hand too. I put my mouth close to Sasha's head and shout, 'What's Lynsey drinking?' The smell of the cologne's stronger than ever now he's hot from dancing. 'She's only twelve.'

'Cordial!' Sasha shouts back. 'And look at Mo.' He turns me round with his two hands on my shoulders and points towards the girl in the 501s. She's pouring herself a glass of something from a white bottle you can't see through.

'How old is she?' I shout. When I twist round to make sure he can hear me, my back presses against his front.

'Twelve,' Sasha says. 'Ish.' He's not really shouting now. He's close enough so that he can say it straight into my ear. His breath is hot.

'What is that she's pouring?'

'Peach-flavoured cordial.' Sasha turns me again and puts his arms round me as a slow song comes on.

———————

I don't know why we stop dancing or whose idea it is to play Postman's Knock. I do know it's quiet in the pool room now. The tape's finished and no one gets up to put on a new one.

'I don't think I know how,' Jellifer says.

'One goes out,' says Morag. She's lying back on a beanbag with her legs straight out in front of her. Her hair's pushed back off her sweaty face and her mascara's in panda rings halfway down her cheeks. 'That's the postman. And he knock-knock-knocks. And when he says who the letter's for, that one goes out.'

'And then that one's the postman and they knock-knock-knock,' says Rosalie. 'And then someone else goes out.'

'How is that a game?' says Jellifer, and the rest of them – the rest of us – split into peals of laughter.

'Because you pay for the letter with a kiss,' I say, bold with them now although I don't know why. 'That's the rule. You have to kiss whoever comes outside to get the letter.'

'It should be called Telegram Boy's Knock,' Jellifer says. 'It's telegrams you pay for at the door. Nobody pays the postman for letters.'

The other girls laugh so much that Morag cries rivulets of mascara down through her panda rings all the way to her chin. Then Rosalie – lying next to her, sharing a beanbag – tries to rub them off with an ice cube out of her drink and loses it down Morag's top.

'Maybe it's Christmas,' says Ramsay, ignoring them. 'You tip the postman at Christmas.'

'And the binman,' says the beardy boy. 'Hey, let's play Binman's Knock. It's the same as Postman's but dirtier.'

'Who's first?' Morag says. After a long silence, Lynsey giggles.

'Oh, go on then,' the beardy boy says, getting to his feet and weaving unsteadily towards the door.

'This isn't going to work,' Jellifer says. 'Too many sisters and brothers. Too many cousins.'

'Oh, no,' says Sasha. 'That is where you are dead wrong, Jelly. We have worked this out with graphs and charts, haven't we, lads? This is absolutely planned down to the last drop of shared blood. Do not worry.'

When the knock comes on the door, the three girls giggle. Lynsey giggles too but a half-beat too late. She looks tired and I wonder what time it is. Light is still slicing in through the gap in the middle of the curtains but it's orange light, no real brightness in it.

'How do we decide who's going?' says Morag. 'Not me, obviously. Buck's my brother.'

'Jelly-bean,' says Sasha. Someone wolf-whistles and someone else makes a long, squeaky kiss-noise.

'Says who?' Jellifer's blushing.

'Says the birthday boy,' Sasha tells her. 'Go on.' Jellifer mixes herself another drink from the bottles on the pool table on the way to the door. She holds the white bottle upside down over her glass but only a few drops come out.

'Good grief, Morag,' she says.

'It's nice,' Morag says. 'It tastes like peaches. I'll taste like a peach for the postman.'

'Good grief,' says Jellifer again.

We wait in silence for a few minutes after she's gone. I'm thinking about how it would feel to kiss that boy with the scrubby beard.

'Who's next?' says one of the tall boys. The one with the nice skin but the long piece of hair over his face anyway. Paul, I think.

'Naw, naw,' says Lynsey. 'That's not how you play it. That boy comes back in and the girl stays outside and she knocks and then another boy goes out.'

'That's not how *we*'re doing it,' Sasha says. 'Paul's next.'

'Fine by me,' the boy with the hair says. He wiggles his eyebrows at the dress girl as he goes out and she stands up before he's even knocked.

'It's not you, Rosalie,' Sasha says. 'Paul's the youngest boy so he gets the youngest girl. That's Peachy Morag here. You still with us, Peaches?' Sasha pokes Morag with his toe. She rolls softly away from him.

'Who gave you a badge and a whistle?' Rosalie says. She goes out and we can all hear them giggling as they run along the corridor.

''S not how you play it,' Lynsey says.

'Right,' says Sasha. 'No point me hanging round in here if no one's going to do what they're told anyway. I'm going outside and I'm not going to tell you if I'm a postman or a binman. You'll have to wait and see.'

He gets to his feet and staggers about a bit before he's balanced.

'Have you got pins and needles?' says Lynsey. She sounds drowsy. 'Have you got a dead leg?'

'I've got a *third* leg,' says Sasha. Ramsay guffaws, then smothers it.

He raps out a shave and a haircut on the door before he's even closed it behind him. 'I've got a package for . . . Carmen,' he says.

'You don't have to go,' Ramsay tells me. I stare at him, trying to work out if he's asking me to stay. But it can't be that, because Lynsey and Morag are in here too.

'I don't mind going,' I say, getting my feet under me. 'Will you be okay, Lynsey?' She doesn't answer. Her eyes are closed. Maybe she's sleeping. Morag definitely is.

I make my way to the door. I'm sure I can feel lumps of food inside me, floating on a rough sea of Pimm's.

He's not there. There's no furniture in the hall and nowhere for him to be hiding. I look owlishly from one end of the corridor to the other where the stairs rise up. Maybe he wants to sit down and kiss. Or even lie down. Binmen, I think with a giggle, are dirty.

I check the room opposite, a big living room with three settees round a fireplace and an oval table in a bay window overlooking the front garden. And I look in the dining room again, where the pile of presents is still sitting on the wee table. What kind of person could get to this time on his birthday and not open his presents yet? What kind of parents are Anna and Oliver, going out before everyone's gathered round, watched him opening his presents and sung 'Happy Birthday'?

Suddenly I'm as tired as Lynsey and I don't want to go back into that dark room and have them all laugh because he ran away rather than kiss me. If Lynsey wasn't here, I would leave by the front door and start walking home.

For sure, I need the fresh air. The lumps of chunky salad have all stuck together in one big ball now, bitter with olives and salty from that black stuff, and it's right at the top of my stomach. I swallow hard. Maybe a drink of water would help. But when I think about that kitchen and the flies on the dirty dishes, I start to sweat.

Where did my mum say the downstairs toilet was? Somewhere at the back. I bang through a half-glass door and find myself in a cramped little hallway with a narrow staircase. So many doors. One opens onto a short corridor with cupboards and drawers, then there's a scullery with a washing-machine and an ironing board set up. I suck my breath in hard and clench my teeth. There's nothing for it now. I'll have to go out the back into the cobbled yard and hope there's a hose to wash it away after. I blunder down the side of the staircase and I've just started scrabbling with the heavy latch when a door to the side opens and there he is. There he is. There he is, standing there staring at me.

'How was I supposed to find you?' I say.

He's pale now, and the razor-burn on his jaw stands out like when Lynsey scratched her chicken pox. He looks back at me glassily.

'I needed a slash,' he says. 'But you found me in the end. C'mere.'

But he doesn't give me a chance. He comes towards *me*, his breath sour with the sick he's been getting out of himself, clashing with the cologne. He pushes me against the wall, so my head whips back and makes a bumping sound.

'No,' I try to say, but it comes out as a burp. He steps away from me then and, grabbing me by one wrist, he swings me round like he's doing a hammer throw and sends me spinning and lurching into the bathroom. I can hear him laughing at me as I start to retch.

123

I only realize I'm still wearing the party hat when it falls off my head into the toilet. I squeeze my eyes shut. I hear him laughing but I see nothing.

Even once I've rolled away from the toilet and I'm leaning back, I keep my eyes shut to stop the high bathroom walls from closing in around me as they spin.

When I come out at last, when I'm feeling better enough to stand up and walk, he's waiting with two water glasses, smiling at me. I groan and take one. He laughs again, watching me realize that it's not water.

'No point stopping now,' he says.

'Right,' I say. I want Lynsey and I want Mum. Close-up, his crooked teeth with bits of white food stuck in them make me feel queasy again. It's rotten of me to think that because I haven't rinsed my mouth out either, but I can't help it. I hold my breath and take a big glug of the vodka.

This time, I don't even get the door locked and I can feel him rubbing my back and murmuring at me as I heave. 'There, there,' he says. 'Better out than in.'

Then everything's gone. Like anaesthetic at the dentist. It's different from sleeping and coming back is different from waking.

When I *do* come back, drifting down out of my head into that bathroom, with the floor rock hard even under the towels I'm lying on, I shuffle until I'm propped up against the wall and I finally use a gulp of the vodka like mouthwash. But I've got nowhere to spit it. I don't want to spit it into the glass or on the floor and look like a pig. Mum told me not to show her up and Sasha's still here. He's at the door, his body still in the bathroom with me but his head poked out into the hallway. I swallow the vodka down.

'Of course not,' a voice is saying. 'She's my *cousin*, Sasha!'

'The kid's not your cousin.'

'The kid's twelve!'

'Don't blame me. Blame Paul.'

'Is that Sasha?' Someone else is coming. 'Have you been in the bog this whole time? Rosalie's having a meltdown. We need to phone Anna and Oliver.'

'No way, José.' Sasha's laughing.

'Someone needs to take the little one home.' That's the first voice again. 'She's as pissed as a fart and she's crying for her mum.'

'Fuck's sake,' says Sasha. 'It's supposed to be a party.'

'And she should be playing Pass the Parcel and blowing out candles.'

'If you take her home now, we'll never hear the end of it,' Sasha says. 'Tell her to stick her fingers down her throat and give her a pint of water. What the hell's wrong with Rosie?' He slams out of the bathroom, without looking back at me. Whoever he's been speaking to leaves too, one of them out the back door and one of them up the narrow stairs. I can hear the racket of feet on the bare boards.

It seems like a minute later that I sit up slowly and look around, except that the light's changed again and nothing's spinning now. I feel like a bag of cement as I pull myself up and look in the mirror. The stupid dye from the crêpe paper looks like bruises all over my eyes and I can't tell if it's gone that way or if it started like that and I've looked like a clown right from the start of the party.

Lynsey.

I push my hair behind my ears, splash my face and dry it with bog roll. All the towels are on the floor, like he made me

125

somewhere soft to lie when I was down there. I creep out into the quiet house on my tiptoes, listening for movement and looking round corners.

The pool room's empty. Someone's knocked over all the bottles and the booze has soaked into the felt, filling the air with a sickening stench. The big living room's empty too. The two little rooms on either side of the front door are deserted. And there's no one in the long dining room. I can't face the kitchen.

Upstairs is silent but it's a different silence. I walk to the other end of the corridor, listening, then push open a door at the far end. It's a mum-and-dad room, stale and cluttered. The furniture is carved dark wood and the footboard of the bed is so high I have to walk right up to it before I can see over.

Buck, the boy with the beard, and the girl called Jellifer are lying there. They're naked, with the sheets pushed to their waists. He's got hair on his chest too and she's got heavy breasts that have slid to each side and tremble as she snores. I'm turning to leave when I realize the boy has opened his eyes and is staring at me.

'I'm looking for my sister,' I say. I'm surprised by the rasp of my own voice.

The boy nods slowly. 'She went home.'

I don't believe him. Lynsey wouldn't leave without me. 'When?' I say.

'A bottle and a half ago,' he says. Then he sticks out his elbow and jabs the snoring girl. 'Jell? That's right, isn't it? The little one went home?'

'Wha'?' says the girl. Her eyes open a slit and she pulls the sheet up to cover her breasts, then turns onto her side, groaning. 'Jesus, I feel like shit.'

'Lynsey, the little girl? She went home, right?'

126

'Yes! I told you! She was walking home, right as rain. She didn't want anyone to go with her.'

I don't believe this either. It'll soon be dark and Lynsey's scared of the dark. By the time I speak, the girl's snoring again. I don't think she'll know I was ever there.

'But was she okay?' I say. 'Was that you at the bathroom door saying she was crying for her mum?'

'No,' says the boy.

I believe that. His voice sounds different from the ones I heard while I lay on the towels and Sasha argued with them, his head round the door.

'Anyway,' he says, 'she'll be home by now if she went before Sleeping Beauty here came back upstairs.' He pokes Jellifer with his elbow again, but she's fast asleep.

I walk away.

The next bedroom's got three single beds, jumbled and covered in clothes. It stinks of boy but it's dead and empty.

I can hear whimpering in the next grown-up room, but it doesn't sound like Lynsey. She's always either shrieking with laughter or bawling with outrage. I've never heard her whimper. I knock softly on the door.

'Morag?' comes a girl's voice.

'It's Carmen,' I say, pushing the door open and entering.

'This isn't a good time.' That's definitely one of the two boys I heard speaking. He's sitting on a low oblong kind of settee with no back, and he's got his arm round the girl who's not Morag. Rosalie. She's crying hard, quiet steady tears dripping off her cheeks and hitting the skirt of her dress.

'Sorry,' I say. 'I was looking for my sister. And I heard you. Are you okay?

'She's gone,' the boy says. 'I think Ramsay took her home.'

That makes more sense. If she couldn't find me, maybe she *would* get someone else to go with her.

'Okay, thanks,' I say. 'This is . . . a lovely party but I think I'll head off if my sister's gone.'

Rosalie lifts her head and stares at me. Her face is swollen like a bee-sting. 'A lovely party?' she says.

'I mean thank you for having me. And Lynsey too.'

They stare at me so I leave. But I don't make it as far as the stair head. From inside the dark little room where they were playing when we arrived comes the noise of someone choking and gulping like a blocked drain. I go battering in and stop dead. It's the Morag girl. She's changed into her nightdress, as if the party's definitely over. She's lying on her back on the floor, sobbing too hard to puke and retching too much to cry. The stink of the peach stuff is enough to make my stomach roll over and rise up, but I manage to wedge my foot under her back and flip her over onto her side. I even take the time to pull her nightie down a bit to cover her up. I run out before she gets going, though, knowing I couldn't watch it without joining in. I tell myself I'm racing to find Lynsey but really I just want to get away.

Outside in the garden, the stars are piercing the navy blue up high, but the sky's still pink at the edges, long shoots of dusky light shining through the trees and dappling the grass, where the other one of the two tall boys is lying on his back with a cigarette in his mouth looking straight up at the sky.

'Where's my sister?' I say. It's beginning to feel like some kind of prayer that doesn't work, like some kind of spell that I haven't learned right.

'Hey!' says the boy. 'Miranda, right? We thought you'd gone.'

'Carmen,' I say, and only realize he was kidding me when he laughs. 'Do you know where she is?'

'Don't worry. She went home.' But he points to the gate in the garden wall that leads to the beach path.

'That's not the way.'

He can hear the worry in my voice and he sits up. But his face goes grey behind the mess of his skin and he lets himself drop back slowly until he's flat again.

'Maybe it's a shortcut.'

'It's not.'

'Scenic route? I'm sure she's all right.'

'Are you Ramsay?' I say. 'Your brother said *you* took her home.'

'I was going to try,' he tells me, 'but I'm so wasted.' At least he's honest. I wish I had stayed in the pool room, like he said. In the same room as Lynsey.

'Anyway,' he says, 'she's not alone. Sasha stepped in.'

I have no idea why I start running. Only that our house is absolutely the other direction from the beach. It's inland. There's no reason at all for Sasha to take Lynsey towards the sea. I can't get his words out of my head. 'The *kid*'s not your cousin.' It's like a drumbeat inside me. 'The *kid*'s not your cousin.' And then it's not just in my head any more. My blood's beating to the rhythm of the words and my feet are rapping them out on the ground. I fling myself through the gate in the wall and feel the trees close over up above me.

Under here, the sinking day is gone completely and it's far too dark to run on this steep path. So I feel my way, checking my footing before I step forward. Once I trip, but I don't fall. I cry out though. And he hears me.

'Who's that?' His voice comes from a long way down.

129

'Paul, is that you, ya chicken? Is it you, Ramsay, ya big fairy? Well, you owe me one!'

I'm running now, heedless of falling. 'One what?' I shout. 'Where's Lynsey? What have you done?'

Then there's silence. I plunge down and down, ignoring the sudden lurches as the path drops away from me. He's hiding. At the top of the sand, at the edge of the trees, I stop and hold my breath. He's in there somewhere, crouched in the brambles and nettles or standing behind a tree. He can't be more than a few metres off. But as I sweep my gaze round again, looking for movement, I catch sight of something from the corner of my eye. A bump where there shouldn't be a bump, a smudge of dark in the middle of the rippled gold tide in the bay.

Lynsey is walking into the sea.

I knock off my shoes and start running, ignoring the thrashing noises behind me as he comes out from his hidey-hole and scuttles off up the path.

She's deep enough that her hair is floating out behind her, long silver ribbons of hair streaming out from under the paper hat that's still jammed on her head, that's jammed on so low it must be covering her eyes like a blindfold. And she keeps on walking away.

Chapter 10

'A beach picnic,' I said. 'But grand. Think Edwardian.' I had copied the idea from one of the posh hotels on the island. 'It's all down there already in hot boxes and chillers.' Chicken legs and strawberries. Frittata and fruitcake. I had prepared most of it in advance, bought in the rest and ferried it in two trips. I liked that there was a back drive to a parking space handy for the kitchen. It meant we could hide the rigging and set up the show for maximum impact. We had a key to the slipway barrier in case any of our guests ever brought a boat. It was strictly against beach rules to take a car onto the shore for any other reason except towing a boat in or picking it up, of course, but the beach cottages didn't overlook the track and no one had seen me.

'Won't the gulls have eaten it?' said Sasha. 'Or the local peasants?' They were waiting for Peach, but they'd decided to do their waiting in the breakfast room, while I stacked the dishwasher. I should have known the guests would gravitate towards the kitchen. It happened at every party. The monitor was off and I'd made sure an oven glove was hanging in front of it.

'It's safe,' I said. 'It's a private beach.'

'What if it rains?' said Sasha. Rosalie huffed out a sigh of exasperation but I was glad someone had brought it up. I like showing off about The Breakers. We worked hard on it.

'There's a pavilion,' I told him. 'Open to the sea at the front, but with a waterproof blind you can unroll if you need to.'

'Lovely,' said Rosalie.

'Eating lunch huddled in a beach-hut?' Sasha said.

'Yes, Sasha,' said Rosalie. 'It's a treat. A beano, an excursion, a jolly, a spree.'

'Why do you always say fifteen words when one is too many?' said Sasha.

Paul laughed. 'Ha! See, Rosie? It's not just me.'

'For merriment, joy, diversion and delight,' said Rosalie.

'What is *wrong* with you?'

'She drives me bonkers with it,' Paul said.

'I'm taking the whole weekend off the live tournament,' said Rosalie. 'With penalties racking up for lost turns. You can't expect me not to practise. Acionna's streaking ahead as we speak.'

'Who the hell's Acionna?' Sasha said.

'My Scrabble nemesis. I think she's Russian but she's a complete ninja in English. So stop acting as if you're the only one who's got a life elsewhere, Sasha, and be here and now. With us. We're going on a picnic.'

'And does Peach need to take a flask?' Sasha said. 'Or is there booze laid on? Oh!' he added, as Peach appeared in the door from the back hall. 'There you are.' But he must have heard her. The rest of us had.

'Sasha, if you're going to keep making digs and pulling stunts until I break down and say I'm a miserable alkie with a ruined life, I'll do it now,' Peach said. 'Because it's really boring for everyone.'

'Yah-boo, sucks to you,' said Paul, putting his thumb to his nose and wiggling his fingers at Sasha. 'You've spent so long swishing about your little empire with all your under-lings bowing and scraping, you've forgotten what it's like when people don't revere you.'

'I suppose it must look like an empire from where you're standing.'

'Oh, for God's sake,' said Rosalie. 'Why don't you all slap your todgers on the table and settle it once and for all?'

'Not with ladies present,' Sasha said. 'Peach, Kim, why don't you step outside?'

'What's that supposed to mean?' said Paul. 'What about Rosie?'

'Ignore him,' said Rosalie. 'He's trying to provoke you.'

'Yes, ignore me,' Sasha said. 'Let's all go and have some jolly fun on the beach at Knockbreak Bay.'

In the silence that followed this, we heard Buck and Ramsay coming, Ramsay taking the stairs in little sets of three, like a kind of dressage, and Buck plodding after him.

'Where is everyone?' Buck was saying. Then when he appeared in the doorway: 'There you all are! Let's go!'

––––––––––

'Operation Laptops,' I said to my mum. I was upstairs trying to make my bed, which wasn't going too well with the phone tucked into my neck. 'I'm going to search the whole house and come clean if I can't find them.'

'Of course you'll find them,' she said. 'There's no need for all the drama.'

'I'd rather have the tiny drama of a house search today than the major drama on Monday when we find out they've been nicked. We'd be up Shit Creek with the insurance if we don't notice for two days.'

'Donna, are you seriously telling me there's been a break-in?' She sounded strained and it tripped my guilt-switch. I wasn't the only one working hard on my own this weekend. The convention centre sounded packed to the rafters again.

'Okay, no,' I said. 'Not a break-in. More of a mix-up. I'll track them down.'

'They went for the picnic idea, then, if you're on your own?' It wasn't like her to check. She never gives way to anxiety. She was the one talking me down from ledges on the long journey to where we were today. 'They're all pals again? No atmosphere?'

'Equilibrium,' I said. 'Or . . . a Mexican stand-off, at least.'

'Doesn't sound like much fun.'

'It's going really well, Mum. I didn't mean to worry you.'

But her anxiety had infected me and, around the back corners of my brain, a whispered chant had begun, about how much we'd ploughed into this venture, even on top of Grandpa's money. I had wondered if it would cause a rift: Grandpa leaving the hard cash to one of his two kids, only bequeathing his watch and his good golf clubs to my uncle and auntie. But they didn't care. They came over for the funeral, all suntan and mangled vowels, then couldn't get back to Sydney quick enough. I got the feeling Grandpa's money was loose change to them. My auntie said something about it being my mum's just reward for the grunt work. As if *she* wouldn't have bothered helping us clear the house to get half of it.

'So why do you sound so off, if it's going so well?' my mum was asking me.

'They're just a weird crowd,' I said. 'Kind of competitive. Kind of . . . cruel.'

'Cruel?' It must have seemed like an extreme word to someone who'd never met them.

'Not all,' I said. 'Not the brother that didn't bring his wife. And the client's sister-in-law's working her arse off to keep the peace. But, yeah, some of them are cruel. The husband's a bit of a . . . I think his wife needs someone to talk to.'

'Don't get involved,' my mum said. 'She's surrounded by people to talk to. Anyway, in a year's time you won't even remember their faces. God knows the brides and their mothers are all starting to blur up here. Oh, listen, Donna, there might be a couple coming for a look on Monday. But not till after work and they know we can't stage the house for them. I should be back, but in case I'm not . . . If you *did* have a chance for a bit of a tidy round? It's a Mark and a . . .' I heard her rifling through papers '. . . an Erin. Okay?'

'You're a marvel,' I said. 'I'll make a batch of fairy cakes and crack a half of cava.'

But first, I told myself once I'd hung up, where were the bloody phones? Who was in the room this morning when Sasha moaned about not being able to get hold of Jennifer? I screwed my eyes up, remembering. Kim had rushed out; Peach had rushed out after her. Rosalie had gone to see if they were okay. All the men were there. And none of them had admitted to hiding the damn things. Would they have? I thought so: it was a moment of cooperation.

So one of the women must have them. Peach was far too drunk. The stash would be in either Kim's room or Rosalie's. It was worth starting there anyway.

When I saw the state of the master bedroom, I was glad I'd come snooping. The Breakers isn't a hotel and it's always hard to say whether people in a holiday let are going to clean up after themselves or expect to be waited on. Kim and Sasha, clearly, didn't do *anything* for themselves. The curtains were still shut, except where one had been dragged away from the window and hooked over the edge of the dressing-table mirror – I guessed to let Kim do her make-up. The bed was a twisted mess of covers and pillows. I noticed they hadn't taken the bedspread off and they'd slept on the decorative cushions instead of the proper pillows with their white linen pillow slips. That always drives me kind of nuts. I used to shudder, when I was on room service, to see some fat salesman sitting up in bed topless with the bedspread clamped under his hairy armpits, and more than once when I was chambermaiding I'd seen mascara or even spit on a velvet cushion someone had fallen asleep on, while the real pillows lay discarded on the floor. I wondered if I could do a turn-down, folding bedspreads over a chair-back and piling cushions up on its seat. I'd start with the next booking, maybe. It would seem like the rebuke it was if I suddenly did it tonight.

It didn't take long to check the wardrobes and the blanket box. Kim didn't have the stash anywhere in here. What she did have, hanging on one of the beautiful moleskin padded hangers I had chosen so carefully, was a floor-length white-cotton nightgown with a ruffled neckline and pink ribbon threaded through its cuffs and collar. This was as well as the skimpy lavender-coloured satin teddy she had worn last night that I had just folded under her pillow for her.

I smiled. I like believing people are happy, and it was good to think the sexy lingerie she had brought – or maybe Sasha had brought – for her anniversary had been cracked open a day early. Also, it was endearing to think that Kim, with her expensive hair and her platinum eternity ring, wore such uncool nightclothes normally.

I went into the bathroom, trying not to groan out loud at the litter of towels on the floor. I knew I should have gone for white. Every website I'd looked at about running a holiday home said to go for white towels because you can hot-wash them with bleach and they never fade. But I wanted to carry on the lavender theme from the bedroom and now my lovely bath sheets were lying on the floor, one with a dirty great footprint on it. Sasha must have tromped right over it when he got back in from the garden the night before. I took a photo of it and emailed it to my mum, subject line: *When you're right you're right.*

But before I hit send, I found myself standing still, skin tingling.

I bought the towels to go with the décor and Kim brought a slinky teddy to go with the décor too. The pink and white cotton was the anniversary treat. From the man who had married her when she was sixteen.

I tidied the bathroom as quickly as I could, swallowing hard on the sour taste in my mouth, trying to forget the feel of his lips and the smell of brandy when he kissed me. If he reckoned I was only twenty, same as his sister did . . .

In five minutes, I was out of there. I let my breath go and sucked in a good deep one from the air in the corridor, which suddenly seemed a lot cleaner than the air inside that bedroom.

Paul and Rosalie's room couldn't have been more different. It was the flash one, for a start. We'd had to hold our noses to kit it out and, God, it was awful. But some people like the Bond-villain look. For another thing, it was immaculate. Rosalie had made the bed, tight and smooth, and there was nothing out of place in the bathroom. She'd even dried the taps. It took me no more than a minute to check all round.

Buck and Peach's room was strewn with clothes, every flat surface sprouting detritus – coins, lens solution, toiletries, crumpled receipts, water glasses, coffee cups, chocolate wrappers. I hoped they were both guilty. If one of them was fastidious, a weekend sharing with the other would be torture.

Where next? The empty room that should have been Peach and Jennifer's yielded nothing. The snug neither. Nor Ramsay's room, except for the news that he was as neat as a pin, making me wonder if *Paul* had dried those taps. If it was a family thing.

It was easier to search downstairs: no wardrobes, no chests of drawers or dressing-tables, no low beds to shove things under. I started in the kitchen and worked round. When I got to the billiards room, I was beginning to have wild thoughts about intruders again and my mouth was dry. If we got stung for compensation this early on, we'd never recover.

Then, with a whoop of relief, I saw what I'd forgotten. There were great big deep built-in cupboards in here – full of deckchairs and parasols since this room faced west to the terrace. I should have thought of it. Who would want all those machines in their bedroom overnight? One of them was bound to chirp or beep at an incoming message or start, near morning, to hoot the melancholy warning that its charge was running low. I threw open the cupboard doors, convinced my search was over.

The smell caught me in the back of the throat, sending me reeling away with my hand over my nose. It was sweet and chemical and vaguely familiar. I took a deep breath, held it, and clicked the cupboard light on. A knife, looked like one of my best kitchen knives, was sticking out of the back wall, pinning a gob of sodden coloured paper to the panelling. Whatever the paper was soaked in was causing the stink. Perfume, maybe. Hairspray? It dripped out, staining the wall in a long smear. And what *was* that blob, saturated and reeking? I poked a finger at it. It was too dark to be writing paper, too small to be a napkin and too flimsy to be anything else I could think of. I pulled my phone out and snapped a picture of it.

Right after the click, the sound of someone coming in the front door made me fumble the cupboard shut and start away from it. I was racking up the balls in their frame when I heard a whistle.

'Donna?' It was a man's voice, but from that one word, I couldn't tell whose.

'In here,' I shouted.

'I knew this shutdown would be impossible to stick to,' Ramsay said, entering the room. 'We need to look up the tides and whatnot.' He sniffed but said nothing.

'Why?'

'We've found a lobster pot and Kim wants it as a souvenir.

I say it's abandoned because it's far too far up the beach but my brother reckons it'll float at high tide and we should bait it and try to catch a lobster.'

'Actually, I'm not sure I've got time to cook a lobster. Sorry to be a kill-joy.'

'More for the thrill of the chase,' Ramsay said. 'What larks.' He sniffed again. 'Have you spilled something?'

While I was deciding whether or not to answer, he spoke again. 'What must we all look like to you? Jennifer, for instance. God knows what you think of her. And Peach! The way Buck goes on.'

But he was skirting round what he really wanted to say, I could tell.

'I don't think anything. I'm just trying to make sure everyone has a nice weekend,' I said. 'You know, for TripAdvisor. It's worrying to think The Breakers isn't the kind of house where people feel happy.'

'It's nothing to do with the house,' said Ramsay. 'The house is lovely.' But I remembered Buck's arm bristling with goosebumps as he walked in through the front door and I remembered Peach saying she wouldn't sleep alone. 'When we were here before,' he went on, 'things went a bit far. At Sasha's party. Lots of pranks and dares that didn't go well. If we hadn't all been cousins we'd have thankfully dropped each other.'

'Sounds bad,' I said.

He blinked and tried a laugh that didn't quite work. 'I overstated it a bit. There are some memories we'd rather forget. That's all. Where better than a beach to wash them away?'

'Wash them? Were you thinking of swimming?' I hadn't considered it. I hadn't put any towels down in the pavilion.

140

But Ramsay was laughing. 'God, no! Buck's pretending he might, though, as a wind-up, so Peach is having hysterics and of course Kim doesn't understand what's going on. I volunteered to come back up and do the admin, more or less to get away from them.'

'Strange wind-up,' I said. I was thinking of the gob of soaked paper and wondering if I should show him. *That* was a strange joke too, if it was a joke. And Ramsay didn't seem like a joker. 'Peach said something last night. I thought she'd had a bad dream.'

He nodded and gave me a thoughtful look. 'About swimming?'

'About someone who *went* swimming.'

'There was a story,' Ramsay said. His top was made of that feather-light technical fabric and it was fluttering now as his breathing quickened.

'Is this the ghost? The one Peach doesn't believe in? The one the Ouija board would be for contacting?'

'Telling tales out of school, Ramsay?' It was Sasha. He was standing in the billiards-room doorway and we couldn't see more than his silhouette. 'That's not cricket, you know. That's not the spirit of manly honour than runs through every red-blooded British male. '

'Is this you outing me again, Sasha?' Ramsay said. 'Am I supposed to go and sob into a lace-edged handkerchief now? How many times do you need to hear me say I'm not gay?'

'Once with feeling would do it,' Sasha said. 'Or bring a girl to Christmas dinner. Get married. Give your poor parents some grandchildren. There's lots of ways, really. Grab the fair Donna right now and make her swoon with your caresses.'

'Uh,' I said. 'That's not included in the package.'

Ramsay burst out laughing. 'You're like something from a panto.'

Sasha took a couple of steps forward into the room, then stopped dead. 'What's that smell?' he said. He swallowed hard. 'Where's it coming from?' His chest was rising and falling too fast for someone standing still, and I was sure his face had paled. All of a sudden the line of his top lip looked clearer than before. 'What are you cooking up, you two?' he said. 'Tell the truth. What did that hysterical bitch tell you to do?'

'Which hysterical bitch is this?' said Ramsay. I was glad he had asked, because I genuinely didn't know.

'Kim,' Sasha said. 'It was her that brought us all here. Who else would buy—' He jerked his head away to the side, biting off his own words. Then he turned and stalked out.

'Blimey,' I said.

'That was interesting,' said Ramsay. 'Don't you think he's protesting a bit too much?'

I frowned and shrugged.

'How many times has he said he didn't know we were coming here and Kim organized everything on her own? And then you know what I think just happened? I think he was going to say she'd bought . . . something that hasn't come to light yet. It was a slip. He's behind it all. He's blaming Kim for . . .'

'Shits and giggles?' I suggested. 'What is she *doing* with him? Is he rich?'

'Not rich enough,' Ramsay said. 'He'd have to be Croesus for me to touch him with the Eiffel Tower.'

We both laughed for a minute, and then I think maybe he remembered that Sasha was his cousin and I was a complete stranger. I know I remembered that he was a client and I was a so-called professional.

'Well, anyway,' I said, 'about the lobster pot. It's probably got a tag on it with the owner's business name. If it's Irish go for it. But if it's from round here, if it's Stranraer or Kirkcudbright, I'd leave it. Folk pick them up and hand them back for a tenner. It wouldn't look good if you carted it off.'

'Look good?' he said. 'On TripAdvisor?'

I smiled and we went our separate ways. I hadn't forgotten about the soaked paper. I was going to check my knives and see if that really was one of mine. But I left it where it was in the meantime because, if Sasha was being wound up, that was fine by me.

It was the computers I'd forgotten.

————————

Mid-afternoon, I heard them come back and go to their rooms but I didn't see them and I was too busy, even with the switch to the easy menu, to go looking. I ironed the tablecloth and napkins and starched them crisp. I polished the candlesticks that had gone cloudy in the cupboard – that damp salty air at its tricks again. I sliced lemons for fingerbowls and rubbed the skins off peas to halve them as decoration for the *amuse-bouches*.

'God knows we can't have whole peas in their big ugly skins rolling around the plate,' I muttered to myself. 'Everyone'll throw up.'

At teatime – anchovy toast, from the hamper, and the anniversary cake – I plastered a smile on my face and headed for the drawing room.

'Tea is served,' I said, bumming open the door and turning with a flourish to display the tray.

'Jesus, more food,' said Sasha. I didn't react and I didn't see anyone else so much as glance at him but he went on, 'Sor-reeee. I meant to say, of course, oh goody. I'm absolutely famished. All the fresh sea air has whipped up my appetite for *at least* another two meals today.'

'No one's ramming it down your gullet,' said Rosalie. 'Ignore him, Donna.'

'Ignore who?' I said. It went against my training but Kim snorted and Kim was the client. 'I'll be back in a minute with the teapot.'

I listened in on the monitor while the kettle was boiling.

'It's not Marmite,' Peach was saying. 'It's anchovies.'

'It's fucking disgusting, whatever it is,' Sasha said.

'Don't be such a brat!' That was Rosalie.

'I like it,' said Buck. 'I'll eat your share.'

'We're paying good money for this pathetic joke of a so-called posh weekend.' Sasha's voice was rising. I could hear him faintly along the corridor as well as through the machine. There was a tiny delay, so it sounded like an echo.

'Tea,' I said, entering the room again, hoping my cheeks had died down a bit. The big bay window was open wide and the sea louder than ever. 'Brrrr. Aren't you cold?'

'I was sharing the delicious food with the adorable rabbits,' Sasha said. I frowned and looked out. There was a black rabbit there, right enough, and there was a gob of something brown lying on the edge of the grass.

'Sasha didn't care for the anchovy toast,' Paul said, 'so he threw it out the window. Do you have any plastic you could put down under his high-chair at dinner, Donna?'

'I'll close this,' I said, going over. 'It's getting foggy. Can I bring you something else instead, Sasha? Or will you make do with a slice of cake?'

'*We* all love it,' said Buck.

'What a sycophant you are,' Sasha said. 'Has no one ever told you not to suck up to the staff? They might have trained themselves to smile those supercilious smiles, like tarts faking the big O, but they despise you for it.'

My trained smile faded. But I didn't have to think of anything to say because Sasha was just getting started.

'Perhaps *Ramsay* would like something else,' he said. 'Ramsay doesn't care for fish, do you, cupcake? Oh, Lord, that's a thought. I hope there aren't any oysters planned for our wondrous dinner tonight. That would never do for Ramsay. Or mussels, either. I can't see Ramsay with his tongue in a mussel shell.'

'What are you even on about?' said Paul. Ramsay was staring at the carpet.

'Your loyalty does you proud,' Sasha said. 'Not to mention your scrupulous PC attitude.'

'Well, I'll leave you to it,' I said. 'Dinner's at eight. Drinks and nibbles in here at half seven, okay?'

'Nibbles?' said Sasha, giving a mirthless laugh. 'God almighty! *Nibbles?*'

'Yes, Sasha, nibbles,' said Rosalie. 'You know. Appetizers. Snacks. Hors d'oeuvres. Edible equivalents of openers, pre-ambles, prefaces, prologues, preludes.'

But Sasha wasn't listening. He pointed at the cake. 'Who did that?'

'I made it,' I said. 'It's a Victoria sponge. And butter icing.'

145

'Did you do *that*?' He jabbed a finger so close he nearly poked it into the piped message. 'Who told you to write that?'

'Um,' I said, with a glance at Kim.

She had her head in her hands. She didn't see him lunge forward and swipe up the whole cake, draw back his hand and make to throw it out of the window.

'Let's see if the fucking rabbit can help us choke this down,' he shouted. He sounded ragged, as if he was halfway to sobbing.

'Sasha, cool your jets,' Peach said. 'What the hell is wrong with you?'

'And please don't try to throw the cake out onto the grass,' said Buck. 'Because the window is shut and if it splats on the carpet I will still eat it and it won't be pretty.'

Paul laughed at that and laughed even harder when Sasha wheeled round and ran towards Buck, only stopping when the cake was about an inch from his wide-open mouth.

'I know you probably mean this to be frightening,' Buck said. 'But if it was my wife in skimpy nightie it would be my number-one naughty daydream, so it's slightly backfired, Sasha, my old bean.'

Sasha threw the cake down on the plate, pretty much missing it. The icing message was just about gone, but he smeared his hand over it to obliterate it completely. Then he took a long breath and looked over at Buck.

'Your wife in skimpy nightie?' he said. 'Jesus Christ, if we don't get rid of that image *none* of us will be able to eat our dinner.'

It was the first time I had seen Buck's face without a smile about it anywhere.

'Watch it,' he said.

'Or what?' said Sasha. He was himself again. 'Are you going to set your wife on me? In that case I surrender. She sat on my lap last Christmas, you know, and my back wasn't right till Easter.'

'She sat in your lap?' Buck said.

'Rosalie, you saw it,' Sasha said. 'You arrived just in time to stop me getting groin strain from Ten Ton Tessie's lap-dance. You'll—'

'Oh, just shut up, Sasha,' said Rosalie. 'Buck, she did nothing of the sort.'

'Anyway, don't worry, Buckaroo. I wouldn't have done it. Obviously. She'd have as much luck with Ramsay.'

I picked up the tray and got out before I had to hear any more.

Chapter 11

I had saved my best black and white for tonight: a stiff linen shirt with a nipped-in waist and a pair of glazed-cotton cigarette-pants that I wore with spike heels. My feet would be killing me by the end of service but I reckoned it was worth it to make their special night elegant in every way. Of course, that was before the slanging matches and threat of food fights. Still, I wound my hair into a chignon and put on eyeliner and red lipstick anyway, out of solidarity with Kim. Or pity, maybe. Or to look so good that Sasha would regret being such an arse to me.

That was probably how he had got Kim, now I came to think about it. Acting like a total shit to the world at large, then turning on the charm just for you is hard to resist. I'd been caught that way once or twice. But I hadn't married it. I added a layer of lip gloss and admired myself. Then I jumped as someone knocked softly at my bedroom door.

'Come—' I began, then thought the better of it. 'Who is it?'

'Buck,' came the reply.

I went to the door and opened it.

'Wow,' he said. 'You look great.'

'It's my "Fuck off, Sasha" look,' I said.

Buck nodded. 'Well, that's the thing. Peach is in the bath and Rosalie's in the bath and Kim might be in the bath too, but at any rate she's crying her eyes out in her bathroom. I heard her through the wall. So we all wondered if maybe you would pop in and see if she's okay.'

'Who all?' I said. Buck jerked his head so I stepped out onto the landing and saw Paul and Ramsay standing there in a huddle.

'Where *is* Sasha?' I said. 'Isn't he in there with her?'

'No,' said Paul. 'Sasha seems to have fucked off, to use your excellent phrase. I'll be sure and mention your way with words on TripAdvis— Christ, I'm only kidding. Your face!'

'Has he gone as in gone?' I said. 'Jennifer-gone? Taken the car?'

'If only,' said Ramsay. 'No, he's just stormed off in a huff about something. Else. Jesus, if he was gone, we could have a wonderful evening. Rosalie could start drafting a divorce petition for poor Kim ...'

'You could come out of the closet,' Paul said.

They were still enjoying it in a twisted kind of way, I thought, as I went along to the master suite and tapped on the door.

'It's Donna,' I said. 'Can I come in?' There was no answer. I pushed the door open and stepped inside. They'd managed to trash the room again since that morning: the bed disarranged, drawers hanging open, more towels on the floor. I gave another soft knock on the bathroom door.

149

'Go away and leave me alone!' Her nose was blocked and her voice sounded hoarse. She must have cried pretty hard to get like that in the time she'd had.

'It's—'

'I don't care who it is,' she said. 'I'm sick of the lot of you.'

'I'm not one of the lot,' I said, edging round the door. 'There's just me. Let me help you.'

'Oh, fuck, Donna,' she said. She was sitting propped against the bath, in her underwear – bright pink polka-dot scanties, threaded with black ribbon – holding an almost empty tumbler.

'Good for you if that's water,' I said. 'If it's gin, even better.'

She didn't laugh but she lifted her chin, acknowledging the joke. 'It's water.'

'What happened?' I sat down on the edge of the bath and put a hand on the top of her head.

She slumped against my legs and let a huge breath go. 'What happened?' she echoed. 'I was working as a waitress in a . . . Well, no, I wasn't.' She laughed and it was the bleakest sound I'd ever heard. 'I was working on a hairband concession at Princes Square in Glasgow. One of the little barrows? And I met a charming, handsome, well-off, funny, apparently kind man, who was nearly over his horrible ex. I walked right into the forest with him. Not a backwards glance. So now I've got my own store in Pollokshields, great credit with the wholesalers because Sasha's a guarantor. Gifts, kitchenware, accessories, jewellery. No more hairbands for me.' She lifted the water glass and toasted herself in the full-length mirror.

'What exactly does Sasha do?' I said. 'No one's ever mentioned . . .'

'No, God, no. They wouldn't have. It pisses him off if you

150

get specific. He's an executive. He's CEO of Mowbray's. He's a captain of industry.'

'Is it something embarrassing?'

'Wouldn't that be lovely?' said Kim. 'No, just dull. Wholesale chilled and frozen food distributors.'

'That's not dull,' I said. 'I'd have been interested in a conversation about that – supply chain, perishability and everything – if . . .'

'If Sasha wasn't such a knob?' She almost laughed, although it went a bit ragged. 'You never think you should drive to your own tenth anniversary weekend in separate cars in case you need to get away, do you?'

'I can give you a lift to the station in the morning,' I said, 'but you've had it tonight. Maybe you could borrow Rosalie's car. Or Ramsay's.'

'His sister? Her brother-in-law? No way. I'm the outsider. I don't suppose I could borrow *your* car?' she said. 'I'd leave you collateral.' She glanced around until her gaze fell on the diamond engagement ring. Then she started crying again.

'Shush,' I said. 'Shush now. We're going to mend your face, but it'll be easier the sooner you stop crying. And you're wrong about them. They're all worried. They came and got me and sent me in here.'

'Don't be stupid,' she said. 'One of them has done this. Don't you see? I know they're all pretending to think it was Sasha. But I'm sure it wasn't. He was thunderstruck when he saw where we were.'

'Either that or he's a great actor,' I said, thinking of the way he jabbed at her so quick and sure and the way she fell over and bounced right back up again as if she was used to it. 'But even if *you* didn't tell him, did you tell a friend that might have told him? Could he have asked one of your friends what you were planning? To make sure . . . Oh, I don't know . . . that he had the weekend free or that he didn't plan something else that would clash?' I had worked in hospitality long enough to know all the ways surprises could go wrong. I'd never seen the Holy Grail – someone dropping dead from a massive heart attack when everyone jumps out and toots the noise-makers – but I'd seen nearly everything else.

'The only person I told was my pal, Tia. But she's a book-club pal. Sasha doesn't know her.'

'Doesn't know her well, or doesn't know her at all?'

'Wouldn't know her if he tripped over her,' Kim said. 'We don't have joint friends. That's why our anniversary is all his cousins.'

I gave her my best rueful grin. That was kind of pitiful, when you took a square look at it. 'And you don't think much of his *own* friends either, eh?' I said. 'If you didn't include them?'

'His friends!' Kim said. She hawked hard and then looked around. I whirled a handful of bog roll off the holder and gave it to her to spit into. 'Sorry. Gross. His friend Matt is the only one he ever mentions and I'm fifty per cent convinced it's short for Matilda.'

'And he wouldn't . . . I mean, I've never been married but have you got a password on your email?' There had been approximately a thousand million emails from her about this weekend. My mum had set sticky keys to churn out screeds of fake responsiveness, like her own little hospitality bullshit generator. 'Maybe he snooped.'

Kim shook her head. She was watching me redo the fold and fan on the end of the toilet paper. I couldn't help it. 'It wasn't Sasha. I know him. It was one of them. And I don't even really believe it was *one* of them. I think they did it together. Maybe not Peach or Rosie. But the men. It's one of their side-splitting jokes. They're like a cult.'

'But what do you think they did?'

'They hijacked my anniversary to settle some old score with Sasha, of course. From that party that's got them all up to ninety.'

'But how did they find out you were coming here?'

'No, no, no, it goes back farther than that. Ramsay's got the know-how. Buck's got the appetite for it. And Paul? Well, Paul loathes Sasha. Loathes him.'

'Know-how?'

'Oh, what do you call it?' said Kim. 'Search . . .'

'Engine optimization?' I said. I knew all about that: starting a business that lived and died by website clicks, we had got sick of thinking about it.

'Ramsay could definitely have hacked into my computer and made sure I found this place when I started looking.'

'Well,' I said, 'Home From Home probably worked pretty hard on making sure you'd find it too. And did Ramsay even know you were planning a get-away?'

'Rosalie did, so no doubt everyone did. And they brought the locked box and the doctored picture. Sent the hamper.'

And ordered the message on the cake and soaked that paper and stabbed it with a meat knife, I thought. It made sense. 'And has something else happened since teatime?' I asked her. 'Why did Sasha get upset enough to storm off again?'

'He wouldn't tell me. I was in here doing my hair and he was getting dressed and then suddenly he came in and came

153

right up behind me and shrieked at me. What had I heard, who had been speaking to me, or did I do it myself.'

'Do what?'

She shrugged. 'I don't know and I'm sick of trying to work it out. If you won't lend me your car, Donna, will you at least bring me a bottle of wine and a big bag of crisps and tell them all I've got something catching?'

'No,' I said, standing up, 'but I'll do that thing you were talking about yesterday where you cough it up and I hold it for you. You can get through tonight, Kim. You might even have a laugh. Okay, your marriage is a bust – you need to face that. But this weekend could be a riot of a funeral. *This* could be the story you tell at dinner parties for the rest of your life, with your actually kind, maybe not rich, but a lot less psycho second husband. What do you say?'

At first I wasn't sure what the noise was. I thought she was choking. Then I realized she was coughing. She was coughing up all her misery and humiliation. She chewed on it for a bit, while I watched her in the mirror, then I held out my hand and she spat.

It was only a metaphor. I knew that. But I swear I felt my hand drop from the weight of it and I felt a sick shudder at the thought of it: all that cruelty, all those twisted games out of her and into me.

She shook her head and sat up. 'See?' she said. 'It works. It's freaky but it works. I feel like a . . . helium balloon.' And right enough she sprang up from that cold bathroom floor as if she was on a string.

'Let's fix your face,' I said. 'What are you wearing? Does it need to go on now or—'

'Zips up all the way,' she told me. 'It'll be fine.' She sat on

154

the edge of the bath and blew her nose with toilet paper, while I soaked a flannel with cold water to press into her eye sockets.

'The trick, when you've been crying,' I said, 'is to embrace it. Put a ton of kohl pencil on and some purple contour, and if your lips are swollen, draw them even bigger with a liner and put on double gloss. Do you mind if I pull some strands out of your do and muss it up a bit?'

'Can I see?' she said. I handed her the shaving mirror. 'Wow. I look like a very bad girl. Sasha's going to hate it.'

I laughed. 'Yes, you'll have to wash it off before you put—' I bit my lip.

'Before I put what?'

'Your wardrobe door was ajar when I came in to make up your room earlier,' I said. 'I saw your Little Clara.'

'My what?'

'From *The Nutcracker*? Your nightie?'

'Donna,' she said, 'what are you talking about?' We both looked over towards the bedroom. She started walking first. 'Something in the wardrobe? Because it was when Sasha went to get dressed that he suddenly blew up and went completely ... Oh, my God! Whose is that?' She lifted it out on its hanger and held it up, staring.

'It's not yours, then? Not your anniversary present from Sasha.'

'Or his from me. Who the hell put it here?'

'Sasha?' I said. 'To wind you up?'

She shook her head. 'What's the wind-up if I don't understand what it means?'

'So it's one of the others,' I said. 'It's a dig at the age difference.'

155

'But what about what he said,' she asked. '"What have you heard? Who have you been speaking to?" Who's that?'

I didn't get what she meant by the last bit. I hadn't heard anything. But a low answer came from outside in the hall. 'It's Rosalie. Are you okay?'

'Come in,' Kim called, as she stuffed the nightie back in the wardrobe.

Rosalie was dressed in a silver sheath of a dress, with a high halter at the front and, we saw as she turned to close the door behind her, slashed to the bum behind.

'I like the look,' she said, turning back with a wave supposed to take in Kim's face and hair as well as her pink undies and high heels. 'Bit chilly, though.'

'I'm glad you're here,' said Kim. 'It might take three of us to get me into my frock. It zips from the hem on a twist.'

'Present from Sasha?' Rosalie said. 'Bit of BDSM?'

Kim flashed a questioning look at me. I shrugged.

'Since you kind of sort of nearly brought it up,' Kim said, 'weird though that is, have you any idea why someone might have put this in my wardrobe, Rosalie?'

Kim pulled the nightie out and held it up against her. I kept my eyes on Rosalie's face and, although she got a hold of her expression pretty quickly, I didn't miss the flare in her eyes, the quick swallow, or the way she paled behind her party make-up, giving her a yellow tinge and leaving her blusher like two clown patches on her cheeks.

'No,' she said. She tried to say more. I could see her casting around for something – anything – to serve up.

'When you and Peach were mucking about with the idea of swapping rooms,' I said, 'yesterday, before everyone got here? You didn't get as far as moving any clo—'

'Oh!' said Rosalie. 'Yes, of course. That's it. It's Peach's. I'll tell her you've found it.'

And, hobbling a little on her stilettos, she hurried out again.

'No way,' Kim said. 'This would drown Peach. It would drag on the floor. Quick, help me get this stupid dress on. I want to get out there and find out what's going on.'

We stuffed her into it and I hiked the zip round and round like a helter-skelter, then Peach came in, in a sequinned dress and low-heeled shoes that were already making her feet swell.

'Rosalie says some of my stuff ended up in here,' she said. She sounded just right: breezy and a little bit harassed. 'You look lovely, Kim, by the way.'

'Here you go,' said Kim. She slipped the hanger out of the ruffled neckline and held out the bundle of white cotton to Peach.

I didn't imagine it. Peach hesitated before she reached out. She literally had to force herself to touch the thing.

'Ta,' she said. 'See you down there.' And she scuttled off.

'What the . . .?' Kim said.

'On it,' I answered, and sped away, running on pure nosiness. The corridor was empty, but a voice came from the tartan room.

'Shit!' It was Ramsay, at a guess. 'You swear this wasn't you?'

'On my dog's life.' That was Buck.

'Shit.' Ramsay again.

'And it wasn't me,' said Rosalie. 'Or Paul. I guarantee that.'

'What are we going to do with it?' That was Peach. 'I can't sleep with it in the room.'

'Oh, come on,' said Buck. 'It's sick, I'll grant you, but it's not going to rise up in the night and float across—'

'Shut up!'

'It's not going to reach out with its empty cuffs and take hold of your neck in cold wet invisible fingers and—'

I opened the door. 'I'll take it off your hands, if you like,' I said.

The four of them froze. Rosalie was the first to come back to life. 'It's all right, Donna,' she said. 'I'll take it to Sasha and try to convince him we've had enough pranks. Buck, you're a bastard. Peach, ignore him. See you all downstairs for drinkies soon. Kim has pulled it together and looks like a million dollars, so don't do anything to spoil it all again. Okay?'

The men followed her out, still with their bow-ties undone, grabbing their dinner jackets as they went, jamming in the door to get away from me.

'Can I help you with anything?' I said to Peach when they had gone. It had worked on Kim. And Peach, although she wasn't crying or sitting in her underwear on a cold bathroom floor, actually looked a bit worse. She looked tired and ill. I had put her at forty yesterday when she rolled up but I'd believe she was fifty now, with that grey cast to her face and the way her shoulders slumped.

'I can't face them,' she said. 'Tonight's going to get ugly – can't you feel it coming? – and I'm not sure I can take it.'

'Give some of it to me,' I said. 'You know, like Kim mentioned yesterday? I could hold on to the worst of it and then you'd be able to cope.'

She was shaking her head and her face was even greyer, her lips almost blue. 'Don't,' she said. 'Don't mess with that. It's evil, Donna. It's dark stuff. Don't even joke about it.'

'Evil?' I said. 'Dark? You're a doctor!'

158

'And I prescribe myself a large glass of vodka and grape-fruit juice to take the edge off,' she said. 'Can you sneak me one up the back stairs? Don't say you're too busy.'

'Coming up,' I told her.

The drinks tray was in the drawing room but no one else was there yet and I managed to flit in, fill a tumbler and flit out again without anyone seeing me. I stopped to rearrange the heap of presents that was gathering on the low table and clicked a snap with my phone. It was second nature: getting The Breakers ready for the website going live had left me with a compulsion to turn every collection of objects into a close-up. I still made it back to Peach in good time.

'Angel,' she said.

'I've got to go now, though,' I told her. 'Dinner and all that.'

———

There's a moment in the middle of getting any decent meal to the table, a state of total focus, where everything else falls away.

'Basting is folklore,' I told myself, listening to the sizzle from the oven. I always talk myself through busy bits and crises. 'Life's too short to curl butter,' I said. I shoved the little butter dishes back in the cupboard and cut straight slabs of it. I'd put it in salty ice and glare if they questioned me.

I could hear the clack, clack of someone in heels coming down the stairs, stepping on the painted edges instead of the carpet strip where their stilettos might jab through the weave. Time to take the champagne in, and the caviar-stuffed quail's eggs and fried oysters. 'God bless the hamper!' I said.

Whatever planet I'd been going to make miniature cheese choux buns on, my rocket ship had fallen far short in the end.

'And he better not throw any more out onto the lawn or he'll get my boot up him,' I was saying, as I backed out of the kitchen door with the ice bucket. Kim heard most of it, since she was passing, but she only laughed and asked me if I needed a hand.

'Nope. I'm all over it like a rash.' The low clicking from the billiards room told me where the men had gone when they rushed away from me and I expected the drawing room to be empty, so I didn't bother to watch what I said as I walked in. 'Forget about everything and have a wonderful evening. Let me pamper you. You deserve it.'

'Spare me!' said Sasha. He was sitting in the corner of the long couch, one leg slung over the other in a study of nonchalance, but his jaw was too tense for it to be true. '"You deserve it." "Let's have some pampering." The banality of you all makes me sick.'

Rosalie came in in time to hear the end of this. 'Sasha, if you've written an anniversary love poem for Kim at least wait till we're all gathered before you recite it.'

It wasn't until she snorted that I noticed Jennifer, sitting in the little sofa behind the door.

'You're back!' I said.

'Another outpouring of erudition,' said Sasha.

'You're . . . the . . . waitress, aren't you?' Jennifer said.

Kim and Rosalie both laughed at that, although I managed to keep my professional front intact.

'Oh, Jelly, it was a very long night and it's been a very long day,' Kim said. 'Donna's more or less one of us now.'

'How could *that* go wrong?' said Sasha under his breath, and I watched their faces darken as though a cloud had swept across the room.

'Nothing's going to go wrong, Sasha,' Kim said. 'But I can't let you make up poems for me without returning the favour. Ten years . . . what rhymes with years?'

'Tears, fears, queers, smears,' said Rosalie. 'It's writing itself.'

Peach was coming along the corridor as I ducked out and headed back to the kitchen.

'Thanks for the stiffener,' she said. 'Sorry about my little mini-meltdown.'

'Don't mention it. Hey! Jennifer's back.'

Peach took a deep breath and nodded. 'Lovely. No more upsets.'

I tried to find words to agree with her. She tried not to notice me failing. In the end, I just smiled and bobbed through the kitchen door for the hors d'oeuvres tray.

'"Roses are red,"' came Peach's voice through the intercom. '"Violets are blue."' She was up to speed with the game already.

'"Sugar is sweet,"' Rosalie added. 'And so is the fact that there's no pre-nup.'

'Jelly Belly!' Buck's voice was so loud he made the monitor buzz. 'You came back to us. How's your tum-tum?'

'My tum-tum's fine but I'm regretting my return already,' said Jennifer. 'Could you please stop using that ridiculous, insulting name?'

'Jellifer?' said Buck. 'How is that insulting? Hm? Jelly and custard? Jelly on a plate? Jelly Baby?'

'Shut up, Buck,' said Peach.

'It's not as if you're fat,' Buck said. 'I'm fat. You're as svelte as you were when you were a nubile little jelly still in her packet. Before we poured on all the hot water and put you in the fridge to set to a wobble.'

'Shut *up*, Buck,' said Peach. 'I'm glad you're back, Je–ennifer. We're four and four again.'

'Jesus,' came Sasha's voice. 'Four and four again? Peach, are you absolutely hammered already?'

There was a long silence in the drawing room. Jennifer broke it. 'I got a little perspective and advice. From my goddesses.'

'You prayed for guidance about coming back?' said Kim. Peach snorted.

'It's a support group,' Jennifer said. 'Six goddesses. Women I know.'

'How . . .' said Rosalie. Peach snorted again. '. . . stirring.'

'We look after one another.'

'And that makes you divine, does it?' Sasha said.

'I'm the goddess of the chalk,' said Jennifer. 'Teacher, you know. And there's a goddess of the gold. She's a banker, down in London. And a goddess of the grain. She works in a distillery near Inverness. And the one I was speaking to today, the goddess of the deep.'

'Plumber?' said Buck.

'"The deep" could be MI5,' said Rosalie. 'I'd be goddess of the briefs!'

'Goddess of the flesh!' said Peach. 'Can anyone join, Je–en?'

'Could Kim join?' said Sasha. 'Goddess of the pricy tat?'

'It's not a joke,' said Jennifer. 'Sedna's a marine biologist. She works on dead kelp.'

162

They all tried hard not to laugh and they almost made it. But then I heard a noise like a steam whistle and knew that someone had caught someone else's eye.

'It's all single women without children anyway,' Jennifer said.

'Of course it is,' said Sasha. 'Where are the glasses for that plonk?'

I started into action along in the kitchen, gathering eight flutes in one hand – it was a skill; I could go to ten if I had to – and a tray in the other.

'Give me that,' Buck said, when I entered the drawing room, 'and you take over from Paul before he has someone's eye out.'

Paul was unwinding the wire on the bottle of champagne. In my experience, men hate being outed as crap at opening wine – champagne included – almost as much as they hate not being able to carve a joint of meat or reverse-park a car, but Paul shrugged and handed the bottle to me. 'It's true,' he said. 'Racing track ejaculation every time. I'll be Santa instead, shall I?'

He lifted one of the parcels from the pile on the footstool and read the gift tag. I watched him while I wrapped the cork and eased it out. He'd been rummaging already. My lovely photo-shoot arrangement of presents was ruined from someone planking the biggest one on top of a load of smaller ones.

'With love from Auntie Verve and Cousin Jennifer,' Paul said, holding out a parcel the shape of a shallow hat box. Kim looked to Sasha to see who'd open it, but Sasha only rolled his eyes.

'Thank you for coming back, Jennifer,' Kim said. 'And

thanks for bringing this.' She slid one of her long fingers under the flap at one end, broke the tape and opened the paper. 'Very swish,' she said, uncovering a pressed-paper drum and easing the lid off it. 'Oh, lovely! Look, Sasha! What a lovely idea. It's tin plates.'

'They're picnic plates from Chatsworth,' Jennifer said. 'Replicas of the Sèvres and Limoges originals. Painted on tin.'

'Genius!' said Rosalie. 'Oh, I do like those. We must get some.'

Jennifer preened a little

'And we're such tin-plate people!' said Sasha. 'Not a Saturday goes by without us sitting on a tartan blanket with a packet of sandwiches and a flask.'

Peach's sigh was gusty enough to make the petals on the nearest flower arrangement shiver.

'Don't mention it,' said Jennifer, understandably I suppose, but so prissy even I wanted to smack her.

'And is going in with your mum on a joint present more of the good advice from the spinsters?' Sasha said. 'You're forty-three years old, Jennifer. Isn't it time to grow up? Or at least cough up?'

'My mother isn't well enough to shop so I added her name to my present,' said Jennifer.

'Oh, that's right. I forgot,' said Sasha. 'You've got power of attorney, haven't you? That must be a nice little cushion.'

'Time for another pressie,' said Kim, talking over him. 'Thank you, Jennifer. These are lovely.'

'Anna and Oliver,' said Paul, holding another parcel out to Kim.

'Oh, God,' said Rosalie. 'Let's see what the parents have come up with this time. It was matching remote-holders for our armchairs for Paul and me last Christmas.'

164

'Do you *mind* if I open it, Sasha?' Kim said. 'Your parents after all.'

Sasha stared coldly at her.

'He can open the next one,' Peach said.

I poured the wine – so cold it didn't foam at all – and passed the flutes around, setting Kim's down at her elbow while she tackled the parcel.

'Wow,' she said, when she had the box open. 'A bird feeder. It's official, then. We're old.'

'You're not old,' said Buck. 'But Sasha's bloody ancient.'

'Will this heavy parcel be okay on your old knees?' said Paul, taking the big one and handing it over.

'I like encouraging wildlife into the garden,' Peach said. 'But it's not a thrilling gift.'

'No sign of the black rabbits tonight,' said Rosalie, looking out of the window, 'speaking of wildlife.' Sasha was picking irritably at the paper. 'Rip it, darling, or we'll be here for ever.'

'A tin,' said Sasha, as he pulled the paper off.

'Tin! You see?' Rosalie said.

'What's in it?' Sasha shook it and wrinkled his nose. 'What's that God-awful stink?'

'Nothing in it except more tins,' Rosalie said. 'A set of three.'

I set off back to the kitchen. I don't know if it was a premonition, or if the combination of tiny little details had added up in my subconscious, but I was braced for it when I pushed open the door. It came almost immediately. Kim's voice through the monitor.

'Oh, God. Oh, God! Tell me it's not.'

'Oh, Jesus!' That was Peach.

I wheeled round and ran back. Sasha was sitting with the

parcel in his lap, staring down into the box. His face was white and his eyes wide.

'What's happened?' I asked.

'A rabbit,' said Kim. 'A poor little black rabbit. Someone's killed it and stuffed it in a box and—'

'Kim,' said Rosalie. 'I promise you that thing wasn't in there when I wrapped the parcel.'

I went over and lifted the tin, feeling the weight. The rabbit looked pitifully tiny, curled tight with its ears folded back and its eyes shut. Its mouth shone here and there as though wet. 'It wasn't in there twenty minutes ago,' I said. 'I rearranged the gifts and this box was light then.'

'You "rearranged" them?' said Kim.

'Don't be ridiculous,' said Sasha. 'The B-and-B people wouldn't have done that. It's got to be one of us. One of you.'

'What are you talking about?' said Paul. 'Why would any of us have killed a rabbit and hidden it in a present? It's insane.'

'Have you looked at it?' Sasha said. He stood up and plunged his hand into the box, grabbing the little body and lifting it up. Kim moaned in her throat.

'Fuck's sake,' said Buck.

'*Look* at it,' Sasha said. He held it by the scruff of its neck and shook it in Buck's face. Buck grimaced and turned away, and Peach put a hand over her mouth as though she was going to be sick. But *I* looked. Because something about it was wrong – even more wrong than a baby rabbit, dead and stiffening. Its mouth wasn't wet after all. Those winks of something shiny were fishing gut.

'It's had its mouth sewn shut,' I said.

'Stitched lips,' said Sasha. His voice was tremulous. 'It's had its lips stitched.'

166

'First the locked box,' Buck said. 'And now the stitched lips.' But he wasn't using his spooky voice. He was dead serious and he sounded terrified. 'Who?' he said.

'For God's sake, will you stop waving it around?' said Rosalie.

Sasha dropped it onto the pile of unopened presents where it lolled horribly. Kim started crying and Rosalie went over to her and rubbed her back.

'Pranks are like close magic,' Ramsay said. 'Or comedy. It's all in the timing.' He paused but no one spoke. 'Where you just went wrong, Sasha, was "noticing" the stitches when everyone else was still gagging.'

Paul was carefully unzipping a cushion cover and tipping out the pad. 'You don't mind, do you, Donna?' he said. 'I don't know if there can be fingerprints on rabbit fur but it's worth trying. It's gone too far now. We need to report this.' He turned the cover inside out over his hands and grabbed the rabbit through the fabric.

'Here, let me help,' Rosalie said, drawing the cushion cover over the body and then closing the zip. 'Although I think that's a case of too much *CSI* on the telly, don't you?'

'Ro-Ro, how can you touch it?' said Peach.

'Does anyone else think I did all this?' Sasha said. No one spoke. 'The hamper, box, rabbit, nightie?'

'Actually,' I said, 'there's something else too. And it's got a better chance of fingerprints than the rabbit fur.'

They all turned to gaze at me.

'What better chance?' said Sasha.

'In the cupboard at the back of the billiards room.' I was watching them closely as I spoke, watching for the one face that didn't look mystified, the one face trying to hide knowledge and maybe failing. But I swear every one of them was blank.

'It's not another . . .?' Peach said.

'No,' I said. 'It's paper. That's all. More or less. But there's a knife. That'd be great for prints.'

Paul and Buck shared a look and a nod and together they went out. We waited a few moments, then Buck came back. 'Sasha?' he said. 'You need to see this.' He coughed. 'Actually, you need to *smell* this!'

'Oh, God,' said Peach. 'What *is* it?'

Sasha, his eyes narrowed, looked around all of us, then left.

'What smell, Buck?' said Rosalie. 'What is it?'

'Nothing horrible,' I said. 'Just too strong. It's like someone's doused tissue paper with a whole bottle of perfume or something.'

'It's a party hat,' Buck said. 'A paper party hat, soaked in—'

Then a shriek interrupted him.

'Sasha?' said Rosalie, leaping to her feet.

I was first to the door and got there in time to see him streak along the corridor to the vestibule and go crashing out into the night.

Chapter 12

1991

I hold on hard to her, but she keeps thrashing and kicking, still trying to swim away, so I smack her on one cheek. It shocks her so much she stops paddling and her head goes under the water for a split second. When she comes up again she wails my name. She puts her arms and legs round me and hangs on like a monkey. If we were further out she'd drown both of us but I'm only a couple of lunging strokes from getting a foothold on the sand, and within a minute I'm lumbering up out of the water, holding her.

It gets harder as I haul us further and further out of the tide. When the water's down to my knees and I'm bearing all her weight, I drop her and fall down beside her and we sit there in the shallows. I put my arm round her and pull her close. She moves easily, nearly floating as another wave comes in and washes over our laps. The water's warmer than the air now, like it always is when the tide's high at the end of a sunny day.

'Carmen,' she says. 'Don't tell Mum.'

Then she moans low in her throat and leans away to the side. I hold her round her waist as a huge gush of liquid comes pumping out of her mouth. It's just about clear at first but then the second big heave looks like egg-drop soup from the Chinese carry-out and the third brings out white chunks of potato and red flecks of pepper from those horrible, horrible salads the flies feasted on, and I have to let go of her to lean over the other way and empty myself out too. It feels wonderful. The sea washes all the mess away and I take a mouthful of salt water and feel the sand scrape against my teeth as I swish it round. I spit it out in a spout and Lynsey giggles.

'Let's move along in case our sick comes back on the next wave,' she says, getting up on her hands and knees and crawling along the wet sand with her dress sagging, clinging to her pipe-cleaner legs and her little round bum.

'I've got a better idea,' I say. 'Let's get out and go home.'

'No!' She plumps down again, her skirt billowing up around her like a jellyfish cap. 'I'm staying here till I'm clean.'

'Lynsey,' I say, looking down through the water. I can't be sure because the afterglow of the sunset is still pink and gold on the wavelets. 'Where are your knickers?'

She sniffs deep in her throat and spits hard. 'They fell off in the water.' Her party hat has disintegrated and she's picking shreds of it out of her hair as she speaks, rolling them into balls and flicking them.

'Lynsey,' I say again. 'What happened?'

'Nothing,' she says. 'Don't tell Mum. Nothing happened.' Her voice is turning singsong the way it does whenever she plays pretend. 'I didn't go to that party you got invited to,

Carmen. I stayed at home with Mum and watched *Blind Date*. I'll be in my bed when you get back. I won't even wake up.'

I put my arm round her again. She's shivering. '*Blind Date* isn't on. Because of the football.'

That's when she starts to cry. She hides her face against my neck and sobs. I can feel her snot on my skin because it's so much warmer than the seawater. And her tears are warmer still. Her little tears are hot enough to spike when they trickle down through my goosebumps. We sit there till the tide's gone so far out that not even the bubbly edges of the strongest waves come anywhere near us.

I sing to her. I start with Madonna hits, because I know all the words, but Lynsey wriggles and shakes her head. What I really need is a lullaby but I can't remember more than the first verse of any of them. So it's inevitable, I suppose, that I end up singing bloody Bryan Adams to her, telling her it's all for her. Which isn't so stupid, actually.

When I've been right through it twice, I stand up and tug Lynsey to her feet.

'Are you still drunk?' I ask her. 'Do you still feel woozy?'

'Was I drunk?' She sounds surprised. 'Was that cordial not cordial? Don't tell Mum.'

'Can you remember what happened?'

'Uh-huh.' She takes my hand as we walk up the beach. When we get to the pebbles, I slip my shoes off and put them on her little feet, buckling them a bit tighter to try and make them fit. Her toes are bright pink with the cold. 'Everyone was gone except that plooky boy. Then he went away out too. And I asked if we were still playing Postman's Knock. And the girl – the fat one with the jeans – said he was her cousin so she couldn't go. So I went outside. And he said, "How old are you?" And I said, "Thirteen," because I will be on my birthday, and I said, "How come? How old are you?" And he went away and . . . I forget but the next thing was I was crying and I heard him banging on a door and he was talking to someone.'

The pebbles are killing my feet. I stamp down hard with every step to make it hurt as much as it can hurt. I heard him talking. *The little one's crying*, he said. *She needs her mum.* And I lay there on the bathroom floor and let *him* go to find her.

'And then another one came. I hid under the table. The big table with all the food on it? But that food smelt so bad I thought I was going to do a sick, Carmen. I burped. That's how he found me.'

We're off the beach now. The boat barrier's down and there are nettles growing close in on either side. I wriggle through, then turn to help Lynsey. She winces and tries to hide it.

'Are you sore?'

'Don't tell Mum. She'll kill me.'

'What happened after he found you? Under the table?'

'I ran away,' she says. 'I ran outside but I couldn't go to the path home because there was a boy lying on the grass and he would see up my skirt and I didn't have any—' She catches her lip. 'Then *he* came out and said he would go with me.'

Under the trees it's as black as night. I keep my head down and watch my white feet against the tarmac. I watch them until it makes me dizzy to see them flashing into view over and over again, the dark ground disappearing under them. I feel as if I'm falling. And when I look up it's not as dark as I thought anyway. The mouth of the lane glows, the leaves of the bushes on either side bright and clear. I shake my head, not understanding.

'Someone's coming,' says Lynsey, as the glow becomes a glare and the headlights pin us there. The two of us in the middle of the lane, wet and bedraggled, our faces streaked and our clothes clinging. I turn to Lynsey to see if maybe we just look a wee bit tired from too many party games, if maybe we can laugh it off, but as she lifts an arm across her eyes to shield them from the light, I see a strand of seaweed hooked on the armhole of her dress. As if she drowned for real and came back from her watery grave to go haunting.

The car's brakes squeal as it stops. Then the headlights click to dim and a door opens.

'Girls?' says a voice. There's no *r* in the word. English. That same English voice. It's the woman they all call Anna. 'Are you . . . Is everything . . .?' She sounds tired and kind of wary.

The other door slams and the man's voice comes too. 'Is that the two village girls? What on earth have you been doing?'

It's his voice that does it. He's annoyed and amused and the words he chooses – 'two village girls' – make out like we're from the olden days.

'I'll tell you what the city girls have been doing,' I say. 'Morag's drunk all your peach booze and puked it up on the floor. Rosalie's crying her eyes out. And Jellifer's passed out in your bed.'

'Oh dear,' says the woman. The man gives a bit of a snort. I can't tell if he's laughing. I can't really see either of them. Standing against the headlights, they look like aliens. As if this is a close encounter. 'Well, we asked for it, I suppose,' the woman says, sighing. 'Although I did think the Leslies were

173

old enough to be responsible and Jennifer too. Do you want a lift?'

'Don't let them take us home,' Lynsey breathes into my neck. 'We'll never get in without Mum hearing if a car drives up.'

'Ask me what the boys have been doing,' I say.

'Swimming?' says the man. 'With you two? Our lads do tend to head for water when they're in high spirits.'

'Guess again.' I don't know where I'm getting the nerve to speak to them like this. Maybe it's the way their headlights are shining on us, so bright they're making my head hurt. And my sore head's making my stomach start to roll again.

'I'm not sure I care for your tone, if I'm honest,' the man says.

'Shut up, Oliver,' the woman says. She walks closer. I can pick out her features when the bulk of her body blocks the headlights' beam. 'What are you talking about, dear?'

'Never mind,' I say. She's not threatening or anything. She looks kind and tired, and she's got her bag on across her body like a sash and her mascara's run and she smells like smoke. I don't think she's had much of a night either. 'We just want to go home, eh, Lynsey?'

'But— Good grief, where are your shoes?' the woman says. 'Aren't you cold?'

'Made of sturdy stock, these country girls,' her husband puts in.

'And what's that?' She bends close to Lynsey. I think she's seen the seaweed, but her eyes aren't on Lynsey's dress: they're on her legs.

'Mud,' Lynsey says, moving so she's standing half behind me. 'We went swimming.'

The woman crouches right down and peers even closer,

like Lynsey's some kind of insect. 'Oh! My dear, you're hurt! What happened? Oliver, turn the car. Turn the car round. We need to get this girl to a doctor.'

'Oh, come off it!' says the man. 'I can't drive to a hospital, Anna. I'm way over the limit. I'll get done. What's the problem anyway?'

'I'm fine,' says Lynsey. 'Bit cold. I need a shower.'

'I'll drive you home,' the woman says. 'And we'll see about the doctor, eh?'

'God's sake,' says the man. 'Don't you think we should go and see if our own children and our nephews and nieces are in alcoholic comas or burning the house down? These two are clearly used to being out and about on their own.'

I'm darting glances all over Lynsey, no idea why the woman's taking such a flaky. Then I spot it, bright and shocking in the headlight glare. Lynsey must be numb with cold not to feel any pain. And now I understand why she wouldn't get out of the saltwater. I didn't see it when I put my shoes on her, or maybe it hadn't started again by then, but now the blood is streaking down both her legs and seeping along the tops of my sandals.

'Don't tell my mum,' she says. 'She'll kill—' Then she stops and turns, distracted by a noise behind us. Footsteps are slapping along the lane and the light from a torch is bobbing like a karaoke ball.

'There you are!' It's the big girl, Jellifer, up out of the bed where I saw her, flushed now and panting. She stops and puts her hands on her knees. That's when I notice the water dripping off the hem of her skirt. 'We thought you'd drowned!' she says. 'No one saw you leave. Why didn't you say you'd gone home, sillies?'

175

'Jennifer,' says the woman. 'You were supposed to be looking after them. You're eighteen years old. We thought we
could trust you.'

'What?' says the girl. 'It's not my fault they took off.'

'Why is Ro-Ro crying?' the woman says. 'And why did you
let Morag drink enough peach schnapps to be sick? And why
were you sleeping in my bed?'

'What?' says the girl again. 'Who told you that?' Her eyes
are wide and her mouth's open in an O-shape. She looks like
a cartoon of a choirboy on a Christmas card. I can't believe
the woman's buying it. Then a smile spreads over her face.
'Oh, wait. Carmen, you've got the wrong end of the stick.
Morag *spilled* the schnapps. It does stink a bit, but it didn't
bounce off her stomach, thank God. Yuck! And I went into
your room, Aunt Anna, to close your curtains and turn down
your bed for you. Least I could do after you let us take over
like that. I don't know why Rosalie was crying, but she's all
right now. She's at the beach with the rest of us, laughing her
head off. Listen. That's why we never noticed this pair had
sneaked away.'

And when she stops talking we can all hear the sound of
them larking around. It comes through the still night like
wildlife cries. Like foxes. The woman looks at us, then at the
girl who's called Jennifer, of course, then over at her husband.
He's leaning on the bonnet of the car, smoking what I think,
from the smell, is a cigar.

'My period started,' says Lynsey. 'That's why we left.'

'Oh, no!' says Jennifer. 'What a time for it to happen.'

The woman lets out a high, nervous laugh. 'Oliver, next
time you tell me I'm being too dramatic, don't let me argue.
Poor little thing,' she adds.

I say nothing. Lynsey hasn't started her periods yet. Ten girls in her class have and she's one of three still waiting.

'I should have something,' says the woman, scrabbling in her bag. 'I don't suppose you use . . .? No, of course not. But I might have a liner.'

Lynsey flashes me a look. If they find out she's got no knickers on the whole story will fall apart again. 'I just want to go home,' she says.

'Me too,' says the man, flicking the rest of his cigar into the verge and getting back into the car.

'I'll chum you as far as your gate,' says Jennifer. 'I've had enough swimming.'

And they leave. The woman gets back in the passenger side and we stand at the edge of the lane to let them drive off, watching until the red rear lights disappear around a bend taking the sickly glow with them.

As soon as we're back in the dark, Jennifer kneels down. She puts her hands on either side of Lynsey's face. 'Are you feeling bad?' she says. Lynsey nods, dragging the girl's hands.

'I want you to do something for me,' Jennifer says. Lynsey waits, watching. 'I want you to take the horrible, sore, sad, nasty feeling inside – can you feel it?' Another nod. 'And I want you to turn it into a little black stone. As small as you can get it. Is it heavy?' Lynsey gives a small nod, one up and one back down. 'Where is it?'

'Tummy,' Lynsey says. She's beginning to sound like a toddler, her voice uncertain and piping.

'I want you to cough it up,' the girl says. 'Cough it up into your hands.'

Lynsey nods. Then she takes a deep breath and makes a sharp hacking sound. She's got her two hands cupped in front of her.

'There,' says Jennifer. 'Doesn't your tummy feel better now? And doesn't that feel heavy in your hands?'

Lynsey looks down and says nothing.

'You can get rid of it, you know. You can give it to someone else to hold instead of you. And it'll never come back. Wouldn't that be nice?'

Lynsey stretches out her cupped hands towards the girl, who rears back. 'No, sweetheart,' she says. 'Not me. Give it to your sister. Your sister loves you and she'll be there in case you ever have to cough up any more. She'll hold it for you, won't you, Carmen?'

Lynsey turns and gazes up at me, holding out her hands.

'Of course,' I say. 'I'll carry it home for you and then we'll decide what to do with it after that.'

'But she said you'd keep it,' Lynsey says.

'Of course she'll keep it. If that's what you want.' The girl's voice is wheedling. 'She loves you. She'll do this for you. Won't you, Carmen?'

I reach out a hand and watch Lynsey carefully slide the invisible stone into it as if she's separating an egg. And I can't deny it: my hand drops an inch or two and I flex the muscles in my arm to hold it steady. I mime putting it in my jeans pocket.

'Don't do that,' Lynsey says. 'What if Mum finds it when she's doing the washing?'

'I'll take it out before I put them in the wash.'

'But where will—'

'If you hide it somewhere it might find its way back to poor little Lynsey,' Jennifer says. 'You need to hold it inside yourself, really. For your sister.'

I tell myself it's a load of crap anyway and it doesn't matter so long as it helps her. Then I throw it up into the air, duck my head and catch it like a seal in the wild-water show, swallowing it whole and cold and feeling it hit the pit of my stomach and die there.

Chapter 13

'We're one down for dinner, then,' said Buck. 'All the more for the rest of us.'

'I'll go after him,' Jennifer said. She fished her keys out of her pocket and strode out of the front door. We heard her slamming into her car and taking off down the drive in a spray of gravel.

We'd come to be standing in a ring, all of us with our chests heaving. Rosalie had her hands over her mouth and her eyes were still wide with shock. Paul and Ramsay looked more alike than ever. Buck had taken it in his stride. Peach, half drunk already, was buffered against most of it. But Kim was gulping and had tears running down through her heavy eye make-up. Still, it was her that laughed first.

'We've been played,' she said. Ramsay turned a curious look on her. But Rosalie clapped her hands and laughed too.

'How, in particular?' said Buck. 'I mean, I'm prepared to believe it, but how?'

'Jelly's not going after Sasha,' said Rosalie. 'Why would she? She's just scarpered again without admitting it.'

'I don't blame her,' said Kim. 'That poor rabbit.'

'Do you want my phone?' I said. 'Are you serious about reporting it?'

'I want *my* phone,' Ramsay said. 'This black-out is beginning to get to me.'

'About that,' I said. I felt sweat on my palms at the thought. But I couldn't hide it any more. 'I need to talk to you all. Cards on the table. Can we hold dinner a bit?'

I turned towards the drawing room but Kim put a hand on my arm. 'I can't,' she said. 'Not with that thing lying there. Even inside a cushion cover.'

'I'll take it outside,' said Paul, and pushed ahead of us. We all waited, even the other two men, for the sound of the French window opening, but what we heard was the rustle and thump of him rummaging among the parcels and wrapping paper, cursing. I knew what he was going to say before he said it.

'It's gone!'

'What?' Buck was first in but we all crowded in right after him. The bare cushion pad was back on the couch, the box in its burst-open wrapping was still on the table, but the rabbit in its zipped shroud was nowhere.

'He's really messing with us,' Rosalie said. 'He must have doubled back and nabbed it.'

'Sorry, Kim,' said Ramsay. 'I know he's your husband and, Rosalie, I know he's your brother, but he is a total dick, isn't he? How can he still think these games are worth playing?'

'Look,' Peach said, going to the window and looking out. 'Footprints to the beach gate. He's going to go and fling it in the tide, then try to tell us it never happened.'

'Good luck telling *seven* of us it never happened,' Kim said. 'That only works one at a time. As I know.'

'I bet it was Donna talking about fingerprints that's made him rush to get rid of the evidence,' said Ramsay. He was almost laughing, then caught my eye as the same thought struck both of us at once. I raced across the hall and into the billiards room.

'Too late,' I said. The garden door was open and the party hat was gone. 'If that was one of my knives I'm adding it to your bill. I love that knife.'

'Oh, God,' Ramsay said. 'Let's all have a drink, shall we?' He put a hand in the small of my back and steered me out of the room again. 'You too, Donna. Sit down and have a glass of champers. Let's all drink to Sasha breaking his neck on the cliff path.'

'Or falling on the knife,' Peach said.

'Or,' said Kim, 'having all his orifices stitched shut by the angry ghost of that poor bunny.' Rosalie raised her eyebrows but Kim was adamant. 'I don't care. I've fucking had it. I've been flogging this dead horse of a marriage for a good two years. This weekend was my last ditch.'

'What are you drinking to, Donna?' said Buck.

'Forgiveness?' I said. 'I haven't got your devices.'

They looked blank again. It *had* to be Sasha, I decided, unless one of them had a poker face that could break the bank at Monte Carlo.

'I didn't pick them up from outside your rooms last night,' I said. 'But someone did. And I've got no idea where they are. I searched the house while you were all out today – that's when I found the nightie and the party hat – and they've vanished.'

'*Fucking* Sasha!' Ramsay said. 'If he's tipped my iPad into the sea I'll sue the arse off him.'

182

'Don't be a chump,' said Rosalie. 'He's probably locked them all in his car.'

I let my breath go. Of course! It was such an obvious solution I was ashamed not to have seen it.

'Kimmie,' Rosalie went on, standing. 'Have you got a key? I'll go out and check while Sasha's off playing silly buggers.'

'I *have* got a key,' Kim said. 'But it's gone. The bastard's taken it out of my bag. House key too.'

'He took your *keys*?' That was Ramsay.

'*Takes* my keys,' Kim said. 'If he thinks I might bolt.'

'That's not legal,' Ramsay said. 'That's . . . What is that, Rosalie?'

'Unlawful detention,' she said. 'With intent.'

'It's not even the worst thing he does on any given day,' said Kim, and I thought of the way she had been standing, then suddenly had been on the ground. Her quick recovery and the way she hopped into the moving car. Practised, now I thought about it properly.

'Fucking hell,' said Buck. 'Why on earth do you sta—'

'Do not finish that sentence,' said Peach. 'Or so help me . . .'

'Okay, well, maybe I can finish this one, then,' said Buck. 'Have you got my keys, Peach?'

'Have I got your *car* keys? No. Why?'

'Funny you should say that,' said Paul. 'Rosie, I was going to ask why you'd snaffled mine. I wanted to get my penknife out of the glove box and I couldn't lay my hands on them.'

'So,' said Rosalie. 'We think Sasha has purloined all of our car keys, do we? Ramsay, can you check yours?'

He nodded and left the room.

'But it's not as if we're on some island only joined to the

coast by a tidal causeway, is it?' said Rosalie, while we waited. 'Donna's got a car and a phone, haven't you?' I nodded. 'And it's only a few miles to the nearest neighbour.'

'It's kind of pathetic, actually,' Kim said. 'It's needling for needling's sake.'

'And, really, sweeping off isn't much of a wind-up if the people you leave behind are all sick of you,' said Paul. 'Sorry, Kim. Sorry, Ro.'

Ramsay was back. 'Car keys gone,' he said. 'No sign of the white nightie either.'

'It's all pretty well choreographed, isn't it?' said Rosalie. 'Pretending to slam out, then creeping back.'

'Well, fuck him sideways,' said Buck. 'Donna, it's time to party. We're ready for our dinner. If Sasha comes back he can have bread and cheese in his room.'

'And really, Donna, do join us,' Kim said. 'We're kind of past the formalities, wouldn't you say?'

I resisted and resisted, but there were six of them and they were determined. So, after I dished up – shoot me – I sat down and troughed into the smoked salmon, wafer thin and sweet.

Peach groaned. 'God almighty, this is the best thing I've ever had in my mouth.'

Buck snorted and Rosalie threw a piece of bread at him. I knew they'd come to food fights in the end. Their sort always do.

Mad as it sounds now after what had just happened, and considering what was coming next, for a few hours there we had a magical evening. I felt like I'd known them all my life, except that I didn't know any of their stories. And so they got to tell me, showing their best sides.

I heard about Buck's children and how his eldest was nearly born in a taxi on the M8 and the driver fainted when his wife's waters broke. So Buck had to drive the taxi to the hospital with both of them laid out in the back of the cab.

I heard about how Paul always pretended to be divorced at work because no one trusts a happily married divorce lawyer and how Rosalie kept pictures of Peach's children on her desk because no one trusts a childless family-law specialist.

'I'm tempted to flick some cream of mushroom on my suit jacket some days,' she said. 'Pretend it's baby sick. Really get them on my side.'

'Didn't you ever want them for real?' said Kim.

'I'll tell you after another bottle of wine,' said Rosalie. 'Each.'

I heard about how Ramsay pretended to be gay at work – in the online marketing department for a magazine group – to stop women asking him out.

'It just makes them more determined. Can't really complain. We pump out a hundred and eighty pages a time across seven different titles, telling them they're beautiful and powerful and the sky's the limit. No wonder they've got delusions.'

I heard about how Peach gave a talk about being a casualty doctor to Ramsay's magazines' executives' away-day, and there were more complaints than the time the Christmas night out ended up in a lap-dancing club.

'So I asked Buck to come and do the talk the next time,' Ramsay said.

'Why? What do you do for a living?' I asked.

'I'm a *nurse!*' Buck said. 'We see it all before it's cleaned up

185

and the doctors get there. I made someone cry. Remember, Ramsbum? I made that one cry telling her about the women who fed her—'

'No!' A chorus of voices shut him down.

Kim wiped her eyes with her napkin. 'Oh, God, I haven't laughed so much for years.'

'Now you,' said Ramsay. 'Tell us your proudest moment.'

Kim shook her head and waved them off. 'I've got nothing to top that. I'm in retail. Can I ask you all a question, though?' She went on without waiting, 'Did you come here this weekend to watch a car crash?'

'No!' said Peach.

'Partly.' That was Ramsay.

'Fifty-fifty,' said Rosalie.

'Sixty-forty,' said Paul.

'Buck?' Kim said.

'Absolutely not,' Buck said. 'I came to watch a train wreck and I'm not disappointed.'

'Fucking hell,' Kim said, when she had stopped laughing. 'What a mess. Lucky I know a good divorce lawyer.'

Paul gave one last chuckle, then cleared his throat. 'I don't know, Kim. He's my brother-in-law after all. But I can promise you I won't take him on as a client. How about it?'

'Bullshit,' said Rosalie. 'Kim, of course he'll do your divorce. Sasha deserves it. Bringing us all back here and freaking us all out.'

'He didn't know,' Kim said. 'Honestly. He had no idea until we got here.'

'Of course he knew,' said Paul. 'I bet Ramsay'll be able to check your email account – if the stupid bastard ever gives us our stuff back. I bet he's been stalking you online as long as you've been married. Sasha always did like to be the boss. Hey, Buck, remember . . .'

And they were off again.

Eventually, when we were finished with the venison and even Buck had stopped pouring gravy onto his plate and wiping it up with bread, when we were full and getting drunk, when we were beginning to laugh a bit less and talk a bit more, I spoke up.

'Can I ask something?' They were owlish with booze but in the candlelight they still looked pretty glamorous. It wouldn't be till they were looking at themselves in their bathroom mirrors that the full effects of the night would show. I had chosen the lights in the bathrooms; I should know.

'A swat?' Peach said. 'Ass. Ka-watt? Aw, shit, I'm pissed.'

'Hard to argue,' said Rosalie. 'Are you going to be okay?'

'My spozzer's going to kill me. Kill me dead.'

'Your what?' said Kim. 'Jesus, Peach, don't tell me you've got one of those implants that gives you alkie poisoning if you—'

'Sponsor, I think she meant,' said Buck. 'Right, Peachy-pie? Your AA sponsor?'

'Thalassa,' said Peach. She made an effort, but only managed 'Sposser,' then giggled and leaned against Buck.

'The last one?' said Rosalie. 'Peach, are you on some kind of final warning?'

'Her name is . . .' said Peach, articulating carefully '. . . Thalassa.'

Rosalie laughed quietly, shaking her head, and Buck stroked his sister's hair back. 'She's probably called Theresa,' he said. 'Or Alicia. Oh, God, Peach.'

187

'What did you want to ask, Donna?' Ramsay said, leaning across the table and upending an almost finished bottle of wine into my glass. 'Go for it.'

I flicked my eyes to the mantelpiece. 'It's about the picture.'

'The picture!' said Buck. 'The one tease that is mysteriously still there. It hasn't vanished like everything else.'

'I really do think that was Jennifer,' said Paul. 'I think she was trying to be nice. That's why it's still there. It wasn't part of Sasha's big head game.'

'You're not going to ask why I was wearing that hideous frock, are you?' Rosalie said. 'That was my bloody mother overcompensating as usual. I wanted a pair of jeans and a Breton T-shirt, like Peach had.'

'Borrow 'em,' murmured Peach.

'Overcompensating for what?' I said.

'You're all the woman I'll ever want,' said Paul, dropping a kiss on her shoulder. 'And don't ask for an explanation of my hairstyle either. First proper puking hangover I ever had – God, I can still smell the hair gel as I hung over the bog!'

'Lovely,' said Rosalie. 'How drunk are you, exactly?' She pushed Paul off her and stared at him. 'Jesus, your eyes are like pinpricks. Donna, did you give us your secret peyote sauce?'

'I'm not drunk,' said Paul. 'How very dare you?' But he put his head down on the table as he spoke, starting off another round of jeering.

'What did you want to ask?' Rosalie said.

'The kids who've been Photoshopped out,' I began. 'I don't get that. Why would Jennifer – why would anyone – do that?'

Paul sat up again and let his head drop back, watching me from under his lashes.

188

'I agree,' said Kim. 'I could see the point if it was Sasha rubbed out. That would be genuinely creepy. But random locals? Who were they anyway?'

'They were siblings,' Rosalie said.

'Sssh,' said Paul. His voice was so slack I thought at first he was just breathing noisily. 'Locked in a box, Rosalie.'

'Sissers,' said Peach.

'Stitched lips,' said Buck.

'They were invited to . . . Well, to . . .' said Ramsay. 'At least, one of them was.'

'Stop,' said Paul. 'We were supposed to go to our—'

'They were here to round out the numbers,' Ramsay said. 'There were four of us boys, you see. Sasha, Paul, Buck and me. And the three girls. Jennifer, Peach and Rosalie. So we invited another girl. To play all those excruciating party games that need an even match. Do they still play those games at parties?'

'But I still don't understand,' I said. 'Why are they blanked out?'

'Well,' said Rosalie, 'not to be too blunt about it –'

'Stop talking, Rosie,' said Paul. 'You're pissed.'

'– but the one who was invited brought her little sister. Far too young to be unsupervised and . . . she . . . died.'

'What?' said Kim. 'No.'

'She drowned,' Rosalie said. 'It's true. We all went swimming. And this poor girl went in and sank like a—' She swallowed the word and took a big drink of water.

I waited to see if one of them was going to crack and start cackling. When the silence had stretched thin, I spoke at last. 'I don't think so,' I said.

'We wouldn't joke about something like that,' said Ramsay.

'No, of course not. I believe you believe it. You nearly told me this afternoon and Peach blurted it out last night. But I think you're wrong is what I'm saying.'

'What do you mean, Donna?' Paul said. '*We* were here. You weren't even born.'

'No, but no one's ever drowned swimming in Knockbreak Bay. We did research before we—' Bought this place, I was going to say. Basic suicide check, my mum called it. I pulled my phone out of my back pocket and Googled 'drowning, Galloway, 1990s'. There was nothing. I knew there wouldn't be.

'Iss been hush up,' Peach said.

'What are you all on about?' I said. 'This is only twenty-odd years ago, right? Not the olden days. I mean, I know Galloway's backward but even then they had a proper police force and the Coastguard and a – a local newspaper and all that. If there had been skinny-dipping after a wild party and some drunk girl drowned, people would know.'

'That's not what happened,' Rosalie said. 'She didn't go skinny-dipping.'

'Sssh, Rosie,' said Paul.

'And then I brought him back here?' said Kim. 'No wonder he's going crazy.'

'But it didn't happen!' I said. 'There's nothing online. What was her name and I'll search again?'

'I dunno wish one was wish,' said Peach.

'It was all so nuts that night,' Paul said. 'We went to the beach and lit a fire. We thought she'd gone home. But we were all right there on the beach when she drowned and we were so pissed we didn't even know.'

'Jesus,' said Kim. 'What kind of sixteenth birthday party *was* this?'

'More sex than this one and not so many dead rabbits,' Ramsay said.

There was a long silence and then every one of them started gulping with guilty laughter.

Not me. Questions pinged in my head, like high scores on a fruit machine. Could an accident or even a suicide be kept that quiet? If the Glasgow and Edinburgh press didn't hear about it, would the small-town back-scratchers on the local force bend the rules that much, keep it out of the local rags too? Could a family – three rich families of doctors, lawyers and the like, used to getting their own way – bury a death that deep? Put it in a locked box, stitch their lips and—

'What *was* her name?' I said. 'To make sure.'

'I can't remember,' Buck said.

'Okay, I can do this,' I said. 'I'm hopeless with names so I know all the tricks.'

'What? You're wonderful with names,' said Rosalie. 'Eight of us and you never faltered.'

'Close your eyes,' I said.

'Mine are closed,' said Peach.

'And don't try to remember the names, just the tune. The rhythm. So, like Rosalie is Dum-de-dee and Ramsay is Dum-dee.'

'Dum-dee and Dum-dee,' said Paul.

'Dum-dum and Dah-da,' said Buck, then opened his eyes. He pointed across the table at me. 'Burn the witch.'

'Close your eyes again,' I told them, 'and put your hands flat on the table.'

'I'll have to, for balance,' Paul said.

I told them their left forefingers were the big sister and their right forefingers were the little sister and then I started chanting the letters of the alphabet, clear and slow.

'A, B, C . . .' Five forefingers rose up.

Ramsay and Kim both opened their eyes then.

'E, F, G, H, I, J, K, L . . .' Rosalie and Paul's fingers rose.

'I don't want to do this,' said Rosalie. 'It's too much like—'

'Carol and Laura?' I said.

'One was quite exotic and one was bog-standard,' said Rosalie. 'I remember thinking they didn't go together.'

'Carol and Lettice?' said Ramsay.

'Other way round, wasn't it?' Paul put in.

'Clotilde and Laura?'

'Wait,' said Paul. 'The funny name was musical, wasn't it?'

'Stop it,' said Rosalie. 'We were supposed to take it to— We pledged. We vowed. Together on the beach after she died.' She screwed up her eyes. 'Wait. Was it *Linda*?'

But suddenly the food inside me felt like a sandbag lying in the bottom of my stomach. 'It doesn't make any sense,' I said. 'You make it sound like *Swallows and Amazons* or the Famous Five or something. If a kid died, how could another gang of kids on a beach decide to keep it quiet? Where were the adults?'

'They took us away,' said Rosalie. 'Our parents bundled us all away first thing the next day and told us not to talk about it. But it's true, Donna. There were two sisters.'

'Locals, right?' Buck said. 'Not holiday-makers?'

'Locals,' said Rosalie. 'Something musical and maybe Linda. And one of them walked into the sea.'

'I'll clear,' I said, standing. I didn't know I'd barked it until I saw them all startle, saw Paul knock his wine glass over. 'We need a break before pudding.'

I blundered out of the dining room and went to splash my

192

face with water. I didn't know what was wrong with me. Why had I tried to hypnotize them into remembering something that couldn't be true anyway? I stared at my reflection in the mirror above the sink. If there was no official record of a drowning in Knockbreak Bay, it couldn't have happened. But what about a missing person? Had a child ever disappeared? What if this lot were the only ones who knew what had happened to her? And their parents had hustled them away to get them out of trouble. What if the kid's family were still looking for her all these years later and this bunch of spoiled twats had known all along there was no hope of her ever coming home again?

I dried my face and made my careful way to the kitchen. I was drunker than I'd ever been, trying to waitress in spike heels with my own china I'd have to pay for if I dropped any. And concentrating only made it worse. I could see trails of sparkles when I turned my head. It would be a bloody miracle if I managed to make crème brûlée without burning the house down. I'd chosen it because it was easy, but I'd never used a blowtorch drunk.

Even at the thought of it I could feel my stomach rolling. I'm not a picky eater. No one who's ever worked in a hotel is a picky eater. Maybe it's from standing there with our pens poised over our order pads while diners practically call in the UN to help them decide between steak and fish, then change their minds four times and still sigh when their plate comes. For whatever reason, waiters will chow down on anything that's slapped in front of them unless the maggots are still wriggling. I eat kidneys, capers and tapioca. I eat sweetbreads and steak tartare. The only thing I've never been able to swallow is crème brûlée.

I took my heels off sitting on one of the breakfast-room chairs and dug my phone out of my back pocket.

'Donna?' My mum picked up on the first ring, her voice harsh. 'What's wrong?'

'Nothing,' I said. 'How are you? *Where* are you?'

She groaned. 'Back at the hotel. Next time I'll pay extra and get one closer to the convention centre. How am I? Knackered. My head's fizzing. My feet are stinging. If I have to admire another diamond ring or look at another thumbnail of a white dress, I'll go stark raving mad.'

I laughed. She was never a romantic.

But my laugh didn't fool her. 'Okay, for the second time,' she said. 'What is wrong?'

'Nothing,' I said again. 'But only because the clients are so chummy. I joined in with dinner, Mum, and I'm pissed.'

'You?' my mum said. 'You joined – you mean you sat down and—?'

'I know,' I said. 'I'm sorry. You're working your arse off up there and I'm down here eating the profits.'

'How did they taste?' she asked, and I giggled. My mum never made a fuss about anything.

'The salmon was amazing. They must cut it with a laser. The beetroot and chilli jelly was ridiculous, like all good *amuse-bouches*. The venison was spoonable and it's completely finished. And I'm bunking off of the pud, obviously, because it's boak brûlée.' Now she was laughing and I started to forgive myself. 'Maybe I'm not pissed,' I said. 'I've been scunnered since this avvy. I saw something weird when I was looking for the computers – which I still haven't found by the way.'

'Weird how?' she said. 'Oh, my feet!' I heard the sound of lapping water. She must be soaking them.

'In the cupboard in the billiards room. A party hat drenched in perfume. God, it stank.'

'A what?'

'Yeah, I know. I didn't know what it was. It just looked like a lump of coloured paper, but it was spiked to the wall with a knife. My meat knife, I think, although I haven't had a minute to check yet.' I craned my neck but couldn't see my knife rack from where I was sitting.

'*What?*'

'I know! They're a very strange bunch. Really into the kind of practical jokes that aren't the least bit funny. Everyone thinks it's the husband behind it all, but he took a complete benny when he saw the hat and he's disappeared. That's why there's so much spare food and why I ate it. Doesn't explain why I drank so much, mind you. If I immolate myself trying to use the blowtorch, you can have my leather jacket.'

'What stage are you at with it?' said my mum. 'Why don't you just dust the top with a bit of something, shove on a raspberry and call them vanilla pots? Did you use the vanilla sugar?'

'Of course.'

'Or plain cream pots if you didn't.'

'I *did*. What am I telling you? But that's a great idea. I think I will. I'll email you a photo and then crash out.'

'A photo of what?' my mum said. 'I've seen crème brûlée before. And God knows I've seen your wee white face when you're hammered.'

'I took a pic of the party hat,' I said. 'Seriously weird.'

I uploaded the photo to an email and then said, 'God, I nearly forgot why I phoned. Mum, no one's ever drowned in Knockbreak Bay, have they?'

'Eh? Not that I know of, but that doesn't mean it's safe to swim at night if they're pissed and full of venison.'

'No, it's a specific person,' I said. 'A wee girl. Someone from when they were here before. Did you see anything about that when you were checking this place out?'

'When was this?'

'Early nineties, I think.'

'Sounds like they're telling ghost stories, Donna. No wonder they're getting under your skin.'

'And no one ever went missing?' I said. 'We'd know that too, right?'

'Are you asking me if I sank our last bean into a holiday house where a kid disappeared?'

'No,' I said. 'Sorry.'

'I've got to say, Donna, it doesn't sound like much of a party. Go and shove the cream pots under their noses and go to bed.'

'Vanilla pots,' I said. 'I think I will. I'll put coffee in the drawing room and leave them to it.'

———

I was sure I'd have to puke before I could lie down and rest but in the end I just undid my waistband and bra and crashed onto my bed, pulling the quilt over me.

I woke hours later, my bare feet hanging out and ice cold, jerked awake by a dream or a memory. I lay panting, waiting for the sweat on my body to dry. Something was missing. Not the devices. Or not missing . . . but I'd forgotten to do something. I'd been close to it, then got distracted. I turned my pillow to the cool side and settled down again. What was

196

bothering me? The drowned girl? She didn't exist. It was probably something professional. Crapping out of the burned sugar? No, that wasn't it, although it was close enough to make my brain tickle. It was something to do with the guests. All the pranks. Was it the gift card I'd taken out of the fire and then somehow mislaid? No, but that was even closer.

My knife! I had forgotten to check up on my meat knife. The relief of remembering flooded through me and I swung my legs out of bed.

I realized I was still off my head as I tottered down the stairs, my frozen feet feeling wooden and strange. I clicked on the kitchen light switch and squeezed my eyes shut as more of the little sparkles fizzed at the edge of my vision. I had seen enough anyway. All my knives were there on their magnet, biggest meat knife included. So either Sasha – if it was Sasha – had spent two hundred quid on a knife of his own for his trick or he had slipped in at the kitchen door and returned mine.

'No matter,' I said.

Back upstairs, I set my alarm clock for six, to give me time for clean-up before breakfast, then I cuddled down in bed and fell into a pit of sleep so deep, with walls so smooth, that – no matter the nightmares – there was no escaping.

Chapter 14

But what woke me in the morning wasn't my alarm. Someone was screaming. I opened my eyes onto a brightness that hacked into my skull and sat up with my head lurching like a lava lamp.

She was still screaming – it was definitely a woman – and it was getting closer too. I stood up, ignoring the sick swirl in the pit of my belly. It was coming from the front garden. I stumbled through to the empty bedroom and got to the window in time to see Kim come dragging across the lawn, her feet leaving dark prints in the dew. I knocked on the window and she raised her face, wild-eyed, to see who was there.

'Help!' she said, lurching forward, then falling onto her hands and knees on the wet grass. 'Donna, help me,' she croaked, through sobs, looking down at the ground.

I checked myself, wincing as my eyeballs moved, and found I was still wearing my clothes. I pulled my shirt tail out – quicker than trying to grapple with the side-fastening of my trousers – then headed towards the back stairs, thumping down in my bare feet and jamming on my Crocs at the back door. I hopped and trotted through the house and was out the front when Kim threw herself onto the porch, falling again and stopping herself on her outstretched hands.

'Kim?' I said. 'What's happened? What's wrong? Is someone chasing you?'

'It's Sasha,' she said. She flicked her head to get the wet rats' tails of her hair off her face. 'Donna, he's in the sea. He's floating in the sea. I think he's dead down there.' She was on her feet again and she backed away from the house, looking up at the windows. 'Why is no one else . . .' She staggered a little and took a step forward. 'God, I'm so out of it still,' she said.

'Me too.' I shivered. 'Kim, are you sure? I've been having the freakiest dreams the last few hours. Maybe . . .'

'No,' she said, slow and certain. 'My husband is lying dead in the tide. I didn't dream it.'

But there was something not right about her. It was more than shock. Her eyes looked beady and her colour wasn't the grey of a hangover or the white of being cold and wet, shivering there in the cheerless damp morning.

'Show me,' I said. 'Take me and show me. And if you're right, we'll come back and wake them. But it's probably a tyre or something.'

Kim nodded, then put her hands on her knees and bent over, catching her breath. She was wearing a pair of our fluffy slippers and one of our dressing-gowns. I could see the strap of her pink bra in the wide-open neckline.

'How long have you been up?' I asked her.

'What?' she said. 'What the hell does that matter?' She

199

grabbed my hand and started pulling me across the grass. 'Didn't you hear what I said? Sasha's dead!'

'I mean, when did you last see him?' I said. 'How long has he been gone?'

We slipped through the gate and into the trees, stumbling on the tree roots across the path.

'I didn't see him,' Kim said. 'I couldn't face him. I went to the empty room. Jennifer and Peach's room.'

'But what took you down to the beach?'

'Stop asking me so many stupid questions. Hurry!'

I don't know if it was the hangover or the fog of sleep still clouding my head, those dreams I'd been having – the scuffle of rabbits in the walls and the sweep of headlights showing through the cracks around the edge of the cupboard doors – or even if it was Kim's panic transferred, but nothing about this morning seemed real. As the trees closed in behind us, deadening every sound, I kept thinking about all the stories of girls going into the woods and all the terrible things that ever happened to them there. I had a picture in my mind of Sasha crouched behind one of the trunks, ready to jump out at us. I was half sure I could hear his breathing. Then I thought I could see him, flitting in the shadows.

The beach path got steeper as it went on, though, and I got colder and colder as we got nearer and nearer the sea. And soon the world seemed real again: leaf mould to skid on and rocks sticking up like shark teeth to trip me. Then the canopy started to thin and the ground paled where the sand had blown in, and suddenly we found ourselves standing on the little ridge, not really a dune, staring at the half-gone tide, at the pebbles that were chuckling and glistening as the water sucked at them on its way out, and at the dark shape that was almost beaching as each wave drained away, floating again as the next came washing in.

I would have thought it was a dead seal, or even a broad clump of wrack, except that a bit further up the beach there was a lobster pot, and the lobster pot was full of rocks and a rope led from it to the dark shape.

'Sasha,' said Kim, in a tiny voice.

'We need to phone,' I said. 'Nine-nine-nine.'

Then I blinked. Had he moved? Or was it just the way the waves surged and eddied, lifting him and dropping him again? I squinted harder. No, he wasn't moving. He looked stiff.

'Do you think it's another trick?' Kim said. 'It's another trick. It's not big enough to be Sasha's body.'

'Yes,' I said. 'I think so. I think it's a dummy. And I haven't got my phone anyway. Let's wait till it's beached and then walk out and make sure. Or I will. You don't need to.'

As if she'd needed permission, Kim sank down onto the sand and the tufts of rough grass, her feet crumpled under her.

'Don't sit like that,' I said. 'If your feet are cold anyway, you'll get pins and needles.'

'How long will it take?' she asked. 'For the tide to go out?'

'Minutes,' I said. 'Not long at all. Here, hutch up and let's keep warm.'

She shuffled towards me and I put my arm round her, even though reaching out made me colder than ever and her body was so chilled that no comfort came back from touching her.

'So,' I said. 'What brought you down to the beach?'

'I woke up,' Kim said. 'I was sure someone was shaking

201

me but there was no one there. Felt like death on a stick and I wanted some fresh air. Then I remembered the lobster pot, and decided to go and get it.'

'In your dressing-gown?'

'It's going to sound stupid,' she said. 'But I thought, What's the point of a private beach if you don't go down there in your jammies?'

'Right,' I said. 'Right.' I could feel myself nodding and Kim started nodding too.

'And there was a note on my pillow,' she said, 'saying, "Come to the beach." So there was that.'

For some reason, this struck me as the funniest thing I had ever heard and I laughed until my voice gave out, then I laughed silently. Sometime in the middle of it, Kim started laughing too, rocking and snuffling, trying to catch her breath and choking herself, then laughing even harder at the noises she was making.

Trying to get a proper deep breath before I fainted, I turned away to face down the beach again and managed to stop. I sighed a couple of times and cleared my throat. Bubbles of laughter were still inside me somewhere but tears were closer because down at the tideline the water was starting to look thin over the stones underneath. The dummy, or seal, or bundle of clothes or whatever it was, was barely moving.

'I'm not saying this to be rude,' Kim said, 'but I wish to God I'd never thought of Galloway, never clicked the link to the Home From Home website, never booked this weekend and never seen this godforsaken beach until the day I died. No offence.'

'None taken,' I said. 'Under the circumstances. But you know you didn't click a link by chance. There's no way you *wandered* onto our website, Kim. You do know that, don't you? You do *know* Sasha engineered this?'

'It felt like chance,' she said. 'My book group was reading *Eat Pray Love* and one of the questions was "Where's your next dream destination?" And I said I had this anniversary coming up and not a clue what to do. And we all chatted a bit and then boom. Galloway.'

'I'm so sorry,' I said. 'No one should have to read *Eat Pray Love*.' But the laughter was gone. There wasn't so much as a chuckle from either of us.

'Right, then,' said Kim. A wave came up and fell back and didn't touch the black shape at all. It was just a sodden lump on the sparkling stones. I took Kim's hand, pulled her up and started walking.

The sand was only a strip along the top of the beach, then the pebbles began, little ones first, then big cobbles uncomfortable to walk on, then smaller ones again and finally sharp grit stretching all the way to far beyond the low-tide line. It's the fluke that keeps Knockbreak Bay quiet. If there was sand underfoot all the way, we'd have a car park and crowds.

'Is it?' Kim said, when we were halfway. She was holding on to me to keep her balance on the stones. Her slippers were soaked through now, slapping heavily with every step, and I hated myself for thinking that they'd be trashed and we'd have to bin them. We had budgeted for getting a few wears out of every pair when we went for top-of-the-range instead of the cheap ones.

'It's hard to say,' I said. 'It's not a seal.' I was looking at the head end – a sodden mop of black. It could be human hair, but it could be any kind of wet fabric. Maybe the whole thing was a roll of cloth. The middle could be a dinner jacket, or it could be a bin bag or a big coughed-up clump of seaweed and twine. Except that there was a band of white where the rope was tied round. It wasn't pure white. It was pink where the rough fibres had chafed. It was actually, I could see, as we kept on slipping and slapping over the stones, it was actually red in a line right under the rope, rubbed bloody.

'Oh, God,' Kim said. 'It's not a dummy.' She started to run. I let go of her and let her surge ahead. When I reached her she was standing with her feet spread wide, trying to balance as she bent over and peered at it.

He lay on his front, his face hidden in the sludge of tiny pebbles and pieces of shell. His hands were white and spongy-looking, lying by his sides.

'He's not wearing his wedding ring,' Kim whispered. 'Oh, my God, Donna, it's not Sasha, is it? It's not him!'

'What are you talking about?' I said. I thought over all of them, all the men in their black dinner jackets. Buck Leslie, with his salt-and-pepper hair, Ramsay and Paul Buchanan, both fair. 'Who else could it be?'

'Turn him over! Turn him over!'

Peach with her highlights. Rosalie— I gasped. Surely this body was far too heavy to be Rosalie's. Those hands were too square to be Rosalie's.

I reached down and grabbed the jacket, feeling the squelch as the seawater ran out of the sopping cloth. I tugged until the body was balanced on its other shoulder and then pushed it flat again.

Jennifer's face, bloated and blue, stared up at us out of milky eyes. Her mouth was stretched wide and stuffed with a stone.

'Jen,' Kim whispered, staggering back, away from the sight of it.

My lips felt numb and dry, like they might stick to my teeth if I tried to talk.

'Push her back over,' said Kim. 'We shouldn't have moved her before the police see her but I won't tell if you don't tell. Push her back over, Donna. And let's go.'

Some of the weight was for real. My trousers were wet and my Crocs were full of sand sludge. But that didn't explain how hard it was to drag myself back across that beach and up the path to The Breakers' garden gate. At one point, I went down onto my hands and knees and crawled, grabbing the tree roots to pull myself onwards. Kim was ahead of me, walking like a zombie. She tripped once but didn't put her hands out, just let herself go over on her ankle.

It was almost fully light now. A dull grey day without shadows, without a breath of wind. There was no sign of life at the house. No lights on. All the curtains were drawn shut, except for the gap I had poked at the window of Jennifer and Peach's room.

'I'm so cold,' Kim said, crossing the lawn. 'I'm just so cold. Would it be okay, do you think, to have a shower before we start phoning and telling people? To warm up?'

I was shaking so hard my teeth hurt every time they clacked against each other. 'No, of course not,' I said. I knew it was wrong, although I couldn't say why.

'I'll go and tell Sasha,' said Kim. 'Wake him up and then *he* can phone. I'm just so bloody cold.'

'Do you think he's in your room?' I said. 'Did he come back?'

Kim stopped walking and stared at me. 'I forgot he left last night. *Did* he come back?' She hit herself on the temple with her knuckles. 'My head's not right.' Then she looked past me at the sleeping face of the house, gaunt in the grey dawn. 'His car's gone.'

I turned. The navy-blue Range Rover was missing.

'Why is no one awake?' Kim said.

'It's not even six o'clock yet,' I told her, as we slipped back in at the drawing-room window and I looked at the mantel clock. I turned my head as we squelched across the room. I couldn't bear to see the pile of presents, shoved onto the floor, or the bare cushion pad. I didn't understand how I could still care so much about a rabbit when I had seen a dead woman. Maybe it was from horror on top of horror and all of them worse for all the others.

'Can I get a towel?' Kim said, when we were in the hall. 'I need a clean one.'

'Through here,' I said, opening the door to the back and swerving left to the long bank of cupboards, unlatching the one where the bath sheets and hand towels were stored. I handed a pair to Kim and took a pair for myself.

'Why did she do it?' Kim said. 'She must have done it, right? She brought us all here, played all those nasty pranks and then did that? But why?'

I shook my head, couldn't think of a single thing to say. None of this was real.

'Phone the police,' I said, then stumbled into the bathroom as she trailed up the stairs.

I noticed the wet floor first, strange as that sounds. A

puddle of water in the middle of the vinyl floor of the staff shower room. After that, it was the smell. The smell of the sea: saltwater and weed. Only then did I look up and see the sagging shape hanging there. Black hair, black clothes, white spongy hands and the seawater still dripping from the wet black socks. For one nightmare moment I thought it was Jennifer again. Then I walked round the shape and looked up into Sasha's face, his skin black, his tongue black, his eyes black and bulging, his gaping mouth filled with a huge black stone.

Chapter 15

1991

It feels like three o'clock in the morning but Mum and Dad are still watching the telly. I send Lynsey upstairs and put my head round the living-room door.

'Hiya!'

'There she is!' Dad says. 'Did you have a good time?'

'We went swimming!' I say. 'We're freezing!'

'Swimming in what?' Mum's on her feet and headed my way. They've had a four-pack of beers with their curry. All of it's still sitting on the coffee-table in front of them: smeared plates and ring pulls. I would have said it was a right old mess before I saw the state of the kitchen at the party.

'In the bay,' I say. 'Where else?'

'You know what I mean, you cheeky besom,' says Mum. 'If you've been skinny-dipping and showing me up!'

'We borrowed cozzies. But we didn't have towels. Brrrrr! Lynsey's in the shower and I'll jump in after her.'

'Well, give me the costumes and I'll rinse them

through,' Mum says. 'You can take them back fresh in the morning.'

'Stop fussing,' says Dad. 'You're missing the film.'

'Mum, we left them on the beach.'

'You what? They lent you their good swimming costumes and you left them lying damp on the beach at your backs. Didn't I tell you not to show me up?'

'I'll go back and get them if you want.' I'm kidding but, to my amazement, my mum nods.

'And take some towels in case they need them.'

Dad rolls his eyes at me and I try to smile at him. She hasn't got a clue. She really thinks the drawling drunk man that threw his cigar into the verge and that drip of a woman who doesn't care if her kids get salmonella would be shocked if a cozzie got left on a beach. And now I'm going to have to go back with a load of my mum's towels. Like *I'm* the maid instead of her.

I stamp upstairs to the bathroom and barge in without knocking. Lynsey's standing under the hot water with her head back and her eyes closed. Her cheeks are puffed out as far as they'll go and her lips are pinched shut.

'Puke if you need to puke,' I tell her. 'It'll go down the drain.'

She shakes her head and beckons me over, miming at me to cup my hands.

'It really works, Carmen,' she says, once she's spat it into my hand and I've mimed swallowing. 'I feel fine now.'

'Good. I said we've been swimming but that's all. Okay?'

'I just want to have a cup of hot juice and go to bed.'

So I gather the best of the towels, five new ones Mum got at the street market in Carlisle when she went to meet her

209

sister for a shopping day. She wouldn't want the Mowbrays seeing the towels *we* use for the beach. I know that.

I peel off my wet jeans, in my bedroom, ignoring the sting of them on my cold skin, then drag my top off. I kick it under the bed. If Mum finds it and washes it, it'll hang in my wardrobe until the moths eat it. I won't be wearing it again. The feel of pulling on a soft dry T-shirt and a pair of old stretched-out leggings nearly makes me cry with relief. I put my old rubbers on, ignoring the way my nails catch on the inside of the toe bits. I don't care if I chip the polish now.

'I won't be long,' I say at the living-room door. Then I'm out in the night again.

They might not even still be on the beach, I tell myself, jogging along the lane towards the boat-gate. If their parents read them the Riot Act they might all be back at the house, mopping up spilled booze and doing dishes. But I hear them before I'm halfway there and I see the glow of the bonfire and the pinprick light of cigarettes as soon as I'm round the lane end and onto the sand.

It's so dark outside the ring of firelight, though, that they can't see me. I creep a little closer, drop down behind a wedge of rock and rest my chin on my hands, listening. I hear the popping sound of someone taking a bottle away from their lips. They're still drinking.

'. . . pretty narrow squeak,' Jennifer's saying. 'If I hadn't got you all up and got you down here to the beach in time, we'd have been for it. I thought Anna and Oliver were going to bust a gut as it was.'

'What did the little bitch tell them?' That's Sasha.

'Don't be so horrible,' says Rosalie. 'And pass the wine. I

need more wine. I need to pickle my brain till it's like tonight never happened.'

'She said I was in Anna's bed and Rosie was crying and Peach was paralytic. No reason for it. She just opened her mouth and dropped us all in it.'

'And what about the other little bitch?' said Sasha. 'What did she say?'

'She told them the truth,' says Jennifer. 'She came down to the beach to go swimming, but her period started.'

'Oh, shut up!' says Ramsay. 'I'm still feeling sick from the cocktails. Shut up about periods!'

'I mix a pretty good Monthly Mary,' says Sasha. 'The trick is to get it lumpy.'

'Shut *up*!' That's more than Ramsay now.

'Chopped plum tomatoes.' Sasha hoots with laughter, then adds, 'but I'm making myself feel sick, actually.'

'Hold on, though,' Buck says. He's slurring his words. 'When did she go swimming? Jellifer, you told me she went home.'

'To shut you up,' Jennifer says.

'Yeah, Sasha,' says Ramsay. 'You said you were taking her home. I told her sister that.'

'She asked to go to the beach instead,' Sasha says. 'I passed out. I was a bit worried about her when I woke up. But if you saw her in the lane, Jelly, all's well.'

'Speaking of passing out,' says Paul. 'Peach? Oh, Pe-each! Calling Miss Schna-apps.'

'Morag!' That's Buck. 'She's out for the count this time. I'll take her back to the house.'

'Aren't Anna and Oliver going to wonder why Morag went swimming in her nightie?' Sasha says.

211

'You're welcome!' says Jennifer. 'That was my quick thinking. If we hadn't chucked her in the sea to get the sick off her we wouldn't be able to blame the sisters for the mess in that room.'

'As long as they don't make trouble,' Buck says.

'They won't,' Jennifer says. 'They wouldn't dare. It's our word against—'

'Not the kids!' Buck says. 'I mean, as long as Anna and Oliver don't try to get them to pay for the cleaning or something.'

'Same deal,' says Jennifer. 'Their word against ours.'

'Evil genius,' says Buck, but at least he sounds unhappy about it. He pulls Morag to her feet. She groans but, with his arm round her, he manages to drag her off.

I know I've got to keep quiet. I can't let a peep out. But inside – absolutely silently – I'm boiling over. They're going to blame me for that pile of peach puke, are they? Me, who was all set to go out the back and hose my mess away.

'And what's wrong with *your* face, Ro-Ro?' Sasha says, when the others have gone. 'It's my birthday and you're sitting there like it's a wake.'

'Leave her alone,' says Paul.

'Ooo-ooooh,' Sasha says. 'Paul and Rosalie, up a tree!'

'Shut up, you chimp,' Paul says. 'Honestly, Sasha, why are you such an arse? Come on, Rosalie. Let's go.'

'I know you don't need a spare leg, but I'll come with you,' Ramsay says.

'Playing gooseberry again, eh?' says Sasha.

'Now, now, children,' Jennifer puts in.

But Rosalie holds a hand out to both brothers and the three of them go off together.

'Well, happy fucking birthday to me,' Sasha says, when it's just him and Jennifer. 'Some party this was.'

'We need to put tonight behind us,' Jennifer says. 'The kid's not going to open her mouth. She's scared of her mum getting angry. So as long as *we* don't say anything, everything'll be fine.'

'Why shouldn't it be? What's the problem?'

'For God's sake, Sasha! Gormless as Anna and Oliver are, when they sober up they're going to smell a rat. So here's what we need to do. Visualize the party. Imagine—'

'Oh, not this crap!'

'Take the whole party and put it in a box. Lock the box. And throw the key out into the sea, where it sinks to the ocean floor and is lost for ever.'

'That's not an ocean. That's the Solway.'

'Think of all the music you heard tonight,' Jennifer says.

Sasha starts singing Bryan Adams at the top of his voice.

Jennifer laughs. I turn over and lie on my back on the sand, looking up at the stars. She *laughed*. 'But not only the music,' she goes on. 'Take every word spoken, every sound made, and imagine that you're stitching your lips shut. Big black Frankenstein stitches, crisscross. Okay?'

'Mm-mmm,' says Sasha.

'And now we swear,' says Jennifer. 'Say after me: I will go to my grave keeping the secret of what happened here tonight. I will never picture it – never open the box. I will never speak of it – never cut open the stitches. I will go to my silent grave.'

'Fuck's sake, Jelly,' says Sasha. 'Don't you think you're overreacting a bit?'

'Do *you*?'

'She wasn't even invited. She gate-crashed.'

'Sasha, you need to wise up,' Jennifer says. 'She's twelve. And, as of today, you are sixteen. Yesterday it would have been one thing and today it's a much worse thing.'

'Oh, come off it!' Sasha says. 'They wouldn't bring the hammer down on the stroke of midnight on my birthday.'

'Why are you having such a hard time facing facts?'

'Because she's a total prick-tease. Flirting away all night, then acting like a nun when I went in for a fumble. I could kick her teeth in.'

'Why did you have to "fumble" her at all? What was wrong with the sister?'

'Her *sister* was passed out on the floor of the bog.'

'Put it in the box, stitch your lips and go to your grave,' says Jennifer. 'Seriously. Do it for me. Because I'm in a lot of trouble too. I mean, you should have known better, but I'm eighteen. I was the only adult.'

They're silent now. All I can hear is the sound of the waves and the occasional crack of a twig in the fire, sending up a shower of blue sparks as the salt burns.

I notice the two people walking before they do. It's inky black but they've got a torch. The circle of light on the sand is only metres away when Jennifer says, 'Who's that?'

'Anna,' says a voice. 'And Oliver. We're going to have a conversation with you and if we can't get this thing straightened out we're going to have a conversation with the parents of those two little girls who came to your party.'

The silence lasts so long that I risk discovery to pop my head up and see what's happening. If they moved their torch they'd see me, lying there so close to them. But the torch is pointed straight down, like Anna doesn't want to see the face of her own son.

'What did she say?' That's Sasha. 'Has she phoned up telling tales?'

'She covered for you all,' Anna says. 'But I want to know what happened. Sasha, put that bloody wine bottle down!'

'What's changed?' says Jennifer. 'Since we met in the lane?'

'It's not up for discussion.' It's the first time Oliver has spoken.

'It was very irresponsible of you,' Anna says, 'to let such a young girl get so drunk that she'd ...' She stops talking and starts to cry.

'Go swimming?' says Jennifer. 'Or go swimming with her period?'

Anna makes an incoherent sound.

'Was it you, Sasha?' says Oliver.

'Was what me?' Sasha says. 'I didn't even invite her. She just turned up.'

'She should have been safe at a party full of well-brought-up responsible children,' his father says. 'I'm not going to ask you again. Was it you?'

'I think she helped *herself* to the drinks, Uncle Oliver,' Jennifer says. 'We showed her where the lemonade was, but—'

'Don't!' he barks. 'Stop.'

'We found her underpants under the breakfast-room table,' says Anna.

'Oh, no, those are mine!' says Jennifer. 'I got changed into my swimsuit in the breakfast room.'

'And we found a bed made of towels in the downstairs loo.'

'Yes, I was keeping an ear cocked for Morag. That's why I changed downstairs. *She* was in the loo. I made that bed up for her to lie on until she felt better.'

'Shut up!' Anna says, with her voice breaking. 'Stop lying! What's wrong with you? The child's name is in her knickers.'

'A twelve-year-old child has been assaulted in our house tonight,' Oliver says. 'At best our children did nothing about it. At worst – at worst—'

'It wasn't me, Dad,' Sasha says. 'And I don't think it was Paul. Or Buck. So that leaves Ramsay. If you're serious. Are you really serious?'

'This is going to ruin lives,' Oliver says. Then he pauses. 'If it comes out.'

'I could stop it coming out,' Jennifer says. 'You should let me loose on the rest of them. I've got this three-part method, you see. I can teach it to you. It's quick and easy and it really works. A locked box and stitched lips and—'

'Jennifer, just stop talking,' says Anna. 'I know you're all drunk, and I know these girls might be rough and ready, but for God's sake!'

'Tell them she drowned,' says Sasha, suddenly.

'What?' His father spits the word.

'You want them to take it seriously, don't you? You don't want Ramsay confessing or anyone else blabbing? You want them to lock it in a box and all Jennifer's crap? Well, tell them she drowned and it's our fault for not looking after her. That should do it.'

'How did we spawn you?' says Anna. 'How did we manage to produce two such malformed creatures as your sister and you?'

'Malformed?' Sasha says. 'What's wrong with Rosalie?'

'Get back to the house,' his mother says, ignoring him. 'We're leaving in the morning.'

'Aw, Mu-um,' says Sasha.

'I think that's a good idea,' says Jennifer. She has stood up and she's dusting the sand off the back of her skirt. 'It would be impossible to make them believe she'd drowned if we were still here. I mean, if she really drowned there'd be the Coastguard and frogmen or something, wouldn't there? You can say we're packing up and leaving because a child has gone missing and then you can reveal the big news that she drowned once we're all home again.'

'There's something diabolical about you, Jennifer,' says Anna. She turns and stumbles away, taking the torch.

'Kick this bonfire over and get back to the house,' Oliver says, before he takes off after her.

They're completely silent until the torchlight's disappeared into the trees. Then Sasha makes a noise like a bottle of warm fizzy juice opening, a long, burbling hiss. 'Oh, my God!' he says. He puts on a falsetto voice: *'There's something diabolical about you, Jennifer!'*

'How did we spawn you?' says Jennifer. 'Jesus, Sash, how did you keep your face straight?'

I know I can't move till after they've gone, so I lie there, on my back, looking up at the sky, trying to ignore their cackling voices, letting the tears slide out of the sides of my eyes and fall into my hair.

———

I've drifted off when I realize the tone of their voices has changed from cackles to murmurs, so low that the rustle and rub of their clothes almost drowns it. The tide is at its lowest ebb, far down the bay and hardly moving.

'Sasha,' says Jennifer, in a slow creaking voice, halfway to a groan. 'What are you doing?'

'Claiming my birthday treat,' Sasha says. The crooning of his voice makes me swallow a sour mouthful of spit. I don't know which of them's worse. Jennifer knows exactly what he's doing and she's fine with it, even though she's just got out of bed with Buck. And Sasha— I will my thoughts away from that. And, telling myself they're too busy to notice, I creep away.

Back at the house, Lynsey's curled in her bed in our shared room, with a towel under her head to keep her damp pigtails off her pillow, an empty cup on her bedside table.

'How you doing?' I ask.

She holds out a hand. 'One tiny wee black lump for you.'

I gulp it down. It hardly registers among all the lead in my belly. 'It's over,' I say. 'They're going away in the morning. They won't be back.'

'Good,' says Lynsey, and she huffs over onto her other shoulder. 'Will you sing again, Carmen?'

I begin softly singing to her. I hear the wet smack as she puts her thumb in her mouth.

She's asleep before I've got my clothes off.

She's snoring when I get back from the bathroom.

But when I wake in the morning to the sound of the cars in the lane, as Anna and Oliver drive all their precious children away, she's gone.

Chapter 16

I cleaned the kitchen. There is no explanation for it – none at all – but when I came reeling out of the staff shower room, I went in there for solace and what I found was all of last night's mess. Someone had cleared the dining table, but every glass, every pudding bowl, every coffee cup was sitting out on my teak worktops. So I cleaned.

And when the good crystal glasses were draining upside down on spread tea-cloths and the dishwasher was running, when all the empty tins were in the recycling, and all the rubbish was tied in a black bag and it was taken out to the wheelie-bin, when the worktops were wiped and the floor was mopped, then at last I went to the foot of the back stairs and started to climb them.

And, anyway, there *was* an explanation. Jennifer's death was terrible, of course, but it was down at the beach. When it came out that someone had died right there in the house, we were finished. And it seemed to me that telling Kim – telling anyone – was where that started. Until I told, I could hang on to the dream of The Breakers. Five-star reviews, restaurant critics coming to stay, a second property added, an office manager, articles in the glossies, a recipe book, a TV series, an empire. All of that was going to vanish now. But not until I told someone. Until then it could maybe un-happen.

Then I shook the thought out of my head. Stupid! Kim had already vanished it. She had gone to tell Sasha and he was probably on the phone to the police station already. I shook my head again. There was something wrong with that, but I couldn't work out what it was.

When I stepped through the door to the front corridor, Kim was walking towards me. She was wearing a fresh dressing-gown and her hair was wet and pulled back from her face.

'I can't find him,' she said. 'He's not in our room and he's not in with Buck and Peach.'

I opened my mouth to tell her what I'd seen in the bathroom downstairs, but she was already pushing on the door to Ramsay's room. A cold sweat passed over me, as if I'd been doused with a bucket of ice-water. Suddenly I was sure he would be dead too. All of them were dead, Paul and Rosalie cold and stiff in each other's arms in the silver bedroom.

But it left as quickly as it came. I heard a low groan from the dark. 'Leave me alone, Kim,' came Ramsay's voice. 'What the hell time is it?'

'I'm looking for Sasha.'

'Well, I haven't got him. Sod off and look for him some-where else.'

She came out and wheeled round to go in and check the cherry-wood bedroom, where Jennifer should have been. This time the wave of sweat brought a picture of Jennifer lying soaked and bloated under the crisp white sheets, her matted hair spread out like seaweed on the pillow under her head.

'Ramsay,' I said, knocking softly and going in. 'It's Donna.'

'No,' Ramsay said. He was lying in a sweaty tangle of sheets, naked above his waist.

'Sasha,' I said.

'Isn't here.' His voice was a rasp and his throat clicked as he swallowed.

'He's downstairs in the staff bathroom,' I said.

'Tell *Kim*. I don't care.'

'He's hanged himself.'

I thought for a minute he hadn't heard me or that he'd managed to fall asleep again.

'For kicks?' he said at last. 'With a belt from the back of the door? Did you interrupt him?'

'He is hanging from the ceiling light,' I said. 'He's dead.'

'It might be a harness,' said Ramsay. 'He could be tricking you.'

'I need to call the police.' Even as I said it, I knew I was beginning to wonder. Was *any* of this real? When I closed my eyes I saw two flashes: the first one Jennifer's blue face and her dry lips stretched to splitting around the stone in her mouth, then Sasha's face, black and dull, a glint in his black slit eyes but the stone in his mouth just a deeper darkness.

Ramsay gave a groan that was almost a snore. 'Go and tickle his feet and see if he jumps, eh?'

I crept back out to the hall.

Kim was standing at the head of the stairs. 'Rosalie hasn't seen him,' she said. 'I told her about Jennifer.'

'Did she believe you?'

Kim swung her head from side to side, slowly. 'No. Did that really happen, Donna? Did we really go to the beach? Or did I dream it? *Is* she dead?'

'If we went,' I said, 'then it's real. If we dreamed it, she might be alive.'

Now she swung her head up and down, confirming what I was saying. She was closing one eye and then the other in turn, making her vision jump from side to side. She had stopped listening.

'You're as high as a kite!' It was Rosalie, still caked in last night's make-up and wearing nothing but a red shortie nightie, trimmed with marabou, like something from a saucy seaside postcard. We must have made a pretty stunning picture too – Kim with her face pure white, and God knows what I looked like. I felt as if all my blood had turned to jelly and was pooled in the pit of my stomach. 'Go to bed, Kim,' Rosalie said. 'Sleep it off.'

'I can't find Sasha,' Kim said.

'Count your blessings,' said Rosalie. 'Paul's been snoring all night long and farting every two minutes.' She stretched. 'I don't suppose you've got a sovereign remedy for hangovers, Donna? My mouth's like a junkie's carpet this morning. Could you do something with tomato juice and raw eggs that'll straighten me out?'

I said nothing.

'More sleep would help, of course,' said Rosalie. 'But Kim came sharing her drunk dreams with me and when I'm up I'm up.'

'It wasn't a dream,' said Kim, on a rising note. 'Donna, tell her. I feel as if I'm going crazy!'

'Ssh,' said Rosalie. 'My head.'

'Rosalie,' I said. 'I'm really sorry but it's true. And I'm really, really sorry, Kim, but that's not all. There's been a . . . Sasha . . . I actually don't know how to say this.'

'True?' said Rosalie. 'Jennifer? On the beach? It can't be.'

'What about Sasha?' said Kim.

'He's downstairs,' I said. 'He's in the loo. He's . . . not okay.'

'Well, why are we standing around?' Kim said. She was already running. 'If he's not okay we should be getting help. Fuck's sake, Donna. What the hell's wrong with you?' She threw herself at the top of the stairs and went clattering down, bringing a bellow from inside Ramsay's bedroom at the noise. Then we could hear her slamming in and out of the back rooms down there.

'Not the utility,' I shouted. 'The shower room.'

'Shut *up*,' Ramsay groaned.

Kim was still bashing around. She shouted up the stairs. 'Where did you see him, Donna? He's not here now. Was he injured? If he's wandered off, injured . . .'

I walked down as steadily as my feet would carry me, holding on to the banister and telling myself I wasn't going to faint when I looked at him again. I needed to forget myself and think about his widow and his sister. Even his cousins. I walked towards the bathroom, breathing deep. There were enough doors down here to confuse anyone, between the kitchen, the scullery, the pantry cupboard and this one. She had somehow managed to miss him.

I was still telling myself that when I pushed the door open.

We had chosen cleverly. The glass shade of the ceiling light and the soft-glow lightbulb gave such a warmth to the room. Especially when it was full of steam – if you took a shower with the window shut. I stared up at it. If a twelve-stone man

223

had tied that cord round his neck and then stepped off the toilet seat, it would have stretched or cracked the plaster . . . or something. Surely.

And he was wet when I saw him hanging there. The seawater had dripped off his sodden clothes and made a puddle on the floor. I stepped forward and pushed my toe along the dry vinyl, feeling it squeak.

'You had a nightmare?' Rosalie said, coming up behind me.

'No,' I said. 'No, I wasn't dreaming.'

Kim came and stood in front of me. 'What did you see?'

I put my hands on her shoulders. 'Sasha is dead,' I told her. Rosalie covered her mouth. 'I'm sorry. I came in and saw him hanging. His face was black and he was definitely, definitely dead. He was wet with seawater. It was dripping off him.'

'Seawater,' Kim said. 'You think he killed Jennifer, then came back here and killed himself? Why?'

'And then cut his own body down and hid it?' said Rosalie. She leaned against the wall and wiped her forehead with the edge of a palm. 'It was a trick. Sasha and his tricks. Sasha!' she shouted. 'You can come out now. You've delighted everyone enough.'

Her voice echoed and the silence stole around us again.

'Or it was a hallucination,' Rosalie said. 'Maybe?'

'Maybe,' I agreed. 'Something isn't right.'

Kim was shaking my arm.

'I know what you mean,' Rosalie said. 'I don't feel drunk, but I don't feel hung-over either. I certainly don't feel normal.'

The word hit me with a jolt. Kim and me sitting on the sand waiting for the tide to go down. Kim wanting a shower before she shared the news. Me cleaning the kitchen. None of it was normal.

224

Kim was still tugging at my arm. 'Jen,' she whispered.

We were both running before the thought – the unthinkable thought – had even formed in my mind. 'We'll take the car,' I threw over my shoulder. 'Go through the slipway. I can't scramble down that path again.'

But when I grabbed my keys from the hook at the back door, telling myself I wasn't too hung-over to drive, telling myself I wasn't going insane, I fumbled and fumbled and stopped dead. 'Shit!'

'What?'

I took a deep breath to slow myself down and looked, one after the other, at every key on the ring. 'The barrier key's missing. The boat-gate. We'll have to hoof it.'

I hit speed-dial and speaker, when we were halfway across the grass. 'Mum? Oh, God, voicemail. Mum, I'm in trouble down here. There's been a . . . there's been a . . . Listen, call me when you get this, eh?' I hung up and threw myself through the open gate onto the path.

We slithered and skidded down and down, grabbing at the tree trunks and each other.

'She won't be there, will she?' Kim said.

'I don't think so.' I felt the grip of sand under my feet and looked up and out across the beach.

She was gone. The lobster pot was gone. The rope was gone. Then, into the silence, came the roar of a car engine and the whine of tyres spinning in the wet sand.

I surged forward out of the trees. At the far edge of the bay where the lane rises up, I saw just a flick of navy-blue paint and the wink of a chrome bumper.

Kim started running.

'There's no point,' I called after her. 'Listen.'

And, in between the soft hiss of the slack low-tide waves, we could hear the Range Rover shifting gear and shifting again, and then the noise of its engine fading as it raced away.

Chapter 17

They were all waiting for us in the dining room. Buck, looking as rough as he could without actually bleeding or puking, opened the side door of the bay window and stood back to let us in. He had one of The Breakers' dressing-gowns on. In fact, they all had their dressing-gowns on, and it gave me a wry moment of pride to see how they'd huddled into them, hands in pockets and collars turned up, for comfort.

Peach looked even worse. She had a bad case of the shakes, lifting her water glass to her lips with both hands. Paul and Ramsay had the fair colouring that looks grimmest of all with a terrible hangover. Their eyes were pink and their lips yellow.

Buck sat down again with a long groan. I noticed no one was in Sasha's place. The head of the table wasn't set at all. I noticed too that the dining room was, in some hard-to-pinpoint way, slightly the worse for wear. The flowers weren't wilting, and there were no crumbs on the carpet or dust on the surfaces, but there was something tired about the air. We had definitely made a mistake with this. We should definitely have had a little breakfast room in place of the study or library, or even let the guests sit in the black breakfast room attached to the kitchen. Let them watch me flipping pancakes, let them smell the coffee and hear the bacon sizzle.

'Well?' said Rosalie. I blinked and came back. I had forgotten none of that mattered now. 'Where were you?' I thought she meant in my daydreams, until I blinked again.

'Someone took my boat-gate key,' I said. 'And Sasha's car.'

'Who cares about your *key*?' said Paul.

'Because if someone needed to shift something off the beach they might well nick a key to the barrier,' Kim said, nodding. 'And the Range Rover's pretty roomy.'

'Is that where you went?' said Rosalie. 'The beach?'

'And this is Jennifer, is it?' said Buck. 'This "something" that's been shifted? Is this for real? Because I'm waiting for the punch line.'

'It's for real,' Kim said. She was speaking very slowly. 'Jennifer's killed herself. Or been murdered. And Sasha's killed himself. Or been murdered. And someone took both bodies away. Donna saw Sasha. We both saw Jennifer. There's no punch line.'

'So we call the police,' said Rosalie. 'But can I call Mum and Dad first?' She put her head in her hands. 'This is going to destroy them.'

'We can't tell them over the phone, sweetheart,' said Paul. 'We'll go before the police get here. You and me. We'll go and break the news. Then we can come back. And if the cops don't like it they can lump it.'

Rosalie gave him a twisted smile.

But I saw Buck shift in his seat. 'Actually,' he said, 'I don't think that's such a fantastic idea. I mean, like Kim said, someone moved the bodies.'

'While we were all together in this room!' said Rosalie.

'Still,' said Buck. 'Maybe none of us should go anywhere. Actually.'

The silence was so perfect it made my ears ring. No one even breathed.

'That's . . . ridiculous,' said Rosalie at last. 'Me? Paul?'

'Someone,' said Buck. 'I think we should let the police decide.'

'My brother is dead,' said Rosalie. She was talking as slow as Kim now. 'Kim's husband is dead. Who cares what you think?'

'Poor Jennifer,' said Ramsay. 'Who cares about her either, eh?'

Rosalie blushed a bit at that but she stuck her chin in the air. 'Right, then. The police it is. Donna, can I use your landline? In the study, isn't it?'

'Help yourself,' I told her, then let my head sink into my hands. The unreality of it all was beginning to make me feel dizzy. That one glimpse of Sasha hanging in the dim bathroom was bleeding into all the dreams of the short night as more of them came back to me: not just the lights and rabbits, but the whistling sound of the meat knife hacking through the sugar on top of the party hats crumpled in the fireplace and the whiff of sulphur as I struck match after match trying to light them.

'Someone should go with you,' said Peach.

'*Et tu?*' said Rosalie.

'It's not about suspicion, Rosie,' Ramsay said. 'We need to stick in pairs to vouch for each other.'

'I'm going to phone the police to report my husband's murder,' Kim said, standing up. 'Rosalie, would you like to come with me? Personally, I'd *rather* have someone at my side. I don't really want to be alone in this house any more. Because you're wrong, Ramsay. It's not about "vouching". Or about "suspicion". It's about not being next.'

I didn't look up but the silence told me everything. They were seeing each other with different eyes now. These people who'd been friends all their lives.

'And you reckon I'm safe, do you?' said Rosalie. She sounded angry. 'What makes you think I feel safe with you?'

'For God's sake,' said Ramsay. 'We can all go, if you like. We can hold hands like children crossing the road. But someone phone the police.'

'I'll make some coffee,' I said. 'And breakfast.' There were a few scattered groans. 'Just some scrambled eggs or toast. It's going to be a long day.'

'Shouldn't one of us go with you?' said Paul.

'No,' said Buck. 'No "us", no "you", no "them". I could murder a cup of coffee, Donna.'

'Thanks,' I said. 'For the vote of confidence.'

I swerved by the bay window as if to close it against the draught. What I was really doing was picking up the transmitter. I bolted along to the drawing room to pick up the other one, making sure Rosalie and Kim didn't see me pass the study doorway. When I got to the kitchen my phone was playing 'Mamma Mia'.

'Donna? You sounded terrible on that message,' my mum said. 'What's up?'

'Suicide,' I said. 'Murder. One guest drowned on the beach and one hanging from a ceiling light.'

She was silent. In the background the wedding fair was going on as lively as ever, a cacophony of happy girls and proud mothers still at it, even this early on a Sunday morning. I ripped out the receiver from its place by the side of the stove.

'I need to get rid of the monitors,' I said. 'The cops are coming.'

'Can you repeat what you just said?' My mum's voice was toneless.

'The client's husband and one of the other guests are dead,' I said. 'The police are coming. I need to get rid of the monitors and I don't know where to put them.'

'I'm on my way,' my mum said. She was hurrying, her voice warbling as she moved. 'I'll be there in two hours.' I could feel a hard ache in the back of my throat. Why not? No one would want to get married here now.

'Mum, tell me what to do with these bloody monitors!' I said. 'I can't put them in the bin. I should have chucked them in the sea, but Kim was with me. I don't know . . .'

'Put them in one of the cupboards,' my mum said. 'Why shouldn't we have baby monitors? For guests with babies.'

I nearly laughed. It was so obvious when she put it that way. Listening for movement, I sidled out of the kitchen and along the passageway to the linen cupboards. I opened the one where we kept the lightbulbs and bin bags. And I stared.

On the middle shelf there was a pile of iPads, phones, cables and chargers, jumbled together. Some still had their standby lights glowing.

'Donna?' said my mum.

That ache in my throat had turned into a little nugget of stubbornness. The monitors were unplugged. The missing devices were back.

'You stay put,' I said. 'I can handle this.'

'What are you *talking* about? You've got to be crazy if you think I'd leave you—'

'Mum,' I said. 'I'm not saying this isn't bad. It's a bloody nightmare. But it's *nothing to do with us*. This is their mess, caused by their secrets, their lies. It shouldn't ruin our lives, you and me.'

'You're not making any sense! I can't leave you to deal—'

'Trust me,' I said. 'I've got to go. I'll phone you as soon as there's news. Get back out there to the booth and snag us some bookings.'

'Don't you hang up on me!'

'Mum, if I don't get some caffeine inside me I'm going to drop.' And not only did I hang up but I switched my phone off too.

I met Rosalie and Kim coming back from the study, as I backed out of the kitchen minutes later, with two hot coffee pots in my hands.

'On their way?' I said.

'I had a bit of trouble making them believe me,' Rosalie said. 'Typical plods.'

'Where are they coming from?'

Rosalie shrugged and held open the dining-room door for me. 'They'll be here in twenty minutes,' she announced to the room. That sounded like Stranraer. But the police had changed. Maybe for dead bodies they sent someone from a task force somewhere. 'It would have been ten. But when the genius I was speaking to told me not to touch either of the bodies, I made the mistake of saying the bodies had disappeared and – believe it or not – he asked me if I was pulling his leg.'

'It does sound a bit . . . extravagant,' Buck said. 'It doesn't help that we've got no evidence. I mean, the box and the rabbit and the party hat – they're all gone.'

'Aaaah!' Paul said. 'I get it now. That's why our phones got nicked. To make sure we had no photographic evidence of anything.'

'And, as I recall, that was your idea, wasn't it, Rosalie?' said Ramsay.

'Watch it,' said Paul.

'Thanks a bunch,' said Rosalie. 'That's the second time I've been accused of murdering my brother in the last five minutes. My suggestion was to hand the devices over to Donna. *I* didn't take them from outside our bedroom doors and *I* didn't hide the fact that they'd disappeared.'

'I can't believe we meekly agreed to hand them over,' said Buck, 'and then didn't even wonder where they'd got to. How dumb can you get?'

'Oh, come on,' said Ramsay. 'How were we supposed to know we'd need phones to take pictures of corpses? And I still think it was Sasha. He goaded me. He bet me five hundred quid I couldn't get through the weekend offline.'

Kim sank down onto the nearest chair. 'How can you all still be arguing?' she said. 'Aren't you scared?'

'Because they didn't see them,' I said. She looked up at me, swallowing hard. I reckoned she was remembering Jennifer's face, like I was. Maybe she was trying to imagine Sasha's face. Or trying not to.

'And listen,' I said, putting the coffee pots down on the table and rubbing my hands on my trousers. I had thought those pots were a bargain but the handles were close to scalding after a minute or two. 'First – and I can't believe I forgot to say this before, but what with . . . Anyway, I took a snap of the party hat. In the cupboard. With the knife. So there's that. And also I've found your stuff.'

They stampeded to the back corridor to reclaim their phones and iPads. There were just enough plugs in the kitchen and dining room combined to set them all charging again.

'How did you manage to miss them before?' Kim said.

'I don't know,' I told her truthfully. But that wasn't what was worrying me. I had just swiped up my keys from the kitchen counter where I'd dumped them down, and when I hung them where they belonged, on the hook beside the back door, I saw it as plain as day. The boat-gate key was there again. I felt the floor shift beneath my feet.

Easiest thing in the world, I told myself, to overlook one key on a bunch, in low light, when you're exhausted and terrified and still off your face. Overlooking a pile of devices in a cupboard you've opened to search for a pile of devices, on the other hand? But was I concentrating yesterday when I checked those cupboards? Or was I on the phone to my mum, half my brain on what she was telling me? Did I miss the one where they happened to be? That was a solid possibility I could stand firm on.

I could hear a car. The cops were coming and I needed to think clearly and be clever about this. I'd obviously just missed the computers when I looked for them yesterday. That would explain it.

———

It was a long, grim, exhausting day. If I hadn't had snacks and meals to make, I'd have gone mad.

234

One by one we were all taken into the study, a room I had thought was airy and purposeful, good light on the desk, with no glare, a footstool by the reading chair and somewhere to put a cup of coffee down. I'd imagined businesspeople and writers extending their leases because they were getting so much done and couldn't bear to leave. But put an exhausted cop who didn't want to be working on a Sunday behind the desk and perch a bored PC on the reading chair and my lovely study might as well have been a windowless interview room down at the station. I sat listening to the faint sounds of another two uniforms, who were – with my permission – searching the house and felt the last of my happy hopes for The Breakers leach away.

'I know you're a stranger to all of them,' Sergeant Wilson said, 'but have you gleaned anything over the course of the weekend? Anything that would point to someone having a problem with Mr Mowbray? Or with Ms Mowbray – with Jennifer?'

I tried not to laugh, even though they must be used to hysterical laughter. The sergeant waited with infinite patience for me to gather my thoughts. He was wearing his life like a costume: his hair sticking out in spouts from him running his hands through it when it was greasy, his tie mangled from him tugging at it to loosen its grip, his hands not quite steady either from last night's booze or today's coffee. But his eyes were sharp and his smile was kind, if weary.

'*She* wasn't liked,' I said. 'Sorry to speak ill of—' He held up a hand and shook his head with his eyes closed. I supposed they must be used to that too. 'Well, she was hard to like, to be honest. She didn't really fit in with them all, as far as I could gather. A bit chippy. Bit of a drag. But everyone's got one of them in the family. No reason to kill her.'

'But *Mr* Mowbray?' he said, reading my silence.

'Different story altogether. He got under everyone's skin one way or another. Okay, not always seriously, but to some extent, you know?'

'See, now, this is what's so useful,' he said. 'The family are giving it "united front". As families do. Not a word against him between the lot of them. Talk me through it. Best as you can.'

'He was pretty rotten to Buck, indirectly. He told a mean anecdote about his wife – Buck's wife, I mean. I forget her name – and I got the impression it wasn't the first time. And he was rough with Rosalie. He got physical with her – grabbed her arm. That pissed off Paul. They got into a bit of a slanging match over it. And Ramsay seems pretty easy-going but Sasha kept trying to wind him up anyway. And it was more like they'd picked a scab off a wound and opened it again than like they'd fallen out for the first time. Do you know what I mean?'

He nodded, tugging his tie again. I wondered why he didn't loosen the knot, wondered too how he'd ever get it off at the end of the day without a pair of scissors.

'Then there was a moment at breakfast yesterday. Peach – Mrs Plummer – was drinking. Having a hair of the dog, kind of thing? And Sasha outed her. It was a complete set-up. He pretended to be choking on a bramble and he grabbed her water glass to get a drink and then he pretended to be all surprised that it had vodka in it. But the whole thing was fake. He hadn't choked at all.'

'I see,' Wilson said. 'You're a good witness, Donna. You've certainly got all their names straight in the space of a weekend.'

236

The memory hit me hard, of nearly winkling the sisters' names out of them all last night. I felt my face drain.

'Okay?' Wilson said.

'Yeah,' I said. 'Just the thought of being a witness. If you had evidence, no one would have to— Oh!' I stopped. Sergeant Wilson made a gesture like winding a handle to get me going again. 'Did the others tell you that someone soaked a paper hat in perfume and spiked it to the wall inside a cupboard?' I expected him to look at me as if I was daft, but he only nodded.

'They told us. We smelt it. And we saw the knife mark,' he said. 'Aftershave. Eternity for men.'

'I've got a photo of it,' I said, digging my phone out and scrolling. 'I saw it and Sasha came in and sniffed and asked what the smell was. But he went dead white. And it's not like it's a bad smell, exactly. So there had to be a reason for him reacting that way. Does that make any sense?'

I had scrolled right through my photos without finding it. I went back to the top and started again.

'Yes,' said Sergeant Wilson. 'When you've been at this as long as I have, you'd be surprised what makes sense.' He read over what he'd written, then shared a look with the PC. 'Surprised you haven't mentioned the wife,' he said. 'Kim.'

'He abused her. Did she tell you?'

'Not deliberately. But it comes off her.' He looked over at the PC for corroboration and nodded when it came.

'Well, he really did,' I said. 'He gaslighted her about that stupid nightie for one thing. He hung it in her wardrobe and then he went mental and shouted at her, asking where it came from. She was really frightened of him.'

'Anything physical?' he said.

237

'Does shoving count? He shoved her over on the ground as soon as they got out the car on Friday. I saw it. She fell over hard enough to graze her hands.'

'Shoving counts,' Wilson said. 'Of course, it depends if we can get her to give a statement.'

I thought about the little speck of gravel in my trouser pocket. I could prove that Sasha knocked Kim about. Kim would be a fool to admit to it while the question of a motive for his murder was in the air. 'But even if she wanted to string him up,' I said, 'she couldn't. He's a great big guy and she's normal-sized. Anyway, why would she harm Jennifer? That makes no sense. Ignore me.'

'Don't worry,' he said. 'I'm not going to arrest Mrs Mowbray because you saw her getting shoved.'

'Good,' I said. 'Because this is nothing to do with her. It's all from their childhood. Secrets and old leftover hurt. It's hard to explain.'

'Any joy?' He nodded at my phone.

'I can't find it,' I said. 'I must have deleted it.'

'You didn't need to do that, Ms Weaver. There's no need to worry about handing over evidence.'

'What?' I said. 'You think I sat here and deleted it right now? Under your nose?'

'Has anyone else been near your phone?'

It was one of those moments when you're suddenly peering over the edge of a high cliff. I had felt it before. When I saw my boyfriend's phone left out of his sight and so busy downloading something that it hadn't snapped back behind his password, secret from me, like it usually did after ninety seconds. I could have walked away from the edge then, like I could right now.

That time, I jumped. I pulled up his emails, then his texts, then his photos. What I saw – as I plummeted down – was Rebecca in his inbox, and Bex in his shortcuts, and photos of the same grinning, freckled, wholesome redhead in his photos, who looked as if the name Becky had been invented for her.

I was right on the crumbling edge again now, grit and gravel spraying out from under my feet and spinning away down the cliff, out of sight. This time, I stepped back. There was an explanation for the photo being gone, but I closed my mind to it.

'Sorry,' I said. 'Just one of those things.'

'Well, that's all been very helpful,' said Wilson, dismissing me. 'Unless there's anything else?'

'I've got a photo of the cake I made.' I enlarged it and showed him. 'That freaked him out for some reason.'

'"There's no love like your love,"' Wilson said. 'From the song?'

I shrugged. 'That's what was ordered.'

'Anything else?'

I pretended to think about it. The one thing I hadn't told him was that I'd taken the time, after seeing Sasha, to clean my kitchen. I couldn't say it because it made no sense. I was telling myself the times in Kim's evidence wouldn't match mine. *Then* I'd come clean. Right now, I couldn't tell him, because I didn't understand it myself. It sounded crazy.

'If you'd like to rejoin the others,' he said, 'I'll be there soon.'

———

But it was gone six by the time he was ready to give his summary. The PCs were still searching the house and it was unnerving to hear the faint sounds of doors and drawers. It was hard to keep in mind who it was, when the thought kept washing over me of Sasha's ghost, Jennifer's too, rummaging and rattling.

'A box up the chimney,' Sergeant Wilson said. He was standing in front of the fireplace in the dining room, all of us ranged around the table with coffee cups and brandy glasses and the remains of scratch meals. 'A mysterious hamper. A nightgown hanging in a wardrobe. A paper party hat, soaked in aftershave, spiked to the wall with a chef's knife, a dead wild rabbit with its mouth stitched shut, and finally the drowned body of a female tied by one ankle to a weighted lobster creel and the hanged body of a male.' He looked up from his notebook and gave us all a sharp, clear look, before going on. 'The box seen by all present except Mrs Kim Mowbray, and also by the absent Ms Jennifer Mowbray, but not by the absent Mr Sasha Mowbray. The nightgown seen initially by Ms Weaver, then by Mr and Mrs Mowbray, then by all present and by Ms Mowbray too. The party hat, again Ms Weaver saw it first and then everyone saw it. The rabbit was seen by all. That about right?'

I had lost track among the counts of 'Mr's and 'Ms's but the rest of them murmured.

'And that's everything?' the sergeant said. 'Sounds like you all enjoy a wee joke.' It might have seemed friendly if you didn't know him but I could hear the scorn in his voice. I felt it too. There was nothing funny about *any* of it. It was meanness.

Except I couldn't understand how the box was even mean.

Or the nightie either, come to that. The rabbit was horrific and the party hat was creepy as hell, but most of it was just daft.

'And now we come to the corpses,' Wilson said, turning over another page. 'Mrs Mowbray and Ms Weaver both saw the body of Ms Mowbray on the beach down at Knockbreak Bay as the tide was going out. You watched it for approximately twenty minutes and then walked up to it and made sure she was deceased. Her eyes were open and her mouth was stopped by a stone of some kind. You returned to the house to raise the alarm and that's when you, Ms Weaver,' he turned and gave me a neutral look, 'that's when you entered the staff shower room on the ground floor and saw the body of Mr Sasha Mowbray hanging by the neck, again with his mouth stopped up by some dark object, possibly similar to the stone seen in the mouth of Ms Mowbray.'

He paused, looking at me. I nodded.

'But as I understand it no one else saw this second body.' A few of them shook their heads but none so much as muttered. Rosalie looked as if she might faint. Her face was chalk white, except for dark circles under her eyes, and her hands trembled in her lap. 'After leaving the shower room, Ms Weaver, you went first to the kitchen. Then up the back stairs. You passed through to the main corridor and met Mrs Mowbray.'

I stared at Kim. What had *she* been doing for all that lost time?

'Ms Weaver and Mrs Mowbray went one after the other into Mr Ramsay Buchanan's room,' Wilson said. 'While Ms Weaver was still in there, Mrs Mowbray entered Mr and Mrs Paul Buchanan's room. Ms Weaver, Mrs Mowbray and Mrs Buchanan met on the landing again. It was then that Ms Weaver told the assembled individuals about the hanged man in the shower room. Mrs Mowbray went to see and found no such thing.

'And, most unfortunately for us, there are no photographs of any of the items or either of the bodies,' Wilson said, 'on account of how your phones and computers were missing in an agreed "offline amnesty" from Friday night to this morning, when they reappeared.'

'Are you deliberately trying to make it sound crazy?' said Ramsay.

'Just stating the facts,' he said. 'Although there's one thing that puzzles me.' I felt the room grow still, each of us sitting up a little straighter, waiting. 'Mrs Mowbray woke to find a note on her pillow – a note since mislaid, she tells me – saying, "Come to the beach." Mrs Mowbray said she called for help while ascending the path *from* the beach after seeing Ms Mowbray's body for the first time. Only Ms Weaver heard her and responded. Right?' He looked at Ramsay, then at Paul, and raised his eyebrows. 'You two, and you, Mrs Buchanan – asleep in the front bedrooms – did not hear Mrs Mowbray raising the alarm? And when Mrs Mowbray came into your room' – he looked over at where Buck sat beside Peach, holding her hand – 'and told you that Jennifer was dead and Sasha was still missing, you went back to sleep. As did you, Mr and Mrs Buchanan, and Mr Ramsay Buchanan, who also ignored Ms Weaver's message that Mr Mowbray had hanged himself. Isn't that right, sir?'

It sounded, coming out of his mouth, absolutely insane. The morning had been so odd – so stuffed with horrors and so half asleep and still drunk, so spaced-out and unreal – that I hadn't given a moment's thought to it. But now, hearing it again, at the end of the long grey afternoon, it was ludicrous.

'Right, then,' the steady voice began again. 'So where were we? The time between Ms Weaver leaving the shower room and returning, accompanied by two other people, was a matter of what?'

Forty minutes, I thought. I looked at Kim again.

'Five minutes?' Wilson said. 'Ten? Ms Weaver was in the back premises or on the upstairs corridor, within earshot of any movement in the shower room, except for a few minutes when she was in Mr Ramsay Buchanan's room attempting to rouse him.'

Buck was frowning. 'So where did he go?' he said. The sergeant didn't answer, but he nodded in appreciation of the question. Ramsay was frowning too now. Paul had eyes only for his wife. He was holding her hand and watching her as her closed lids fluttered.

Kim made an odd strangled sound. 'I'm sorry, Donna,' she said. 'I've got to tell him. I had a shower, Sergeant Wilson. When we came back from the beach. I was just so out of it. And I had a long hot shower before I told anyone anything. I didn't tell you before now because it sounds so callous.'

'Don't be hard on yourself, Kim,' Rosalie said. 'It can't have been that long if you met Donna in the corridor.'

'I did the dishes,' I said. 'Speaking of callous. I'm sorry. I don't know why I did them, but I did them.' I glanced at Wilson. 'You don't seem surprised.'

'I'm not,' he told me. 'I'm a wee bit surprised, if I'm honest, that no one else has twigged.'

'Twigged,' Kim repeated. It wasn't a question.

'The milky eyes were a clue,' Wilson said. I saw Kim shiver. 'But the stones in the mouth are the clincher.'

'What are you talking about?' said Rosalie. I was watching Ramsay and I thought I could see the first glimmers of understanding beginning to flicker on his face.

'It's hard to hold your face completely immobile if it's relaxed,' Wilson said. 'But if you've got something in your mouth to bite down on, you can keep most of the main facial muscles tense. Frozen. Mandible muscles anyway. It doesn't help with the eyelids, mind you.'

I was still watching Ramsay and I saw the penny drop. He opened his eyes wide and swallowed. It took me a moment longer and Rosalie a little longer still. It was Buck who spoke.

'They weren't dead,' he said. 'Sasha and Jennifer aren't dead?'

'But we *saw* her,' Kim said. 'Tell them, Donna. We looked right into her dead face.' She stared at me. She saw my certainty start to crack and the cracks spread to her.

'Her eyes wouldn't be milky if she drowned,' said the sergeant. 'Contact lenses.'

'She wasn't dead?' I said. 'God almighty, she must have been shitting bricks when we turned her over. We were supposed to see her from a distance, then run away and call the police, right? But we sat there on the dunes and waited for the water to go down and then we walked over and took a close look.'

'Oh, no, I think you were always supposed to go close,' said Wilson. 'To look into her eyes. Or she wouldn't have bothered with contact lenses at all.'

'She's lucky she *didn't* die!' said Kim. 'In all that cold water for all that time. What a stupid thing to do.'

'So . . . you're serious?' said Rosalie. Tears were pouring out of her. 'He's not dead?'

'Mr Mowbray no doubt had a harness on.'

'Is that what your colleagues are looking for?' Paul said.

'No. I assume Mr Mowbray took it away with him when he left,' said Wilson. 'Well, he'd have been wearing it under his clothes, so . . .'

'So what *are* they looking for?' said Peach.

'Drugs,' Wilson said. 'I reckoned the kind of person who would pull this might think it was funny to get you all into trouble once the coppers turned up. I reckoned whatever he slipped you last night to knock you out would probably be stashed away in someone's toilet bag.'

'I'll kill him,' said Rosalie. 'I will kill him with my bare hands for this. You're seriously saying this is a giant piss-take? What if I'd phoned our mother?'

'You won't be able to kill him if he's in jail,' said Peach, grimly. 'I can't believe I didn't see it. We were *doped*! We were absolutely out of our trees and then we slept through everything.'

'*That*'s why no one woke up when I was screaming in the garden this morning?' Kim said.

'I've never blacked out in my life,' said Buck. 'But last's night's a blank.'

'I had dreams last night like nothing I've ever dreamed before,' Ramsay said. 'I dreamed I was up on the roof. And the thing is, I've got a cut on my foot that I'm having a bit of trouble explaining.'

The sergeant was letting us speak. He looked like he was enjoying it. Maybe he was enjoying not having a double murder to solve.

'Okay, okay,' Peach said. 'Let me think. The combinatiu. of sleepwalking, not waking when disturbed and possible hallucinations . . . that doesn't sound legal. It's not just a spot of Night Nurse.'

'Even if it was f— Night Nurse,' said Buck, 'it's illegal to give it to us, right? Without us knowing?'

'Except if you were all drinking too,' said Wilson. 'It might be hard to argue that you didn't take drugs for a laugh. Bit of coke, couple of mollys. And then downers at the end of the night.'

'We're not your usual clientele, Sergeant,' Rosalie said. 'I'm a lawyer.' Wilson gave her a hell of a look and she blushed.

'But why?' said Kim. '*Why*, for God's sake? Why not just have a nice weekend instead of creeping everyone out and buggering off?'

'Oh, my God,' said Peach. 'And leaving one last little joke behind him, actually.' She was pointing at the mantelpiece. We all looked over and we all saw it at the same time.

I had listed those five things half a dozen times for the sergeant, sitting in the study with him and the PC listening. And I had sat while he listed them again for us all together. The hamper, the box, the nightie, the hat and the rabbit. We had all forgotten that there were six. We'd forgotten the picture.

'Jesus Christ,' said Paul. He stood up and went over. I couldn't have stood if someone had put a gun to my back. My legs were boneless lumps of putty. 'Jesus H. Christ. They've gone.'

And they had. The photo of the party was a strange composition now. Paul and Ramsay stood oddly far apart, no Jennifer between them. And Peach and Buck flanked an empty fireplace. The little table of presents was there but Sasha had vanished.

'Sergeant Wilson,' said Rosalie. 'Do you need to carry on with this? If we're happy to leave it, can we leave it?'

'Well, there's the rabbit,' he said. 'But since the body's gone there's no way of telling if it was killed or if it died of natural causes. The carry-on in the wee back room there and down at the beach are not crimes.'

'Giving us drugs is,' said Peach.

'But, like I said,' Wilson was looking at the floor, 'it would be pretty hard to make it stick. All of you friends and family and all of you drinking as well. If any of you have ever been cautioned for possession – or worse – it would be even harder. I'm averting my gaze, by the way, so I don't catch anyone's eye. But it would be your word against his and you've all got cause to hold a grudge after the pranks.' He looked up again. 'And you'd have to come with me now to the hospital and have blood taken. We can do that, of course. But if I were you, I'd let it go.'

'What about me?' I said. 'I'm not a friend or family.'

'But you're the only one besides me who woke up,' Kim said. 'Maybe you didn't take the stuff. Or not as much. What did we eat less of than the rest? You and me.'

'Honestly, Donna?' Wilson said. 'I'd let it go.'

I took no persuading. I didn't want The Breakers mentioned in a police report on a drug crime.

'Right,' said Rosalie. 'Good.' She stood up and gave Wilson a bright smile. 'We'll let you get back to your family, then, Sergeant. Sunday evening after all.'

'I won't say no to that,' he said. 'Mrs Mowbray, you've got my card. If anything else occurs.'

'They're not dead?' Kim said. I was glad. I needed one more reassurance too.

'They're not dead. Trust me. I've phoned Gartcosh. We've got both indexes flagged for the ANPR and—'

'What does that mean?' said Kim. 'What does any of that mean?'

'They're looking for Sasha and Jennifer's licence plates on the national data base,' said Ramsay. He shrugged in response to Sergeant Wilson's sharp look. 'Once a nerd.'

'It shouldn't be long before we've got news for you.' Wilson gave Kim a warm smile and left. Paul followed him to the door, made sure it was closed, then turned back to face the rest of us.

'I'm not saying he's wrong. Wilson. But we can't leave it, can we?'

'No,' said Ramsay. 'It's time to unlock the box.'

'Unstitch our lips,' said Peach.

'Time to break our solemn promise,' said Rosalie. 'And bring someone back from the grave.'

Chapter 18

1991

This time she's floating. She looks like a star from the way her four white limbs and the long streak of her pale hair are spread out as she lies, quite still, on the surface of the high-tide calm. I shrug out of my pyjama bottoms and wade in, pulling my T-shirt down and tucking it into my knickers as if it can protect me from the sharp morning cold of the water. I feel the ache of it deep inside me, as the waves wash up my body.

'Lynsey!' I shout. 'They've gone. They've driven off. Come out and come home, you wee daftie. They're away.'

I start to dog-paddle as the ground falls from under my feet. My thrashing makes her dip and bob and a wash of water passes right over her face. She doesn't splutter.

'Lynsey?' I shout again, my throat blocking with fear. She wouldn't be floating like that, would she, if she was— Then she blinks.

With one last surge I'm by her side, my shoulders up round

my ears and my neck cramping from the chill. My hands are going from stinging red to that numb yellow-white but when I touch her fingers she's even colder than me. I grab both her hands and kick my legs harder to keep me afloat.

'I'll tow you in,' I say, and turn towards the shore.

'Pull me by my feet,' Lynsey says, her voice almost lost in the shivering. So I put her little feet under my armpits, warming them with the last of my body heat, and strike out for the beach, with her streaming along behind me.

When I'm back in my depth, I stand and go to grab her by her middle.

'No, Carmen,' she says. 'Hold me by my feet.'

I don't get it but it can't do any harm, so I tow her, floating, all the way to the edge, and through the seaweed and sticks, until her back scrapes on the pebbles.

The ash of their fire is only metres away and I remember, with a jolt of guilt that's got relief behind it, that I've left five of Mum's good towels behind that wedge of rock.

'Here,' I say, coming back to Lynsey, putting the biggest one round her shoulders and up over her head like a shawl. 'Wriggle up out of the water and I'll cover your legs too.'

'Mum'll have a flaky,' Lynsey says.

'Mum can take it,' I tell her. 'What were you doing in there?'

'Rinsing through.' It's one of Mum's sayings. *Washing* is what you do to jeans and jumpers and Dad's shirts in the washing-machine. *Rinsing through* is something we do in the bathroom sink to tights and knickers and hand-wash-only underwired bras. Like there's some different kind of dirt that comes out of the three of us.

Lynsey makes a loud HUH! noise, like the start of a cough,

then stops, with her breath held. I brace myself for another howked-up lump, thinking she must be down to tiny pebbles now.

'If you swallow water,' she says, 'it goes right through and comes out.' I don't say anything. I'm busy tucking the rest of the towels around me, trying to work out if my feet would be warmer dug into the gritty sand, or bundled in the damp fabric, or left out to dry in the half-hearted sun. 'So why can't it work the other way? If water goes up you, why can't it come out the top?'

'Is that why I was dragging you by your feet?' I says. 'To get the seawater ...'

'Up,' she says. 'I swallowed tons and sicked it out last night. And I know it can get in and dribble out again, but why can't it go through? Why can't it rinse right through?'

'Have you even *started* biology yet?' I say. I can't remember when we did what in science in the first year.

She shakes her head. All I see is the hood of towelling shift a bit. 'Chemistry,' she says. 'Corrosion.'

'Well, if you keep jumping in the sea I wouldn't be surprised if you rust too.' I'm trying to make her laugh.

'What – my fillings?'

'Oh, Lynsey.'

'But it's wet inside my mouth all the time. Is it the salt?'

'I'm kidding,' I say. 'But you know you're not allowed to swim on your own.'

'I wasn't swimming. I was floating. Rinsing. Don't tell Mum. She'll kill me.'

I haul her to her feet, wrap the bottom towel round her like a kilt and add another one. 'Come on,' I say. 'I'm freezing.'

'Can you sing the song again? And can you hold another

251

stone, Carmen? Or are you full? I can still feel it in my tummy. I didn't wash it away.'

I let the sigh out of myself silently, my mouth wide, as if I'm making smoke-rings. Then I shake one hand free of the towel I've swirled round myself and cup it under her mouth.

———————

Mum's watching out the back window. The kitchen's the only room in the house where the net's scalloped up in a ruffle in the middle, so she can see what's going on in the garden. It must have started when we were wee and playing out, but now we come and go to school through the garden gate and she can clock us as soon as the latch rises. She's usually got the kettle on for a Cup a Soup or the tap running cold for diluting juice before we're in and dumped our schoolbags.

This morning, I can see her wide-open eyes and her mouth moving. She disappears from the clear bit in the scalloped net and the back door goes flying open.

I start first, before she has a chance.

'Mum, I'm so sorry!' I say. 'I forgot to gather up the towels and bring them home last night so we went down to get them. And the tide was up and a couple of them were floating.'

It works. She stops dead in her slippers on the slabs, the scolding forgotten. 'What?' she says. 'They left them lying on the beach? They didn't even take them up to the house and run them through the washer?'

Lynsey, standing at my side, gives such an extravagant shudder that she knocks me off-balance and I have to take a step to steady myself.

'Here, girls, get in and have a hot shower,' Mum says. 'I'm

going to go round there and give that woman a piece of my mind.'

I know they've gone but I *shouldn't* know, so I deliver it as best I can. 'Mu-um! Don't show us up. What if they come back next holidays? Don't go round there and act as if we've been clyping.'

'I'll give you "clyping",' she says, back inside, kicking off her slippers behind the kitchen door and jamming her feet into her trainers.

We're sitting in front of the cartoons when she comes back. Lynsey's bundled in the duvet off her bed, sipping a cup of the baby tea she likes, with too much milk and a wave of the teabag, three sugars only half stirred so there's syrup at the bottom.

Mum plumps down in her armchair and clicks her fingers at me to mute the telly.

'They've cleared out,' she says. 'And you would not believe the mess they've left behind them. There's actual sick on the floor in the wee study upstairs. The carpet'll have to come up. And there's more of it in the downstairs toilet – not the toilet *pan*, I'm saying, but floor, walls, everywhere. I nearly boaked myself, walking in there. There's food stinking to high heaven all over the kitchen, bluebottles laying eggs. The pool room smells like a brewery. There's dirty clothes everywhere.'

Lynsey makes a small mewing noise and I feel her stiffen. 'Carmen,' she breathes. Surely that woman Anna won't have left the knickers with the name tag where she found them.

'If they think I'm doing their washing and ironing and forwarding parcels with my own money,' Mum says, 'they've got another think coming. They've not left me a penny of a tip.'

'So are you going to leave it like it is?' I say.

Mum sniffs hard. 'I couldn't leave that lying the way it is if you paid me in gold bars,' she says. 'No, I'm just here to get my camera and take pictures of it all before I start in.' She laughs. 'They'll not see a pound of their deposit,' she adds, practically purring with delight.

'I'll come and help, if you like,' I say. 'Poor you. You weren't expecting this.'

She gives me a shrewd look. She can sniff out crawling like a dog at the airport.

'Okay,' I say. 'I want to see if he took his birthday present we got him. He didn't even open it, did he, Lynsey?' It's the only thing I can think of and, ordinarily, I wouldn't rely on Lynsey to back up a fib, but she's so out of it today she just nods. 'If it's still there, I'm taking it back and give it to someone else another time.'

My mum treats me to a smile, then turns her gaze to her other child. We're right in her good books this morning, saving her towels and being so much better than those hoity-toities after all. 'You coming along, Lyns?' she asks.

I can see Lynsey's bottom lip trembling and I feel a sudden flash of heat where her leg's up against mine. 'I don't want to smell sick and off food,' she says. Her voice is a tiny peep.

My mum sniffs again. 'All right for some!' she says. 'None of us want to, Miss. I didn't *want* to have both of you down with a bug when your dad was away golfing that time. I didn't *want* two years of nappies from you both and a bin strike in the middle of the summer.'

I feel Lynsey relax. Mum's on a greatest-hits tour now. We know what's coming.

'I didn't *want* to find that bleeping hamster dead in a cornflakes box!'

'Sorry,' says Lynsey. I wait for Mum to wonder why, for the first time ever, Lynsey hadn't taken a case of hysterics, getting reminded of Hamlet that way.

'Will we go now?' I ask. 'It's not going to get any better for drying in.'

Lynsey hands me her empty cup and burrows deeper into the duvet. I click the sound back up and leave her there.

———

How can the house look so different in one day? The grass is still smooth and close, the windows still clean. Yet as I walk into the hall I think of bad breath and blocked drains and crumbs of sleep in the corners of eyes. I pause at the door to the downstairs toilet and feel tears, gritty and grudged, start to prick.

'Don't go in there, Carmen,' Mum says. 'I don't want you seeing the likes of that.' She looks away.

The likes of what? I think. A bit of sick that's probably mine and some towels on the floor?

Anyway, Mum loves filth, no matter what she claims. Her happiest day ever was when she got her first carpet shampooer and could marvel at the grime of her own house. She even likes clearing sink traps, gets narky if someone else does it and spoils her fun.

So I'm surprised that I get the kitchen, once she's taken about fifty pictures, with her mouth pursed up like a cat's bum. I stand in the breakfast-room bit, with my hands on the edge of the tablecloth for three big breaths, before I pluck up the courage to lift the hem and look under. There's nothing there. I stand up again.

The cake's probably fine, but I tip it into a bin bag anyway. I scrape in all the gluey salads, even worse now with that strange, thick dressing curdled into little balls of white and pools of grease. The long strips of fish and the piles of little black dots and the clumps that look like someone's coughed them up? They all smell so bad now – so strong and sharp – I wonder if it was joke and maybe none of it was food after all.

I tie the bin bag shut and take it out to the little yard by the wood store, hefting it up and over the rim of the big bucket with a grunt of effort, catching one last whiff.

Back inside, I run warm water into a shallow bowl and put it in the microwave to steam off the dried-in splatters. Mum would squirt Jif lemon in too but I check a couple of cupboards and can't find any. Then I remember the limes.

Along in the pool room, someone has started the clear-up but abandoned it after minutes. The bottles are all in a box on the floor, but the dregs have seeped through the cardboard so now the carpet's soaked and stinking, as well as the green felt on the table-top. The ice-bucket's still there, though. In it, floating in the melt-water, are two half limes and a wad of spat-out chewing gum. I turn away.

My mum's standing in the doorway. 'This all happened after you left?' she says.

'Mu-um!' It won't do to use the spell too often in case it loses its magic, but one more will be okay. 'I was looking after Lynsey! Even if I *did* drink, I wouldn't drink with my wee sister here!'

Mum looks down. 'No,' she says. 'Of course you wouldn't. I'm glad you went swimming if this was the alternative, I'm telling you.'

We 'go swimming' most days, and most nights too, the rest of that Indian summer. I wake up to the sound of the bedroom-door latch and listen for sounds in the bathroom. If I hear, instead, the quiet turn of the kitchen-door handle, I drive myself out of bed and follow her. Her bright hair picks up dawn, dusk and moonlight, and her little pipe-cleaner legs flash pale against the wet sand, flash brown against the dry sand.

'Why don't you wait for me?' I say, treading water beside her as she floats in her star-shape. 'Wake me and talk to me. Maybe talking's all you need.'

'This is what I need,' she says. 'It's working. I really think the saltwater's working. If I can keep coughing up the black stones – you don't mind, eh, no, Carmen? – and if I can keep rinsing through with all this saltwater, I'll be fine.'

'Rinsing right through?' I say.

She smiles up at the sky, her eyes crinkled against the sun's glare. 'Did you know that when you breathe, the oxygen doesn't just go in and out of your lungs? It gets into your blood! And did you know that when you do a hm-hm, it's not only food that's in it? It's got all the bad things from all over your body! I was wrong, Carmen. It's all connected. There's nowhere blocked off in the middle that you can't get to.'

Then she starts to rumble deep in her throat, and I kick my legs faster and lift my cupped hands.

The last morning, I don't decide not to go. I haven't planned not to go. But I'm feeling like shit and I know I'll feel worse when I'm up. My bed's warm and the air's cold. My pillow's soft and dry and there's drizzle blurring the view of the garden, misting the net curtain where the window's open at the top.

I hear our bedroom door. I hear the kitchen door. I grasp the edge of my duvet to throw it back and then I . . . close my eyes. I even dream about her. It's not drizzle and daylight in my dream. It's inky black night and stars like ice-chips and a cold sliver of a moon. And yet the water's warm and she floats curled up instead of spread out, the waves pushing her beyond the headland, past the cradling arms of the bay, out into the deeper darkness of the endless sea.

Chapter 19

'Because this is so obviously about the kid that drowned,' Buck said. 'Right? I mean, right?' We had drifted through to the library, all of us sick of the dining room after hours corralled there. Now we were down to seven, there was no need to go and spread out in the drawing room. The Leslies sat on the couch. Rosalie and Kim held hands on the long, low footstool, and Ramsay and Paul had the armchairs. I was on the slipper-chair by the fire. Rosalie brought the framed photo and set it on the mantelpiece.

'How many times?' I said. 'No kid drowned. Honestly. Look, Home From Home has only just bought this house and they wouldn't have touched it with a barge pole if there'd been that kind of history.'

It didn't help. 'We were here, Donna,' Ramsay said.

'Did any of you mention it to Sergeant Wilson?' I asked.

'I feel sick speaking about it just to us,' Peach said. 'But we have to. We have to talk about all of it.'

'Or,' said Rosalie, 'we don't. We pack up and leave.'

'Again,' said Ramsay.

'How the hell are we supposed to leave when we've got no car keys?' said Paul.

'And in my case no car,' Kim said.

'Oh, he'll have given our keys back,' said Ramsay. 'No question of that. They'll be here somewhere.'

'Kim, how about if I give you a lift home tomorrow and you just . . . clean out your bank accounts, change the locks and call it a blessing?' Rosalie said. 'Do we have to go poking around working out what he meant? Who cares?'

'You know me,' said Ramsay. 'I'm a technical engineer. I want to take it apart and see how he did it. Because this is the worst prank Sasha's ever pulled – that goes without saying – but it's kind of his best one too.'

'I know,' said Buck. 'If it wasn't for the doping, I'd take my hat off. It's a pretty good wind-up.' He put his hands up in surrender at the looks on the others' faces. 'If it wasn't for the doping.'

'Tell the truth, Buck,' said Paul. 'Are you in on this?'

'I swear on my children's lives,' Buck said.

'Because someone must be.' Paul frowned. 'Someone else must be. There's no way he did it all.'

'With Jennifer, remember,' said Ramsay. I shot a look at Peach and Rosalie. Jennifer's face had turned pale and shiny when she'd realized where she was. She couldn't have faked that. I cleared my throat. But Ramsay went on, 'Jennifer's not the sidekick you'd expect, though. No offence, Buck, but if it was you I wouldn't have been fooled for a minute.'

'None taken,' Buck said. 'And that explains why Jen stormed off. She had to be off-stage taking care of things. Right?'

'I'm not sure,' Kim said. 'Sasha was pretty wired all weekend. Maybe he was panicking because Jennifer bolted.'

'That sounds about right,' I said. 'She came back, you see, late on Friday night. And she saw me in the garden with him.' I gave a short laugh. 'I went out because he said he was going to go for a swim and I thought he needed a minder. Unfortunately, Jennifer came up the drive exactly when he'd decided to come in for a drunken snog and she sort of saw it – saw something anyway – and went kind of ballistic. Drove off again.'

'Sasha made a move on you?' Kim said. 'Well, that says it all. Happy anniversary to me!'

'I've been thinking about the dope,' Ramsay said. 'Sasha's worst freak-out was at tea and then at drinks last night, wasn't it? He wouldn't eat the canapés.'

'How could Sasha get dope into canapés that Donna made?' Buck said.

'I promise you—' I began.

'Oh, for God's sake,' said Paul. 'How can you all be so gullible? How could Sasha have done *any* of it? How could he and Jennifer have done it? A plan that depended on there being a lobster creel on the beach, for a start. A plan that needed Kim to be wakened up when Jen and Sasha were in place? There's got to be someone else. Not Buck. I believe that. But someone.'

'One thing at a time,' said Kim. 'How did he dope us? Where *was* it?'

'Is that you changing the subject?' said Paul. 'The only one of us who knew we were coming here? The one who swears Sasha *didn't* know.'

'I can't swear what Sasha did or didn't know,' Kim said.

'But I swear I didn't tell him. And I swear I've got nothing to do with any of this.'

'You swear on . . .?' said Peach.

'Buck's children's lives,' said Kim.

There was a long silence.

Peach broke it. 'That's enough swearing. So, like Kim said. One thing at a time. Donna, have you washed everything up from last night?'

I grimaced and nodded. 'Every last pickle fork. Everything's been through the dishwasher on a hot wash. But *I* don't see how Sasha could have got dope into the food either. He wasn't skulking round the kitchen.'

'Did he bring anything?' said Buck. 'Kim, did you bring any food with you?'

'*We* didn't bring anything,' Kim said. 'That was you, remember.'

'Wait a minute,' said Buck. 'What's that supposed to mean?'

'We can't pussy-foot around,' Kim said. 'You two brought bags of food. And Peach is the one who knows about drugs. Dosage and everything.'

'Don't be a moron,' said Buck. 'We bought the food in Tesco and brought it straight here. Peach wasn't out of my sight for a minute except to go to the bog and – funnily enough – she didn't take three bags of shopping to the petrol-station toilets with her.'

'So she left them with you?' Kim said.

'This is daft,' said Rosalie. 'Obviously – *obviously* – it was something in that mysterious hamper.'

The truth of this hit us all in a huge wave of relief.

'Of course!' I said. 'And I used the caviar and the foie gras and all the rest of it in the canapés! Which Sasha wouldn't eat.'

'Whose idea was that?' said Peach. 'I don't remember Sasha or Jell suggesting it.'

It was my idea. I remembered clearly thinking the hamper was a godsend to me. I asked if I could use the food. I shot a look around them, wondering if they remembered, and saw Paul staring at me.

'I've been thinking the worst thing about this is feeling you can't trust people you've known your whole life,' he said. 'But then, Donna, we've known you precisely two days.'

'And,' Kim said, 'you were alone in the house for a long time yesterday, weren't you? Much longer than the rest of us. Plenty time to put a nightie in a cupboard and a rabbit in a tin. Plenty time to do the trick with the party hat. And you had months to put the box up the chimney.'

'Why would I do any of those things?' I said. 'I don't know what any of them mean. I had no idea any of you had ever been here before. I'm the only one who definitely didn't know that.'

'You didn't have to know what it means,' Paul said. 'You just had to do what Sasha told you.'

'What are we swearing on now?' I asked. 'How about if I swear on my precious new business that's my lifelong dream and would go tits up if I did anything half this mad?'

'I believe you,' Kim said. 'Sorry, everyone. I just do. But I don't think Sasha masterminded this. He was terrified.' She shivered. 'If I could believe what that sergeant said. If I could believe Jennifer was still alive – instead of believing my own eyes – then I'd believe Sasha was still alive too. But—' She was beginning to shake, big hard judders that went through her whole body, 'Donna, you saw her. And you saw him. And I—' She stopped speaking and her eyes flared. She pointed out the window. I don't know about anyone else but I was sure, when I turned, I'd see Sasha black-faced and streaming with water, Jennifer blue-grey and sodden, both of their mouths wide around the stones.

What I did see – what we all saw – was a cop car coming slowly up the drive.

'They've found the bodies,' Kim said. 'They've found the bodies again.'

She put her hands over her face and bent forward until her head was resting on her knees.

Ramsay went to answer the door as Sergeant Wilson strode towards the porch.

'Sorry to burst in on you all again,' Wilson said. 'But we've got some news. We've located the cars. We got a couple of good clicks on the M8 and followed a hunch. They're at Prestwick airport.'

'Sasha and Jennifer?' Kim said. She leaped to her feet as if she'd been pulled up on a wire.

'No!' Wilson said. 'Sorry. "They" meaning the cars. The cars are at the airport. See, I've got a good friend on the airport security force, such a good friend he didn't mind going out and having a wee scout round the car park for me. There's a navy-blue Range Rover and a mid-blue Escort parked side by side in the long-term.'

'What are you talking about?' Kim said. 'Are you saying Sasha has run off with Jennifer? Left me for her?'

'Looks like it,' Wilson said. 'They're not on a plane. I think the airport car park was a bluff, but . . . off the record, Mrs Mowbray . . . if you've got joint accounts you might want to think about shifting some dosh before he does.'

'My brother's not a joint-account sort,' said Rosalie.

'Well, actually,' Kim said, 'he prefers them to me having my own. And I'll take great pleasure in clearing him out and maxing his credit card.'

'Good girl,' said Wilson. 'Anyway, they were determined. I'll give them that.'

'What do you mean?' said Rosalie.

'The reason we got such a clear CCTV shot as well as the ANPR is they were going very slow, because the Range Rover was towing the Escort.'

'Towing?' said Paul. 'Why wouldn't they drive their own two cars?'

Wilson shrugged. 'Breakdown's the usual reason,' he said. 'Or – possibly – if one of them didn't feel up to it.' He shifted from foot to foot. 'If there was any chance Ms Mowbray was incapacitated,' he said. 'If this was an abduction. It doesn't have to be her next of kin who reports it. One of you could, if you're concerned.'

'If we think Sasha *kidnapped* Jennifer?' said Rosalie.

'Or the other way round,' said Wilson. 'Theoretically.'

'I can't get my head round that,' said Kim. 'Abduction? Is that something that even happens? Apart from divorced dads, I mean.'

'Not often, no,' said Wilson. 'Professional hazard, Mrs Mowbray – casting around for every possible answer.' He smiled and the tension in the room seemed to let go. 'You don't need to decide tonight. If you don't hear from either of them soon, you can get in touch.' He turned to leave, then reconsidered. 'But you shouldn't leave the cars there too long, racking up fines.' And this time he really did go.

'That's weird about the towing,' said Rosalie. 'Why not dump a car if it breaks down when you're only going to

265

dump it anyway?'

'If it was just Sasha,' Ramsay said, 'and he didn't want to leave Jen's car behind ...'

'Why would leaving her car behind be a problem?' said Rosalie. 'Oh! If she's dead in the boot, you mean?'

'Or if Jen's driving and Sasha's dead in the boot,' said Ramsay, nodding.

'Or, like the sergeant said,' Peach put in, 'the Escort broke down at the worst possible moment and they panicked.'

'To be honest,' said Paul, 'Sasha kidnapping Jennifer, Jennifer kidnapping Sasha, either killing the other *or* the two of them holding hands and walking off into the sunset together ... they all seem equally bizarre to me.'

'Sasha and Jennifer up a tree,' Buck said.

'Does any of that change anything or do we go back to where we were?' said Peach. 'Where were we?'

Rosalie tutted loudly. 'That bombshell about the cars put the question right out my head again,' she said. 'We forgot to ask Wilson about the drowned girl.'

'How many *times*?' I said.

'Call Anna and Oliver,' said Paul. 'Not to tell them Sasha's moving on to wife number three, necessarily, but it was them who told us about the kid drowning after the party. It was them who made us promise not to speak about it.'

'And ask them if they can remember her name,' said Buck. 'It's driving me crazy. It starts with an L. And the big one was called something musical that starts with a C ... Oh, God, it's on the tip of my tongue!'

'Ask them if they've got the original of the picture,' said Peach. 'Could they scan it and email it maybe? That might jog our memories.'

Rosalie left the room and we all listened to her heels clip-clopping along the corridor towards the study.

'Meanwhile,' said Paul, 'we need to work out how he did it. Okay, first, he definitely knew we were coming here. Definitely. He had to set it up. He had to put the box up the chimney.'

'When was the first time anyone noticed the picture?' said Buck. 'Was it before Sasha and Kim arrived?'

'Did anyone look in the cupboard in the billiards room before Donna saw the party hat?' said Ramsay. 'Can we narrow down when it got in there?'

'We'd have smelt the Eternity if it was there on Friday night,' said Buck.

'Kim, was the nightie in your wardrobe on Friday or did it appear on Saturday?' said Paul.

'Slow down!' said Kim. 'No point wondering how he did it before we've established that he really did. And I keep telling you I'd bet my eyes that Sasha didn't know we were coming here!'

'He must have,' Paul said. 'He got a sodding hamper delivered before he even arrived.'

'No one knew except me, Home From Home, and my friend Tia from my book group,' Kim said. 'She helped me plan it. She might have found The Breakers actually. Or she forwarded me the link anyway. But she wouldn't have told Sasha. They don't even know each other.'

'Can you phone her and double-check?' said Buck.

But before he could say more, Rosalie opened the door and sidled in. 'They're sending the photo,' she said. 'Hopefully. Once they've dug it out. They might need to call back and be talked through the process. But it's on its way.

267

Against their better judgement and against all their advice.'

'Are you okay?' said Paul.

Rosalie looked at him long and hard. Two tears brimmed and then splashed down her cheeks. 'No,' she said. 'I asked Mum and Dad about the drowned girl. And they were pretty clear. They said there would be nothing but trouble from raking it up, and since the trouble wasn't mine, I should show some family loyalty and let it be.'

'Whose trouble is it?' said Buck. 'We're *all* family.'

'They wouldn't say.'

'Well, can we at least talk about the stuff that's nothing to do with the drowned girl?' Peach said. 'Can I talk about that nightie before I burst?'

'Oh, darling,' said Rosalie. 'Of course. What do you need to say?'

'Because I was wearing a nightie like that, that night,' said Peach. 'I had the jeans and T-shirt on earlier, for the picture. Jesus, I'm scared to look in case I've been zapped.' She squeezed her eyes shut.

'Don't worry,' said Buck. 'You're still there.'

'But when I got drunk on the famous schnapps, blacked out and came to, sprawled on the floor in a pool of peachy goodness, that's what I had on. A long white cotton nightie with pink ribbon. The question is, why did Sasha want to remind me?'

'General rottenness?' said Rosalie. 'Reminding us all of a rough old time?' Her words were casual but her voice was shaking. 'Donna, do you remember I said my over-the-top party dress was my mother compensating?'

'I do,' I said. 'I didn't know what you meant.'

'Well, briefly, my mother bought me clothes like that to

make up – in her mind – for my blemish. My imperfection, my blot, my defect, my deform—'

'Not now,' said Paul.

'My ever so slightly questionable gender identity,' Rosalie said, on a downward beat, like a death knell. Paul leaned forward and cupped her shoulder in his hand.

'Oh,' I said. 'Sorry. I—'

'Nothing to be sorry for,' Rosalie said. 'I didn't know then, of course. I thought I was late starting my periods and for some reason my mother dressed me like a baby doll. I was just about to find out, of course.'

The room had gone quiet.

'In fact, I'll back my "awkward first sexual encounter" against anyone's "awkward first sexual encounter" ever.'

'Ouch,' said Buck.

'But that's not anything to do with his birthday party, is it?' I said.

'Well,' said Rosalie, 'I think it maybe contributed to my mother's extreme . . . What would you call it? "Protectiveness" is the kindest word. "Secrecy" is neutral. "Reflexive defence" is the term, if we're being cynical. Is there just one single word for "reflexive defence"?' She tapped her teeth, looking into the distance.

'Rosie,' said Buck. 'You're not playing fucking online Scrabble. It doesn't have to be one word. What are you talking about?'

'Well, my mother was already rather disappointed in how one of her children had turned out of the mould.'

'Cow,' I said, without meaning to.

Rosalie smiled at me. 'And I think she'd have done any-thing to keep the other one unsmirched. Un-be-smirched?

Inviolate. Sorry!' Buck had heaved an extravagant sigh.
'Also, all psychobabble aside, Sasha's party was when the
awkward encounter took place,' said Rosalie. 'Paul swept me
off my feet.'

'During a game of Postman's Knock,' said Paul.

'You've been together since then?' I said.

'Since we were fourteen,' said Rosalie. 'Except we broke up
between the ages of sixteen and nineteen and then again between
twenty-one and twenty-three and for six months when we were
thirty. In fact, we're overdue for another hiatus, aren't we?'

Paul laughed and pulled her closer.

'Look at that, eh?' said Peach. 'I did everything right.
Waited until I was qualified and found another nice doctor
to marry. And now I'm headed for the divorce courts. Rosalie
bags off with her own cousin at a party and they're all set to
grow old together.'

Rosalie started laughing. 'I can't believe I've never talked
about this before,' she said. 'It took Sasha leaving to get it out
in the open.'

'God, it feels good to get to the bottom of things,' Kim
said. The rest of them shared another of those fleeting looks
that ricocheted around. If I read it right, they knew we were
nowhere near the bottom yet. But Kim's next words showed
that she knew it too. 'So tell me straight. Did Sasha drown
that little girl?'

'No,' said Rosalie. 'But he didn't take care of her. He was
with her. He was supposed to be taking her home. And she
drowned instead.'

'What about the other sister?' Kim said. 'Shouldn't she
have been looking after the little one?'

'She was only fourteen herself,' Paul said. 'And Sasha

started pouring drink down her neck as soon as she got in the door. It was a bad night, Kim. We were hammered. We were all set for trouble.'

'I remember the state of the house the next morning,' said Rosalie. 'We were hustled away before the press got down here about the drowning, but I still remember the state of the house. Flies all over the party food, booze spilled everywhere.' She shuddered.

'I know this is a minority opinion,' I said, 'but I really don't think—'

'Why would Anna and Oliver say she had drowned if she hadn't?' Rosalie said.

I thought about it for a minute. 'To draw a line,' I said. 'Like Sasha and Jennifer's final prank. Dead is dead. Don't you feel a bit more like you'll never see either of them again because you kind of sort of think they're maybe dead?'

'No,' Kim said. 'And it'll be really easy to tell if Sasha's using his credit cards.'

'But if Sasha hacked into your emails to your friend Tia, he's obviously techy enough to hide financial things too,' said Ramsay. 'Ask her at your next book club if she's noticed anything funny.'

'I could ask her right now,' Kim said. 'It's an online group. But it's a hard thing to work up to, isn't it? Asking if—'

'Wait a minute!' said Ramsay. 'Wait a minute! It's online? Do you ever meet in person? Do you ever Skype?'

'No,' said Kim. 'Why?'

'Because what if Sasha *is* Tia?' Ramsay said. 'Or what if *Jennifer* is?'

'Of course they're not! This book group's been running for years. We're friends.'

'How can you have a friend you've never met?' said Paul. 'How could you be so reckless, this day and age?'

'What about what's-his-name from that course?' said Rosalie. 'Ray Ban?'

'Li Ban?' Paul said. 'But he's a genuine person. He lives in Barnsley.'

'But you've never met him face to face?' said Ramsay.

'*You*'ve been gaming with random strangers on the other side of the world since your computer needed two people to lift it,' Paul said. 'There's loads of people I've never met face to face.'

'And what do you talk to him about?' said Ramsay. 'Li Ban.'

'What are you getting at?' said Paul. 'What do you think we talk about? Football, whisky, music.'

'The best ointment for your knuckles if you've scraped them on the ground,' said Rosalie. 'Did you talk to him about coming away on this weekend? You were moaning your head off and then you suddenly changed your mind.'

'He was all for it,' Paul said. 'Actually, yeah. I moaned about it and he was all for it. Why the hell would that be?'

'Listen,' I said. They all fell silent. 'I can hear a fax coming in.'

'That'll be from Mum and Dad,' said Rosalie, standing. 'I knew they'd never get their heads round a scanned email.'

She was studying the picture when she came back in again. 'It's really strange to see it whole,' she said. 'We've been looking at it doctored all weekend.' She sat back down on the footstool and the rest of us crowded round her.

'God, she looks so young,' Kim said. 'She's a baby. It's horrendous to think of her in that cold water.'

'Does anyone remember their names now we're looking at them?' said Buck.

'Carmen and Lynsey,' Peach said.

I stared at the photo. The older girl had her hands held out from her sides as if to stop her top getting crumpled. Her finger- and toenails were a matching deep pink and her jeans were snug and dark. The little one was grinning ear-to-ear and standing half out of her shoes, trying to look taller. They both wore party hats and had dark smudges of eye-shadow but no other make-up.

'I don't suppose you recognize them, do you, Donna?' said Buck, turning round to look at me. I don't know if a spark in my eyes gave me away or if he saw it for himself. 'Oh, my God,' he said. He looked back at the picture and then at me again.

'What?' said Rosalie. Then she seemed to rise up out of herself until she stood, still and light, like a fawn when a twig cracks. 'No,' she breathed. 'No.'

One by one, they all turned to look at me and they edged together until the six of them were standing on one side of the room and I was standing on the other.

'When's your birthday, Donna?' Rosalie said at last.

'End of May.' Nine months after Sasha's birthday. No one needed to say it out loud.

'And was your mum young when she had you?' said Peach.

'She was fifteen when she had me.'

'Fourteen when she conceived you,' said Buck. 'And not quite forty when she killed your father, eh?'

Chapter 20

'But Jennifer and Sasha are still alive,' said Kim. 'We agreed. And the police said so too. They've gone off together.'

She had sunk into a chair, all of them ranged around her like henchmen: Rosalie behind her, swaying and blinking, with a hand clamped so hard on each of Kim's shoulders that her knuckles were white; Peach and Buck close in at each side, slack-faced and slump-backed from the sudden exhaustion that shock can bring; Paul and Ramsay at the edges, stiff as matching gatepost griffins.

I glanced from the six of them before me to the photograph still sitting in its frame on the mantelpiece. Five left behind, strewn around the gaps left where Sasha, Jennifer, Mum and Auntie Lynsey should be. I couldn't quite see the printout in Kim's lap, nine children with party hats and happy faces, before anything had ever gone wrong in their little lives. I took a step forward for a better look, but Paul took a step too, coming towards me with his hand up.

'Stop,' he said. 'Don't move.'

'What? This— It's not me! None of this was *me*!'

'Did you know?' said Rosalie.

I thought about it hard before I answered. 'Twice, today,' I said at last, 'I sort of saw that there must be someone else. And I got close enough to wondering that I . . . And then the names. When you said "Linda". And something musical. But, no, I didn't know. I didn't know. I didn't know. I did—'

'Sit down,' said Buck. 'Put your head between your knees.'

I tipped forward like someone had cut my strings. One of them came over and rubbed my back with a warm hand, but I kept my face buried in my lap, my eyes screwed shut, as my mind reeled.

Home From Home was finished. It was a front. All my hopes were a joke. My life was a joke. Sasha Mowbray was my father. That sneering, drawling, vicious creep who'd grabbed at me was my father. And my mum? My best friend? My mum had drugged me and killed two people.

I sat up slowly, in case the room spun. It was Kim. It was Kim's hand on my back. I reached round and squeezed it. 'So, you need to get the cops back, obviously,' I said. 'Because the rabbit, right? And the drugs, whatever they were? Even if Sasha paid my mum to do all the pranks so him and Jennifer could slip away. Even if that's all it is, you need to phone the police. I get that. I know that. I do. I do.'

'Slow down,' said Buck. 'Breathe.'

'But before that,' I said, 'please would you let me talk to her?'

'And give her time to skedaddle?' said Paul. 'Tip her the—'

'No!' I said. 'Get her here and make her tell us what she did and how she did it. And *why*! For God's sake, why?'

I saw them look at one another then. Not everyone. But Buck looked at Ramsay and Peach looked at Paul.

'In the library?' said Rosalie. 'Like Poirot or something? Except,' she went on, 'that it makes no sense whatsoever that Sasha's accomplice, ally, assistant, co-conspirat— Sorry. It makes no sense that it would be *Carmen*.'

'Oh, no,' said Kim. She was still rubbing my back. 'Sasha's dead. Jennifer too. But I agree with Donna. I want to hear what Carmen's got to say.'

She answered after one ring.

'Donna!' she said. 'God almighty, I've been going out of my mind.'

She was straining to speak over the background noise of the convention centre. It was as busy as ever. Exactly as busy as ever. The same sounds of women's voices. The same blare of the tannoy.

'Switch the soundtrack off, Mum.'

She sighed and suddenly all the hubbub was gone. All the brides and mothers silenced.

'Where are you?' I asked her. I was staring at myself in the bathroom mirror. I looked like a stranger. 'Are you at the caravan? What if I'd popped over for something?'

'You didn't,' she said.

'Where were the drugs?'

'Not "drugs", Donna,' she said. 'Not junkie drugs. Nothing terrible. I bought them in the pub in Stranraer. Plus a few sleeping tablets of my own. Most of it was in the vanilla sugar. Plus a bit in the caviar in the hamper. It was sent to the house by a mysterious stranger, so that seemed like a good idea.'

'You drugged me,' I said.

276

'No,' said my mum. 'You never touch crème brûlée.'

'I ate enough of the caviar to do my head in. I cracked into the hamper for quick hors d'oeuvres.'

'Can I ask you a question?'

'I don't know how to talk to you, Mum,' I said. 'You did all this without asking me and now you make out you need permission for a *question*?'

'How did you work it out?' she said. 'I'm not annoyed. I'm not even surprised. I played fair all the way. Lots of clues. Everyone in the game had a fighting chance to win it.'

'Game,' I said. I was remembering the cold blue of Jennifer's skin and the black swell of Sasha's eyes. 'We all worked it out. They all know.'

'How?' She sounded intrigued, anything but scared.

'They recognized me. Rosalie got her mum to fax through the original photograph from the sixteenth birthday party.'

'Anna,' Mum said. 'Your grandma.'

'My grandma died five years ago.' I leaned my head against the bathroom mirror, fogging it with my breath until my face disappeared, suddenly remembering her. She had been a right wee nippy sweetie, my gran. Not much for cuddling. But she'd taught me to cook and she'd taught me to clean a house until it begged for mercy. She'd taught me that, no matter what my mum said, there was no shame in offering a good service for a fair price. I missed her. 'But I didn't really know her either, did I?' The truth of this hit me in the heart like a physical blow. 'My whole life she never mentioned Galloway once. Or Grandpa either.'

'They were— Well, *she* was ashamed. A daughter pregnant at that age. She never came back here after they moved up to the island.'

They always say the young are self-centred. I could see i. now. I had never asked my gran how long they'd been on Skye, Grandpa Rob and her. Or maybe I had sensed where not to go, where the dark places were. They say that about kids too.

'I thought this house had just caught your eye,' I said. 'On RightMove.'

'It certainly did catch my eye,' she said. 'Because I had an alert on it.'

'You had everything worked out, eh?'

'How about your end?' she asked. 'Have *they* worked everything out?

'How are we supposed to know? How do we know what "everything" is?' I took a breath and got my voice down. 'Look, you need to come over and talk to them. You owe them that much.'

'I owe them nothing,' she said, after a long, silent moment. 'And I won't incriminate myself. They can do without answers. It won't kill them.'

'Won't kill—' I said. 'Mum, for God's sake.'

'Yeah,' she said. Then the silence stretched out even longer.

'So are you coming?' I said at last. She hung up without speaking, but I knew her.

I stood up straight, wiped the cloud from the mirror with my cuff and went back to the drawing room.

We didn't speak much, waiting for her. Paul and Ramsay lit a fire. Paul walked away once it was burning but Ramsay lingered. I thought he was fidgeting with it and I thought there was no need. It was burning beautifully. Then, when he turned, I realized he hadn't picked up the poker to move logs. He wanted a weapon in his hands. I waited for someone to tell him he was being ridiculous, but Paul caught his eye and gave a tight nod.

Paul himself went to the kitchen and came back with one of my biggest knives. He dialled 999 too and left his phone lying open.

Buck found the hot-water bottles stashed in one of the linen cupboards and filled them all. He dispensed them to Rosalie, Peach, Kim and me like medicine, with glasses of whisky. He herded us all until we were in a row on the long couch too.

'The weaker sex, are we?' Peach said, lifting an eyebrow. But she was cuddling the hot bottle like a teddy bear.

A car was coming up the drive, gravel popping and crunching under its slow wheels. I would know the sound of my mum's car anywhere.

'Not all of you,' Buck said, looking out the window.

My heart was hammering behind my jaw when my mum appeared in the drawing-room doorway.

'Hello, Carmen,' said Rosalie, in a steady voice. 'You haven't changed much. Physically.'

My mum took her time, giving all of them a good look. She saw the knife and the poker and nodded. Then she came in and sat down.

'So,' she said. 'Here we are again. Before I start, though ...' She nodded at Paul's phone lying there inches from his hand. She'd noticed that too. '... the voice recorder's not switched on there, is it?'

'Of course not,' said Paul, a look of distaste crossing his face.

'Oh, no, of *course* not!' my mum said. 'How terribly uncouth that would be. And you've always had such lovely manners, haven't you? So well-brought-up and so cultured. Pimm's and caviar at a birthday party. Fresh limes and a silver ice-bucket. Such respectable children. And let's not mention a little girl—'

'Two little girls,' said Peach.

'Would you like a glass of whisky, Carmen?' Kim said. 'It's been quite a weekend for you too.'

My mum shook her head. Then she took a deep breath, blew up into her hair, and nodded. Paul poured it and walked over to the fireplace. He handed it to her with his arm out straight, as if he didn't want to get too close. The hand holding the breadknife was down by his side. My mum took a small sip and shuddered. She hates whisky.

'Why would we be recording you, Carmen?' Rosalie said. 'Why would any of us want a record of any of this?'

'The monitors,' I said. 'You were hooked into them, weren't you?'

My mum lifted her glass to salute me. 'Yes, okay. I suppose it's my guilty conscience making me check about *you* recording *me*. Judging you by my standards. I had devices on,' she said to the others. 'Not in your bedrooms. Just down here. I had to know how it was going. If the balloon went up I'd have thrown in the towel. No hard feelings. No harm done.'

'That's very generous of you, Carmen,' said Rosalie. 'But we're a lot of questions and answers away from "no hard feelings". You understand that, don't you?' She was talking as if my mum was a wild animal or a slow child. And I couldn't pretend I didn't know why.

'Fire away,' my mum said. 'What do you want to know?'

Rosalie blinked. 'What you did, of course.'

280

'Typical lawyer,' said Ramsay. 'I want to know how you did it.'

'Typical engineer,' Paul said. My mum was still looking at Rosalie.

'What is wrong with everyone?' I said. 'Who cares how? We need to know *why*. Why, Mum?' I sent a frantic look around for one of them to back me up but none of them – not even Kim – would meet my eye.

'Were you in cahoots with Jen and Sasha?' said Paul. 'Kim thinks they're dead.'

'Well,' my mum said, 'either way, I planned an elaborate sequence of pranks as a smokescreen, didn't I? Either Sasha and his beloved slipped away, with a big dust-storm of a double murder to help them, or I faked elopement to cover killing. It's one or the other, wouldn't you say?'

'But we need to start at the beginning,' said Ramsay. 'How did you get us all down here?'

'Kim found The Breakers and booked it,' my mum said.

'But how did you *do* it?' said Kim. 'Do you know my friend Tia? She's the only one I spoke to about it.'

'I know your friend Tia very well,' Mum said. 'And Sasha's friend Matt. Matt talked him into the weekend, you know. Tia and Matt between them got you two down here.'

'Oh, my God,' I said, realization dawning, but my mum went on.

'And Sedna, the marine biologist, persuaded Jennifer to come along.' She smiled at Peach. 'Your AA sponsor would have said she thought it was a great idea, Peach, if you'd been in two minds. But you were quite happy to come, weren't you?'

'You're Thalassa?' Peach said.

'Yes, and I feel a bit bad about it,' said Mum. 'I mean, I've studied up and I try my best but I'm not an alcoholic, and I can't help wondering if you'd have been getting better faster if your sponsor was real.'

Peach took a swig of whisky and gave a hollow laugh.

'You've been very resourceful, Carmen,' said Rosalie. 'Which begs the question . . .'

'I *have* been resourceful,' my mum said. 'I've been imaginative, enterprising, ingenious and inventive too. I've been Acionna, your online Scrabble rival.'

'But – but that's been years!' Rosalie said.

'Years and years,' my mum agreed. 'Of course, twenty-five years ago, when the internet was a clumsy toddler, I never dreamed what I'd be able to do.' She turned her head a little and smiled at me. The same warm smile as ever. The smile that said there was nothing I couldn't tell her. 'Donna, I hope you understand. It was pure chance that you came home when you did and got involved. I would have done it on my own, in disguise. Because it was years of planning before I even knew where the plans were leading. When this house came up for sale? And I got Grandpa's money? It was too good to be true.'

She searched out Buck next. 'Speaking of money,' she said, 'Buck, I want to assure you that Samundra has donated every penny you've raised to Operation Smile. Even when we were scraping together the price of buying this place I never kept a bean.'

'Samundra?' said Buck. 'You're Samundra?'

'I am,' said Mum. 'And I'm Li Ban from Barnsley too.' Paul's head jerked up.

'I've been telling all of you all of this for years on end,' said Ramsay. 'None of you take any precautions whatsoever

282

online. Carmen, I think I'm the only one who understands how it was done.'

'Oh, I'm very clear about your level of understanding, Ramsay,' Mum said. 'I know exactly how much detail of Ezli's research to feed you to keep you convinced without confusing you.'

Buck laughed. It was the first time any of them had laughed since Mum walked in, the longest stretch of time without a laugh this whole weekend. 'So you got us all here,' he said. 'Then what?'

'Then,' said my mum, 'if I was helping Jennifer and Sasha run away, it was easy. They were in on it too. They could plant things and then remove them. They could pretend to be scared. Keep the rest of you off-balance.'

'And they could each drive their own car to the airport,' said Ramsay. 'No need to tow. Let's talk about the other possibility, shall we?'

'Well, yes,' said my mum. 'If it was just me working alone, it would have been much more of a challenge. But that's the beauty of The Breakers. So many doors. Six doors in and out. That was the easiest bit – getting things in under your noses and getting them spirited away again, although it helped when you got scared and started sticking together in a pack.'

'Voicemail,' I said. 'You were never there on the end of the phone when I needed you most. Because you were here, right? And couldn't answer?'

'See?' my mum said. 'Clues galore. I played fair all the – nearly all the way. If you'd caught me with the nightie, or moving the hamper, I'd have retired from the field. It was only once corpses got involved that I had to make sure you'd all sleep through it. Hypothetically.'

'Was Jennifer supposed to leave?' said Rosalie.

'No! That was the biggest pain in the neck all weekend, if I'm honest. She kept having to be talked down, talked back in. She knew what she had to lose, see? Well, Sasha knew too, but that's the thing about men and women, isn't it? Sasha was pissed off. Oh, he got scared eventually, but Jennifer was sharp enough to be scared from the start.'

'Eventually,' Paul repeated. 'What did you do to them? How did you—'

'Jennifer was easy. When she slammed out last night she got in touch with Sedna. And Sedna told her to find a nice quiet country pub and have a drink to calm her nerves. And while she was there she met a nice friendly woman who bought her a glass of wine. She never felt a thing.'

Everyone in the room was silent. I could hear the sea and the whisper of ash falling in the fireplace.

'But Sasha? Well, I just sent him an email and said, "Carmen here. Let's talk." He didn't hesitate. Didn't feel anything except anger. Until my hands were round his neck.'

'You?' said Paul. 'You were strong enough to . . .'

'With a little help from a chemical friend.'

'But how did you hang him?' said Ramsay. 'That's the mechanical puzzle. Choking a drugged man is fairly straight-forward, but lifting him up to hang from a light-fitting?'

'We did this place up on a shoestring,' my mum said. 'Did all the work. We painted these high-ceilinged rooms, didn't we, Donna?'

'That's right,' I said. 'We've got a painter's platform. It's in a shed out the back. Bought it secondhand. You crank it like a jack and it goes up and down.'

'Well, I didn't need it to get him down. If any of this had

284

happened, I'd just have cut the rope with the long-handled loppers and let him drop.'

'You don't sound the least bit sorry,' Peach said.

'Neither do you,' said my mum. 'I might have done it. But none of you stopped it. You could have. If you weren't so worried about your own grubby secrets you could have stopped it long before this weekend. If you'd been even the slightest bit curious about other people, you'd have worked it out. If you cared about anything besides yourselves and your golden futures. If *you*'d cared what was going on here in this house, while you were sitting blubbing about . . . What was it, Rosalie? Did you break a nail? If *you*'d got up off your back and taken a little girl home instead of having a nice ciggy and looking at the stars, Ramsay. If you were a normal, close, loving family who spoke to each other – instead of sleeping with your cousins, Buck – you'd have spoken about "the girl who drowned" instead of putting her out of your spoiled, bratty, entitled minds and you'd have worked it out.'

'We were kids,' said Paul. 'We were pissed. And Rosalie wasn't "blubbing" about a "broken nail". God, you're bitter, aren't you? Doesn't it bother you that your beautiful daughter is sitting here hearing this?'

'Doesn't it bother *you* that my mother came back the next morning and cleaned up all your mess?' Mum said. 'I put that fucking disgusting birthday tea into black bags and heaved it all into the bins while my mum was wiping up vomit and stripping beds.'

'But, Mum,' I said, 'that's part of the deal if you work in hospitality. That's what you sign on for. And it's one of the biggest challenges. How to handle embarrassing messes without making the guest feel bad. I kind of love it. It gets you a great tip if you do it well.'

My mum stared at me.

But Buck laughed again. 'Well, Donna, if you're right,' he said, 'if the size of the tip goes with the size of the embarrassing mess . . .' Ramsay gave a short, grudged guffaw too.

'Shut up, Buck,' said Peach. 'Carmen, what did you mean we could "work it out"? Work what out?'

'It's the names,' I said. 'Ezli and Thalassa and all the rest.'

'We thought Thalassa was Peach slurring her words,' said Rosalie.

Ramsay had his phone in his hands. His thumbs were flying.

'Ezli and Thalassa,' he said.

'Li Ban,' said Paul. 'And Acionna.'

'And mine's Samundra,' said Buck.

Ramsay was shaking his head and laughing. 'Ezli,' he said, 'goddess of sweet water. Thalassa, goddess of the seas. Li Ban, god of the ocean. Samundra, goddess of the ocean, Acionna, goddess of wild water.'

'And Sedna,' my mum said, 'Jennifer's goddess of the deep from the support group. Jennifer has needed such a lot of support over the years. Endless reassurance that she's a good person deep down, no need to feel guilty.'

'But what about Tia?' said Kim. 'And Sasha's friend Matt?'

'Donna?' said my mum.

'Tiamat is a Mesopotamian sea goddess,' I said. 'It's my middle name. Madonna Tiamat Weaver. Were you playing this horrible game even away back then, Mum? Were you so angry about having me?' I could feel my throat tightening. 'I don't care about the painting platforms and fake book groups.

I want to know *why*. You never made me feel as if you didn't want me. So . . . why?'

'Donna,' said Rosalie, 'we've been trying to tell you all weekend.'

'She never told you?' said Kim. 'Oh, Donna. She never told you you had an auntie that drowned when she was twelve?'

'Auntie Lynsey?' I said. 'She lives in Australia. She's married and got two sons. She's happy. She didn't die.'

Chapter 21

1991

That last day, the day I fall asleep again instead of following her, I'm dreaming about her the whole time. My sleeping brain is trying so hard to wake me. But I sleep on and on, exhausted, my body outwitting my mind and running the show. I don't even hear her come creeping back into our bedroom, blue and pruny and frothing over with excitement. She doesn't say a word about me staying in bed.

'Carmen,' she hisses. It's a Saturday and Mum and Dad are still sleeping. 'It worked! It's worked! I'm clean right through. I'm rinsed right through! Look!'

I open one eye. She's holding up a finger with a dark smear on it.

'What's that?'

'Blood!' she whispers, and I pull away from the finger, hovering about ten centimetres from my nose. 'It came out of me. It came right out of me. It hurts a bit but it's worth it. I've rinsed right through!'

I sit up and push the covers down. 'Lynsey, you do know what that blood is, right? You do *know*?'

'It worked,' she says, and sets her mouth shut as if she'll never open it again.

Maybe she believes it. Doesn't matter.

Maybe she really believes she's howked up every bit of pain and handed it over to me too. That doesn't matter either. I wish *I* didn't believe I was filled with cold lumps of Lynsey's suffering. I wish I thought it was a game I played to help my wee sister.

Because this autumn morning when I feel too shit to move, I'm scared of all the black poison inside me. I try to move it round my body so it doesn't rot me. And in the winter as I start to drag through my days, when it's more than Lynsey's pain weighing me down and turning my walk into the slow sway of a buffalo, I'm scared that there's not enough room inside me to keep it out of the way.

I've got something else in there now, see, that isn't a cold black stone. It's tiny and pink and warm and it's growing. It's all mine and I love it and to hell with what anyone says about being too young or where I got it. And when it comes out I will be its best friend and it will always be able to tell me anything. And if it's a boy he'll be kind and gentle and never hurt anyone and if it's a girl she'll be strong and brave and never let anyone hurt her. And she won't need to have someone looking after her, gulping and swallowing, treading water, always pretending in magic and miracles. She'll be able to look after herself.

And that means, when the time comes, I can look after me. And the time will come. I've put the black stone far away from her, warm and safe in my belly. I keep it in my head now and it's helping me think.

One day, I think, I'll get even with them. I'll show Jennifer how to trick someone good and proper. I'll show Sasha how to hurt someone good and hard. I'll show all of them how hilarious it can be.

Chapter 22

'So you named your daughter for your revenge fantasy,' said Rosalie. 'And it doesn't bother you at all that she's sitting here – your beautiful, sweet, kind, funny girl – she's sitting here listening to you spewing poison about how much you resent her existing? You don't know how lucky you are, Carmen. If I could get a baby the way you got one, I'd feel touched by angels.' Her voice broke and I saw Paul take her hand.

'What?' said my mum. 'What are you talking about? I'm not bitter about what happened between Sasha and me. I've loved Donna since I felt the first flicker. I'm talking about Lynsey. She didn't die but Sasha poisoned her life that night. Like Peach said. It was *two* little girls.'

'Oh, Jesus,' Peach said. 'In that case, it was three.' She gave an unhappy laugh. 'At least, I think so. I always thought something had happened when I woke up again. I tried not to think about it because I didn't know who it was. But as well as all the horrible things that happened that night, you turned me over on my side, Carmen, didn't you? When I was lying choking in

291

that little room up there? Thank you for that. There might really have been a death if you'd left me on my back.'

My mum nodded. Remembering, I think.

Ramsay took in a breath so deep that his thin nostrils turned white. 'It was supposed to be me, Peach, but I said I wouldn't do it.'

'Because I was wearing a white neck-to-ankle nightie and was face down in my own sick?'

'Because you were my cousin,' Ramsay said. 'That was the point.'

'Oh,' said Peach. 'Okay.'

'Can I ask a question?' said Kim. 'What do you mean it was "supposed" to be you?'

The men all looked at one another and seemed to be deciding who would speak.

'That was the deal,' said Buck. 'Four of us and four girls.'

'Until I brought my little sister,' my mum said. 'And threw off the numbers.'

'I slept with Jennifer,' said Buck. 'I had it off with Jennifer in Anna and Oliver's bed. I did my bit to keep the pact. But I was seventeen and she was eighteen.'

'I went and found Sasha to tell him to call it all off,' said Ramsay. 'Get the party back into one group again because the little one was crying. She was only twelve and she wanted her mum.' He bent over and put his head in his hands. 'It was a really shitty night. I do remember at one point I was lying on my back out on the grass, hanging onto the ground in case it spun me off and Sasha said he'd take the kid home. I had no reason not to believe him, Carmen. And so I let him take her down the beach path. And the next thing we knew we were all being hustled away because she had drowned herself.'

'Well, he didn't take her home,' Mum said. 'He chased her down the path to the beach, hoping for seconds. She walked into the tide to get away from him and she kept walking. But she didn't drown herself. Because I stopped her. I got her out of the sea and took her home. I got her out of the sea and took her home every day for weeks. What Sasha did, with Jennifer helping, what your parents agreed to, was cook up a way to shut your mouths about it all.'

'Twelve,' said Kim. 'She was twelve? And he—'

'Mum,' I said. 'Can I ask you a question? Where did what happened to you happen?'

'In the downstairs bog that's the staff shower room now,' she said. 'Why?'

'And you said Sasha chased Auntie Lynsey to the beach for seconds. Where were the firsts?'

'No,' said Kim. 'Don't say it like that, Donna. Sasha raped Peach in the snug. He raped Carmen in the bathroom. And he raped Lynsey—'

'In the breakfast room,' I said. 'Right, Mum? And that's why you painted it black? Because that never made any sense to me.'

'She was twelve?' Kim said again. 'I've been married for ten years to a man who did that?'

'And I've been drinking for twenty-five,' said Peach. 'Trying not to remember.'

'And we've kept our selfish mouths shut and been very careful not to put it together,' said Ramsay. 'All of us.'

'That's not fai—' said Paul.

'Yes, it is,' said Rosalie. 'All of us. It wouldn't have taken many questions, would it? But we just swallowed them and let them eat away.'

My mum made a barking noise that might have been laughter. 'No,' she said. 'That was me. Jennifer taught my little sister to cough it all up in cold lumps and give to me. I swallowed and swallowed. I remember being scared that all the black pain would hurt the baby. But it didn't, Donna. I didn't let it touch you. And it did no harm to me.'

'No harm?' said Peach. 'Oh, Carmen.'

'What?' my mum said.

'Oh, Carmen,' Peach said again.

'So ...' said Kim. 'Hypothetically, Carmen. You've made it look as if Sasha and Jennifer have run away. Hypothetically, if you've managed to fake AA and Operation Smile and a book group and all the rest of it, would your technological wizardry stretch to making it look as if he's using his credit cards for a while? Until I got a divorce for desertion, say?'

'What about Auntie Verve?' said Rosalie. 'Jennifer looks after her.'

'If there's a nursing home in the country that wouldn't do a better job than Jellifer of looking after an old lady,' Paul said, 'it should lose its licence.'

'Hypothetically,' Mum said, 'the sensible thing to do would be to lay a trail for both of them and then let it fade. Take them to India or Nepal and leave them there.'

'So I'd lose a brother,' said Rosalie, 'and gain a niece? If ...'

'We'd all gain a friend,' said Ramsay, smiling at me. 'If ...'

'If,' said my mum, 'you all agree.'

What would they do? They thought they'd been keeping one secret for twenty-five years. Would they keep another? Would they close ranks against me or would they close ranks around me? Would they, as they had once before, just end the party early and drive away?

'And, hypothetically,' said Paul, 'in the Nepal scenario, Carmen, where would the two of them actually be?'

'They're in the same place in both scenarios,' Mum said. 'They're on their way across the water. They're on a journey starting at our coast, out of the bay into the deep ocean, floating away and away and away.'

We were all silent then, listening to the sound of the waves in the endless, unstoppable sea.

Acknowledgements

I would like to thank: April Osborn, Sarah Grill, Sarah Schoof, Allison Ziegler and all at Minotaur; Krystyna Green, Martin Fletcher, Beth Wright, Rebecca Sheppard, Aimee Kitson, Amanda Keats, Hazel Orme and all at Little, Brown; Lisa Moylett, Zoe Apostolides and all at CMM Literary Agency; my friends and family (as ever); and especially, this time, Catherine and Olivier, whose silver wedding anniversary weekend sparked the idea for a book about a reunion. That said, none of the characters here owes anything to Catherine, Olivier, Sarah, Alastair, Max, Elaine, Caoilte, Eve, Dougie, Evelyn, David, Ian, Rob, Christopher, Caroline or Byam, and there is no such place as The Breakers in Galloway.